T
BIGGE
IN THE

CW01661352

By D

Meet Barry, a deluded Uber driver, saddled with debt and a wife who hates him.

Convinced he's a genius, and that Facebook, Tripadvisor - and just about every other internet giant - were all his ideas, he's determined not to lose out with his latest brainwave by taking it to Silicon Valley himself.

Leaving London with a suitcase full of Non-Disclosure Agreements and a head full of dreams, Barry's confident he's done everything possible to protect his idea and make his billions.

He pitches to deal-crazed bankers, greedy funders, geek-techies - and a shop assistant whose partner's a conman.

All of them want Barry's idea. All of them want to cut him out.

His one savior could be Mickey Roughton, the world famous movie producer who's in town to promote his latest blockbuster.

What starts off as a helping-hand turns to disaster when Barry's idea is broadcast on national TV allowing anyone to steal it - and everyone does. It looks like his unblemished record of disasters remains intact, until slowly the details of his master plan unfold revealing what could be the greatest scam to hit the Valley.

CHAPTER 1

The deluge of reporters hounding me for an interview didn't quite materialise as I'd hoped. Two years of fantiscising them beating a path to my door, and so far, all I've got is a garbled voicemail from Howard, a freelancer from Tottenham who sounds like he's impatient and inconvenienced.

He's heard snippets of my story, partly from googling me, but mostly from the barrage of emails I'd sent him – and half a dozen or so like him. He tells me he'd be happy to interview me, but he doesn't travel outside London and he's going away on Tuesday. Seeing as he's the only response I've had, I make it sound like, at great inconvenience, I've juggled my very busy schedule to accommodate him and meet him today.

Howard seems unconvinced that my likely ban on ever returning to Silicon Valley is enough to make a story, but the fact that I know a world famous movie-producer gives him hope I have some dirt to dish.

I figured if he was any good, he wouldn't be freelancing, so perhaps his choice of what makes a good story is not a good benchmark by which to judge my own.

So here I am, at the end of December, in a snow-covered London, sitting in the lounge of the very posh hotel in which we've agreed to meet.

As he approaches, I'm midway through reading the extensive menu of Light Snacks and Beverages, impressed at their descriptions and shocked at the prices in equal measures.

I assume if I'm giving the story, he's buying the refreshments, and after he's introduced himself, shaken me by the hand, and discretely wiped my sweat from his, I order a Hot Chocolate.

It comes as part of a kit, with tiny biscuits, miniature chocolates and some clusters of sugar, neatly arranged on its fine china tray. It could only have had more presence if it had a brass-band accompaniment. I add four sugars of varying sized lumps to my drink.

Howard is younger than I expected, and though lacking the trilby hat, still manages to present as a journalist. I wonder if he's got a notepad and a pencil that he'll lick before writing. Having never licked a pencil in my life, I wondered why anyone would feel the need to.

It turns out Howard does indeed have a pencil and a notepad. He also has a Dictaphone, which he tells me is necessary because he can't write in shorthand and is likely to miss much of what I tell him.

Proceedings commence with some formalities as he asks me if I'm well, and I ask him the same. He then repeats the question, adding concern to his voice, forcing me to explain I have a naturally grey complexion, and have always been rather sweaty. I don't feel it necessary to tell him I'm over-weight, hoping he's deduced that from his investigative skills and the fact that I'm occupying the entire couch opposite him.

He tells me he thinks my story's unsaleable unless there's a financial, technological or true-life romance that will inspire others – in which case he'll try to pitch it to a relevant publication. I have no recollection of there being any romance in the events I'm about to recount, and wonder if I should perhaps embellish them to include some.

Either way, I'm keen to get started as the miniature chocolates are melting onto the side of my fine bone china mug. As I lick it, I catch his eye and see a look of disappointment on his face. Perhaps I'm not presenting as the person I've portrayed myself in my emails.

Not knowing where to start, I waste the first ten minutes talking about my school life. I'm just getting to why Jason Tapmarsh gave me a black eye, when he interrupts me to ask if my plan started when I was in school.

Having left school at sixteen, and now being forty-eight, it would have been one hell of a long-term plan to have been thirty-two years in the making, not to mention the foresight I would have needed to predict the arrival of the internet, mobile communications – and even computers – all of which were integral parts of my story.

He rips the page out of his notepad, re-sets his dictaphone and explains to me the purpose of the interview.

I start again. This time, I tell him how my ex-wife Marie (may she rot in hell – and may she go there soon) and I were living, unhappily, in Oakwood, North London.

I consider for a moment whether I've just blown any hope of their being any true-life romance in my story.

She was a nail-technician, which is nothing more than someone who paints nails because their owners aren't dexterous enough to do it themselves.

I'm reminded politely to include only the points that are relevant.

I hadn't realised he'd bother writing all that.

I go on to tell him I was a sales rep for a vending company. I knew pitifully little about the mechanics of them, I knew pitifully little about selling them, and by combining both, I made a pitiful living.

We had – and still do have – a son called Danny, who's now twenty-three and living in Nottingham with his much older girlfriend.

I explain, how a decade or so ago, a few years after the first dotcom boom, everyone with an idea seemed to be making billions, and how Marie had a mantra she would spout daily; it was something along the lines of how I was a fat, poor, sweaty failure, and if I was half as clever as I'd told her I was, I would have been riding amongst them on the internet wave.

As vending machines, by their very nature, aren't something that can be moved online, I'd never considered the Internet as anything more than an opportunity for men to book flights and look at naked women. I'd never booked a flight.

As I ease into the flow, I tell Howard how, one day, I had the genius idea for a website where people could keep in touch with everyone they knew, share stories and link with each other.

Everyone I spoke to about it seemed to love the idea, especially as they'd all tired of Friends Reunited, having met with all their old classmates and realised why they'd never stayed in touch.

The excitement of bringing my idea into a reality was so great; Marie stopped beating me up and even found a new admiration for me.

We even spent time together drawing up lists of what features our website would have.

Over the next few months I found forums online where I could talk to techie types to see if they could make it happen.

Around the same time, I spent every hour I wasn't restocking machines with Mars bars, on learning more about the Internet and what it takes to launch a new idea.

I'd spent several hundred pounds that I didn't have, for, amongst other things, a new laptop on which to prepare a presentation for someone to fund it, and the domain name *FriendsAroundMe.com*.

By the time I'd found out how to present to funders, MySpace had come and gone and Facebook was launched.

Howard stops writing and looks up at me. I think he feels my pain.

I continue.
"So Facebook was your idea?" I sense sarcasm in his voice.
"I'm not accusing anyone of pinching my idea directly, but on one of the forums, one of the blokes I chatted with was called Mark, and he seemed very keen on the idea."

Howard returns to his notepad.
Deflated and demotivated, I settled back into the world of coin-operated machinery, and Marie settled back to reminding me how worthless I was.
Then, I had another idea. This time it was a website where you could post photos online for other people to comment.
Once again, I was convinced I'd hit the jackpot. After the lessons of my previous experience though, I'd learned not to talk about the idea in forums. I found a website with a list of funders and how to present to them. Of the two hundred I emailed, only eight responded of which two agreed to meet.
They both pointed identical shortcomings in my plan. I needed to find someone to build the site –a team of acronyms including a CEO, a CTO, a CFO and a COO, each of whom would need the credibility that I lacked. I had to look up what they were when I got home. It turned out they were members of a board I'd need to assemble, with expertise in running the business, running the technology, running the finances and running the operations.
They had also explained the development would probably take a year or two, I'd have to get my own 'seed' investment of between fifty and a hundred thousand pounds, then I'd have to prove the concept works - and finally, if users were signing up at a respectable pace - they might consider investing.

In short, having the idea wasn't enough. I needed the money, time and team to bring it to life. I wondered if Mark Zuckerberg felt this deflated when he realised stealing my idea for Facebook was the easy bit. Being in his twenties, he must have started assembling his team of acronyms when he was still pre-pubescent.
I spent the next months feeling totally dejected. Marie was giving me grief again, and to top it off, the vending company I worked for went bust.
A few months later, Instagram was launched.

Again, I tell Howard I wasn't accusing anyone directly of stealing my idea, but I clearly recalled, one of the funders I'd visited suddenly went on 'holiday' to San Francisco, and that was the last I ever heard of him.

I pause to let Howard come to his own conclusion, and take a sip of hot chocolate, jabbing my cheek with the spoon before continuing.

Sensing his readiness for another wave of disappointment, I give it to him in glorious Technicolor as I talk him through the episode of *seewhatIsee.com* – an idea I had for users to video everything they saw on their smartphone, and broadcast it live to any voyeurs who would select through who's eyes they wanted to see the world.

Having learned my lesson, I had gone to great lengths – and even more expense, to have a legal agreement drawn up. A Non-Disclosure Agreement - or NDA – would ensure anyone I shared my idea with couldn't steal it or even mention it to anyone without my consent.

The lawyer had explained the only proviso needed was if they could prove they'd already had the idea before they signed my agreement, then the document was worthless. I had seven people sign the NDA, and within a month, every single one of them had come back to me telling me they could prove they'd already had the idea.

Was it fluke that shortly afterwards, Periscope was launched? How could I prove they'd only got the idea from me? These weren't the kind of people that gave Pixie Promises or Scout Honours.

Howard raises his eyebrows but continues scribbling. I wonder if he's feeling the same tightness in his chest that I'm feeling by reliving the ordeal.

"Barry, it's unlikely I'm going to be given a ten-page spread for this article so it might be handy if we can move on to where something actually happens – assuming it does. So why do you think you're banned from Silicon Valley?"

I don't want to tell him his business, but I think he's undervaluing the relevance of all this. Nevertheless I move on to the build-up of the big event.

I tell him how, after searching for a new job without success, I finally got work with a chauffeur company, which I absolutely loved. They had long-term contracts with CEOs – a term I had come to know meant Chief Executive Officer, as well as famous actors and movies stars, and a host of other on-spec work too.

For the first two years, I worked for someone who I now consider to be one of my true friends, and who would turn out to be instrumental in the reason I'm sitting here being interviewed today.

The first nine months were spent laying the plan, but it was the last six-months where the real excitement lay.

Other than myself, there were only two people involved directly in the plan, and no one else – especially Marie – had any idea about it.
Howard lifts his pencil to stop me.
"I thought you worked for Uber" he said
"I did" I say "after I stopped work with the chauffeuring company", adding "That was another idea of mine"
He flicks back a couple of pages of his notes, and adds "Uber" to the growing list of other websites I've conceived.
"I've only got one notepad and one tape" he tells me. I'm sure he's already kicking himself.

I move on to tell him about my first trip to Silicon Valley, a little over seven months ago.

* * *

I'd spent three days searching airline websites before I concluded there are no flights to Silicon Valley, primarily because Silicon Valley doesn't actually exist.
I found out it's actually just a label applied to an area within Northern California in which the city of San Jose nestles. Its name's derived from the large number of silicon chip innovators and manufacturers based there. As far as I can find, silicon isn't even mined there, and there are no listings for silicon superstores from which to buy it either.
Within the region lie the corporate head offices of the world's leading tech companies, including the likes of Google, Apple, Intel and HP.
The only direct way to get there from London is to fly to San Francisco, about 40 miles to the South of where the mythological Silicon Valley starts.

As we pull up at Heathrow, I feel like a pioneer as I prepare to fly off in search of the region in which billionaires are spawned. I log the exact time and make a mental note to include it in my Autobiography.
The car's barely stopped as I lean over to kiss my wife, simultaneously kicking the car door open with my foot in my eagerness to get out.
She pulls her cheek away, which frankly, I'm grateful for. I won't have to spend the next ten minutes with the taste of her face-gunk on my lips.

Old habits die hard, and I forget that now we're divorcing, there's no obligation to go through the pretence. Where there was once affection there is now open-warfare. I remind myself I still need her onside, so make an attempt to look hurt. I try several pouts before settling on one, which I think looks the most credible, but she's staring directly ahead so doesn't see it.

The car groans then bounces up on its suspension as I exit. It's like she's even primed the car to insult my weight.

I open the back door and take out my carry-on case, which I place by the kerb before reaching across the back seat to retrieve my umbrella. I'd checked the forecasts for San Fran – like all cool techies, I decide to drop the 'cisco' - and I knew there was no rain forecast, but I wanted to appear quintessentially British and there's nothing more British than walking around with an umbrella. I'd discounted the bowler-hat as it was too cumbersome to carry and I wasn't prepared to walk through Heathrow wearing it.

"Idiot" I hear Marie say under her breath as I slam the back door and she drives off. There's no other exchange or farewell.

I have no idea why she offered to drop me off, but I'm delighted to have saved the thirty-pounds on a cab especially as I've got less than a £120 sterling, a similar amount in dollars, and a questionable amount of available credit left on my array of highly burdened credit-cards.

I've tried to keep the cost of this trip to a minimum by sourcing the cheapest hotel I could find. The reviews I've read make it sound only marginally better than sleeping rough. Tripadvisor rates it number seventy-eight out of seventy-eight hotels in San Jose. I'm less needled by the low rating than I am about Tripadvisor being an idea I had years ago.

I know when I return to London in a few days, I'm going to have to work eighteen hours a day to keep myself afloat until my riches start pouring in. It's only for a few months though. Possibly only weeks.

I imagine the smile forming on Marie's face and the sense of freedom in her heart as she speeds out of sight. I know, because I feel the same.

As I stand by the kerb, I watch as other cars, taxis and mini-buses spill their passengers and luggage around me. I doubt any of them are about to embark on a trip as life-changing as mine, unless of course they're off to Dignitas.

I breathe deeply to see how the air of freedom tastes. I've got less than four days in which to savour it. Something like two-hundred hours on my own. It's what every Creative Genius needs.

It's only 200 yards to the check-in desks, but by the time I join the line, I can feel the sweat under my shirt. I'm still breathing deeply, but it's no longer to taste the air of freedom.

I repeat my mantra. I'm Barry Goodman, and I'm a Creative Genius. I'm not an idiot.

It's fair to say I have the look, behavior, reputation - and even track-record - of an idiot, but that's because the genius within me is yet to be unleashed.

I should rightly have more money than the founders of Facebook, Instagram, Uber – combined, which according to Forbes Rich List is about a hundred billion dollars. I'd probably be worth even more because they were all one-trick ponies with their one-off ideas. I'd have taken them further.

The painful reality is they were all stolen by people I'll never meet, and I'm completely broke.

I have a £1873 overdraft and a long list of other debts including credit-cards, car loans, and legal fees. If I cashed everything in, the proceeds would be somewhere below zero.

I discount the equity in the house as I'm expecting to give it all to Marie in the divorce. I can't think of anything of better value if it gets me away from her.

On top of the mountain of debt, I've got lawyers breathing down my neck for several thousand pounds of outstanding fees, and it's only thanks to Katie's help that I've managed to put them off until I return.

I often wonder if she knows how much of an integral role she plays in my masterplan and how, without her, I'd be sitting in traffic, ferrying someone of no importance to somewhere that's even less so. Without knowing she's there in the background, I'm not sure I could pull it off.

Although I've known her for less than two years – and never actually met her, I think of her often. I imagine how I'll storm into her office with a massive bouquet in one hand, and a huge bottle of champagne in the other, and sit with her as I relay how I implemented the plan we concocted together, step by step.

By the time I return from the Valley, I'm hoping to have enough positive news to delay all my creditors for another few months. By that time, a piffling few thousand will be small-change.

I don't know if it's customary to tip lawyers, but if they stop hounding me until then, I might. I might even give them each a gift too. Perhaps a Ferrari each.

I've kept my communications with them to a minimum throughout the whole process to avoid racking up the fees. I've chosen emails over phone calls and phone calls over meetings.

My emails have been short, and I've talked quickly on the phone. They've replied with wordy responses and deliberated when they speak. I'd probably do the same if I charged by the minute - perhaps even develop a stammer.

I hold no resentment for them though. I would have gladly sold my soul to pay them in return for the freedom they'll help me achieve.

As if one set of lawyers chasing me isn't enough, I also have Messers Barnet Family Law pursuing me for another set of fees, which although far lower, I have the same inability to pay – at the moment. These are my divorce lawyers for which I would gladly sell my wife's soul to pay, but now it feels like I'm paying them to take it.

I've spent too long living a life of hell in the same house as a woman I despise, but I make the effort to keep things as civil as possible, even though I can feel it eating me up inside.

Once we've agreed terms, we can sell the house and finally separate. Until then neither of us can afford to rent anywhere, and neither of us has anyone rushing to let us stay with them. Some people can count their friends on two hands. I struggle to use my thumbs.

Our son Danny moved out to go to university, and never came home. Since he went to live with his older girlfriend, I've been sleeping in his bedroom, wishing we'd had the money to replace his flat-pack single bed. Although I only get the occasional text from him, I still think of him daily, and how I wish I could make his life more comfortable. He's top of my list to compensate for all the tough times and going without he had to put up with.

I'm mindful I don't want to spoil him so I've already decided to cap his gift at five million.

This isn't the first time I've considered the gifts I can throw his way – but unlike all the other ideas I've had, I know this one's got a real chance of succeeding. I'm half-tempted to get him to start looking for his dream property now so he's ready to buy it when his cash comes in. I choose not to though. Things didn't work out well last time I did that.

For as many years as I can remember, I've barely been able to control the steady flow of ideas that rush into my head.

I'm determined my latest big idea is going to stay mine. Having the idea was, I now know, the easy bit. But this time it's different. This is more than an idea. It's a plan – and I'm on my way to the Valley to make it happen.

Putting my plan to one side, I'm acutely aware of the other ingredients needed, not least of all the funding to pay for it.

I'm not sure in which order I need to find them so I've decided to target all of them as aggressively as I can, in the hope I'll hit lucky sooner or later.

I can imagine how – in the not too distant future, the whole world will be embracing my communications app.

Whatsapp messages, texts, emails, - they'll all disappear, along with the confusion of what ping relates to which message type. There'll be just one ping, one message type, and it will combine the best of everything that's come before it.

On paper, I accept it raises more questions than answers, but then so did every online phenomenon before it was launched.

My PowerPoint presentation not only looks awesome, but goes a long way towards demonstrating the simplicity of it, together with the technology behind it. I'm particularly proud of the bright starbursts I've used to get the main points across on the cover page.

All I need to do is bring the team together to deliver it.

As with all good recipes, the ingredients also need time. It can take months - sometimes years - to mature the seed of an idea into a sea of opportunity.

Turns out, I lack that too. I add impatience to my long list of shortcomings and hope, on this trip, I find the single quality of being a creative genius will compensate for all the others I don't have.

Like all the best ideas, I've given mine a project name. This enables it to be discussed as though it exists independently to me, and also I don't have to keep referring to it as 'the idea' or 'my thing'.

The idea of giving a project a codename adds a feeling of secrecy and importance. I therefore changed my project name from My Internet Idea to Project Ronald.

Not long ago, it was all over the news that Facebook had bought WhatsApp for an eye-watering nineteen-billion dollars, which is something like $3 for every man, woman and child on planet earth. Project Ronald is ten times better, but I like to think I'm a realist, so I reduce my expectations to getting no more than thirty billion for it.

After my past experiences, I'm using a totally new approach to make this work. I'm not sharing it on forums, I'm not limiting my search to just investors, and if all goes well I'll get twenty million or so in the next eighteen months, and perhaps a billion or two a couple of years later.

That's because I'm a Creative Genius, not an idiot.

I lie awake at night visualising the orderly line of investors, techies and online monsters vying to be involved.

I've calculated – to the day – when I'm going to actually have my first millions in cash, and it's 181 days - from today.

I'm not entirely sure – or bothered – whether I calculated it in dollars or sterling.

I no longer have to waste my time trying to convince my soon-to-be ex-wife of this idea, and I've all but given up on my son who thinks being an idiot is one of my better traits. I used to blame it on his teenage hormones, but I may have to re-think that now that he's 23.

I'm aware of the long list of gripes he and his mother share about me:

I'm overweight; my complexion is drab and grey – to the extent it's unclear whether a photo of me is in black & white or colour; I look ten years older than my true age of 48.

And they don't like that I look like I'm on the cusp of a coronary – they'd rather I had it.

They also think I dress like an idiot. I have no idea why. My jeans, jacket and trainers combo is the uniform of dotcom billionaires. It's unfortunate that jeans in my size only come with an elasticated waist.

The line to check-in at the long row of Economy desks snakes back and forth.

There's a group of eight or so nuns hustled around one desk. They all look the same so there's probably confusion about whose passport belongs to who.

No one's watching though. Everyone's attention is on the paparazzi encircling the First Class desks. There are stepladders and chairs, and a couple of enterprising photographers are even using luggage trolleys to scoot themselves across the red carpet. They're all desperate to beat the hoards for the perfect shot of someone yet to arrive.

I watch the attractive looking girls behind the First Class desks fussing with their makeup and practicing their smiles. It's in stark contrast to the row of miserable faces I'm waiting in line to encounter on the Economy desks.

The VIP they're waiting for is adept at building the climax. He's probably in his limo stuck on the M4, or perhaps he's not even left home yet.

By the time I've walked up and down four rows within my cordoned pen, reached the front of the line, grovelled, begged and ultimately been rejected for an upgrade, the celebrity they're waiting for is still to arrive.

I hang around for a bit admiring the fuss and find myself fanticising it's me. The world's greatest Creative Genius. The man who broke Silicon Valley. I'm brought back to reality by someone shouting for a fat idiot to move out the way.

As I turn to see who the idiot is, a luggage trolley, complete with photographer rams me.

Humiliated and bruised, I decide to make my way to the departure lounge.

I join another line for security, during which time I check my boarding pass, and take another look at the map of San Jose.

I've circled three venues.

One of them's the Self-Starter Inn ("Basic Bed, Board and Bath") that sixty-three people have reviewed as terrible, mostly on account that there's no worse rating. There's another circle around a Starbucks, one of just six hundred or so in the valley, noted as it's where Zuckerberg used to tap away, bringing Facebook to life, and is now a hub for techies to meet.

The last venue I've circled is The Oat House Meeting Hall. Attached to my map is a print-out of an article from *SiliconValleyNews.com* detailing how the "Oat House Pitch & Present" has established itself as *the* destination for start-ups, founders and funders to find each other. I don't need to read it again, to know anyone can turn up and pitch to the valley's biggest names. It's like the Troubedour is to music, but for tech.

Meetings are the first Tuesday of every month, and as today's Monday the 2nd June, I'm assured of my place there tomorrow – and in the history books.

I make one last check of my phone and see I've got a text from Katie, wishing me luck and hoping I achieve everything I set out to do. She's also asked me to keep in touch so she can be sure everything's going to plan.

I hope she knows how much work she has to do once I return.

CHAPTER 2

Less than fifty-yards from where she'd dropped Barry off, Marie pulled over, still inside the airport perimeter.
Still beaming, she leant over to the glove-box and removed a mobile phone from behind the screwed up parking tickets and tissues, and switched it on.
Within seconds, it beeped with the text.
"Hi Mary, I'm here in the lounge at the Skyline. Looking forward to meeting u x"
She tapped her reply
"Just dropped my idiot husband off. Will be there in 10. Can't wait. And it's Marie not Mary x"
She scanned her emails and saw a dozen or so messages from the dating site, each one from another man wanting her undivided attention.
She salivated at the thought of meeting Mr Right – or at least Mr Right-for-now. She'd spent too many years with the idiot and now she craved the attention and adoration she deserved.

At forty-six, she considered herself still young with more years in front of her than behind, and the opportunity to have the fairy-tale romance she'd hoped for when she was a teenager.
She still felt attractive, albeit with a few more curves and a slight repositioning of her best assets. She'd been in the beauty business long enough to know how to present herself to accentuate her best bits and hide the worst.
Her hair, though shorter now, was platinum blonde, belying the grey, and her makeup covered the cracks. From a distance she was knockout; up close, less so. Unfortunately, no one other than Barry had been up close enough to get to know that.
Eager to find a loving relationship, Marie had spilled her heart out to her clients in the hope they'd have the perfect match with which to fix her up.
When it became apparent no one wanted a relationship which involved picking her up from her marital home, she decided to look online.
After a week or so of toying with the regular sites, she concluded they were too overt and, if her picture was seen on them, it might affect her divorce.

She'd first found the married-dating site when she was searching for information on divorce. The ad that popped up had offered "Passion and Affairs for Marrieds Wanting More".
Unsure of whether it was the curiosity or the desperation, she'd clicked on it and within twenty minutes had written her profile and was receiving messages. Lots of messages.
She felt comfortable in the company of like-minded others, presumably in a similar position to herself, where discretion, secrecy and a desperate need to find attention out-weighed the risk of getting caught.

Within a couple of days, Marie had received more attention than she'd had over the past twenty years, and worked out how to recognise and weed out those who were merely after pictures and those who were genuinely seeking an affair.
She'd learned how to deal with the men who appeared more interested in the size of her chest than the size of her personality, and she'd got used to the photos of middle-aged balding men leaning on their car bonnets. Receiving photos of men wearing nothing but a smile was something she would never get used to.
They all wanted similar pictures of Marie in return.
She received an endless stream of winks and virtual kisses by men either unwilling or incapable of engaging in an exchange.
She wondered whether perhaps there was someone like her, on the precipice of being free and single. Ideally he'd be rich, handsome and fit - and seeking the company of a very appreciative woman until they were both divorced and could then run towards each other in slow motion on the beach.
Ideally he would also live in a large house with a swimming pool, a couple of horses and want his (future) wife to do nothing more than spend her mornings watching Jeremy Kyle on TV and her afternoons shopping for handbags. And shoes.

CHAPTER 3

Luke had been out Ubering since six in the morning. He'd had two cyclists kick his car and one bend his wing-mirror back, which, considering it was almost 11am, was one of his more positive mornings in San Francisco.

Having moved to the city in 2012, Luke wanted to get away from the heat of the Floridian summer, and more importantly, create a fresh start and an opportunity to reinvent himself.

He was only in prison for seven months, but he'd come out to find his wife in a new relationship and friends wanting nothing more to do with him. His kids were polite and distanced, and happy in their new home where mummy didn't cry anymore.

He was sick of the injustice. Everyone loved him when he was making them money. Still, it was their loss, not his. Perhaps a little too literally.

The small apartment he rented was in Tenderloin, ironically named as it was the rump of San Francisco.

He would liked to have been closer to Silicon Valley, but the rentals were extortionate, so he accepted the ninety-minute drive each way until he could afford to move nearer. After five years, he was disappointed to still be waiting.

At 43, Luke looked established, even if he wasn't. His face was weathered and tanned. His teeth were white, straight and perfect and his clothing was smart.

He wore chinos with a sharp crease, a crisp smart shirt, and his loafers were suede and never scuffed.

He carried an air of confidence and the gait of someone successful.

In fairness, he had, on several occasions been successful. His used car dealership was the second largest in central Florida. The claim after the fire was the eighteenth largest in the same region.

His investment business was the fourth largest employer in Pinellas. It was certainly the single largest employer of telesales personnel before the Feds closed him down.

He was hungry for his next venture, and in the seven months he was incarcerated, he'd thought about little else than how he could make his next fortune. Having spent his time keeping his head down and reading the periodicals he was allowed access to, he concluded the easy money was found in the world of tech.

The fact that he had no understanding of technology, or that almost all of the articles he read bewildered him, concerned him little.

He'd learned everything he needed to know about used cars and how to finance them in a few months. He'd spent even less learning about junk bonds and penny shares.

His expertise lay in talking, schmoozing and rain-making. He wouldn't even need to understand technology, just as he didn't understand how a car engine worked, or what a junk bond actually did.

That would be a partner's role – and thanks to the *SiliconValleyNews.com*, he knew exactly where to find one.

Since his first visit to the Oat House Pitch & Present eighteen months ago, Luke had become a regular, with a dozen or so visits under his belt.

After just two visits, he thought he'd found the perfect business - in book publishing. He'd even got two titles on the best-sellers list, thanks to Zach his first tech partner.

Zach had approached Luke outside the Oat House, and complimented him on his snakeskin shoes. Having pet snakes at home and a fascination for the reptiles, Zach had instantly recognised them as Python. He'd also recognised the likelihood that anyone wearing them had a higher chance of appreciating the 'creative' ideas he had to get rich quick.

Over a coffee, Luke learned of Zach's publishing idea, which was nothing more than re-publishing best-selling books, but changing the author's name and title. That way, they could post them in eBook formats under a different name, sit back and wait for people to download them.

It was the same concept as stealing a car, changing the number plates, and re-selling it, except books could be sold multiple times across the world, and all online.

He was convinced once they'd read a book; most people forgot not just the name of it, but often the story too. With a little deception, he could resell them the same book twice, even if he didn't own the rights.

Zach had needed a partner to finance the commercial photocopier needed to copy the books, before converting them to digital format and uploading them.

Luke agreed to it but didn't mention he couldn't get finance in his name, so when the time came they spent three weeks at the local library using the public photocopier and scanning their first three books, totalling over two-thousand pages.

Luke had been quick to point out the benefits - not only did they no longer need to buy a photocopier, they no longer needed to pay for books either.

The scanned copies were then converted by software, into PDF documents, and once the necessary changes were made, Zach loaded them onto various download sites. Within minutes people were buying his eBooks.

For several weeks, the money built up in their on-line account, peaking at $233,040 at the point when Zach was arrested.

Their undoing had come when one of the books they'd copied was downloaded by the original author, interested to read another interpretation of the downfall of the Berlin Wall. Having spent six years studying the German divide, he had hoped he was the leading authority. It was an unwelcome shock to find he still was.

Luke managed to come away unscathed as the police couldn't link his name to the business and the photocopying at the library was paid for in cash. Luke didn't even have a library membership card, nor did he understand how to use a photocopier. Fortunately, his input was limited to agreeing to the idea, and showing Zach a shortcut to bring it to life.

Several visits later, at another Oat House meeting event, Luke met Callum.

At twenty-one Callum's coding skills made up for his lack in social skills, or the ability to dress himself properly.

It was Callum's idea to create buzzme, an app that allowed everyone in a room to see who was there without looking up from their phone. It was clear from the odd angle at which Callum held his head, looking up from his phone was something he'd avoided.

No one else at the Oat House had recognised the potential of the idea that day, so when Luke approached him, Callum was grateful for the interest and agreed to the changes he was told would be necessary.

Luke had seen the bigger opportunity for conferences, exhibitions and big offices, allowing users to see who was in attendance, and which company they worked for, without the need to scour everyone's name badges.

Having lost opportunities himself by wasting his time talking to clerks at conferences and missing the decision makers, Luke could see the potential of such an app.

They made a good partnership, with Callum focused on building the app, and Luke promising to turn it into a fortune.

Unfortunately, Callum also needed to eat, drink beer and pay his phone contract - all of which he assumed would be covered by Luke's promised investment which was always on the cusp of materialising but never actually did.

Finally, after several months of the money failing to arrive, Callum lost interest and felt no guilt as he searched the job sites, looking for a regular paycheck and some appreciation for his coding skills.
It took Luke almost two months to realise he'd given up rather than just gone AWOL for several days - as he had on a couple of occasions.

Luke returned to driving for Uber, but now added the Oat House to the growing list of places he needed to avoid, which included the library.

CHAPTER 4

The entire plane's watching as the crew fusses around the main doors awaiting their VIP. Finally, minutes before we're due to take-off, Mickey Roughton and his entourage breeze on.

He's clearly not in a good mood. I know how much he hates flying, hates the US and his gout's probably playing him up.

He scolds the attendants fussing around him as he settles his large frame into the armchair and disappears out of view. There's one last glimpse of his arm as he raises it to remove two glasses of champagne from a passing attendant's tray.

With only two weeks to his premiere, he's under pressure to do the obligatory schmoozing and record enough TV interviews to create the required buzz. Not that he needs another blockbuster success.

After twenty-two years of producing movies, I'm sure the novelty of these trips has long worn off and they're now a chore he despises.

Safe in the confines of the front cabin, he kicks off his shoes and removes his jacket and wig. He'd given the paparazzi the Mickey Roughton they wanted, and he could now spend the next eleven hours at peace, with his gout.

Four hours into the flight, I've watched two movies and devoured something called Beef Burgundy, which according to the menu is 'A traditional French recipe of chunky lean beef in a rich red wine and red onion sauce with root vegetables and mustard mash' but would be better described as lukewarm lumps of chewy gristle and hot lumps of mashed potato. Whatever it is, it repeats on me.

I've listened to the woman on my left's life story, although I recall none of it, other than something about a surprise fortieth birthday for her son in San Francisco. I can see why he's moved halfway across the world from her.

From my position beside the wing, the drone of the engines is hypnotic and makes me sleepy but I fight to stay awake.

As I puff up my inflatable neck cushion, I notice someone hobbling along the aisle towards me. As he makes his way down, everyone's head turns to follow him.

Despite the awkwardness of his walk and his hair being at an unusual angle, I instantly recognise him.

"Mickey?"

He catches my eye and his grimace turns to a smile.

"Barry! What are you...how are you?"

Everyone's wondering how someone in the poverty cabin can possibly know this 'A' lister. He's so dumbfounded to see me, he's not quite sure what to ask first.

"Great to see you" he says. "Where are you going? Are you still driving? Why haven't you been in touch?"

I'm still preparing my answer to his first question but he keeps firing away.

"Hey, come up front and have a drink with me. Gotta keep walking, fucking gout's killing me".

I jump up and follow him to the back of the plane, past the row of toilets and then up the other aisle. As we go through the curtain at the front, it widens enough for me to walk next to him.

An attendant approaches, presumably to tell Mickey no poor people are allowed up front, but he gestures a wave with his hand and they ignore me.

The bar's got five stools around it, four of which are occupied by Mickey's crew. There's no one else in the front cabin. He's obviously booked the whole lot for himself.

Another hand gesture from him and they scatter.

We sit and chat. It's always good to see Mickey. I haven't seen him since he left to start work on his film a couple of years ago, but he doesn't know how hard I've worked to track his movements to ensure I bumped into him today.

Talking to Mickey's easy. He and I used to spend hours chatting. We both hated our wives, we both had sons the same age who were little bastards, and we both shared a humour I'd not found before or since.

The two years I'd spent assigned as his driver were the happiest of my sad driving career.

I'm grateful he came to the back of the plane, but disappointed he waited so long to do so, nevertheless, the remaining seven hours of the flight slip by.

We talk about everything from his new movie to Project Ronald, whilst we eat, drink, snack and laugh. There's a brief interlude whilst Mickey tries it on with the flight attendant he'd been so rude to earlier, which I assume to be bravado. Everyone knows Mickey pays for it.

Mickey returns his attention to me and after hearing about his latest movie *"Silicon Robots "*, I go into the latest on Project Ronald and he loves it.

We laugh about my past disasters, which I think he finds somewhat funnier than I do, then we chat about my master plan and how, with his help, it can be improved upon. We then spend a short time arguing over whose wife is the most vile. It's a close call, but because I'm divorcing and he isn't, I try to make him feel better by letting him win.

Other than Katie, Mickey's the only person I've opened up to. Even though he now knows every last detail, I trust him enough not to ask him to sign a Non-Disclosure Agreement. I don't consider there to be any risk. Mickey's the richest man I've ever met and he certainly doesn't need to pinch an idea to make him richer.

Ridiculous as it sounds, I feel he's one of my true friends, but I could never consider asking him for financial help for fear it would ruin our relationship.

I assume he feels the same, because he's never offered me anything.

It's just another trait we both share.

We're two creative geniuses, just in different fields. He wants nothing from me other than the opportunity to acquire the film rights to my life – once I've completed my master plan. I know he means it so I insist we agree on the amount now.

I have no idea how to value film rights.

The first figure suggested is five million, countered by zero. By the time we've batted back and forth, we settle on a measly one hundred thousand pounds, which I'm not happy about, but agree the deal, especially as he's now an intrinsic part of the plan.

He begs me to keep him updated and insists I return to San Jose in two weeks to see his movie premiere for myself, all at his expense. I accept, and then wonder if I should have declined gracefully and asked if there was perhaps a cash alternative.

I stay upfront for the landing, and only leave his company when he's ushered off to be whisked through the VIP arrivals area, while I go to join the herds.

Although I already have his mobile number, he insists I take it again, and tells me to contact him if there's anything I need before he returns to London on Wednesday. I know he's genuine. As he straightens his hairpiece, he winks and reminds me about the film rights.

CHAPTER 5

The train from the airport to the San Jose Self-Starter Inn takes four changes and nearly three hours, including thirty-minutes of gorging over a stack of eggs, pancakes and sausages in the Denny's behind the hotel.

It's hot and sticky, and I'm tired. I should be in a foul mood, but I've never felt more excited and alive – if slightly light-headed and a little dazed. I'm also bloated which is presumably eight pancakes fighting with the gristle I ate on the plane.

The entrance to the Self-Starter Inn is more of a hallway than lobby area. There's a small desk with a TV perched on it, and a stool next to it on which is perched a scruffy girl. She has several tattoos, each of a different name and date.

The check-in process feels more like a credit check, and culminates in the handing over of a bronze key dangling from a tennis ball with the room number written in black marker.

My room's basic and looks like the type they use in old movies in which they discover a murdered body. It smells like there's possibly still one here. There are holes punched in one wall, but as I sit on the bed checking the signal on my phone, I'm grateful they spent their budget on the WiFi rather than plastering.

Amongst the newly arrived emails, I see one from Katie.

> By the time you read this, I'll be out of contact, but I just want you to know it's the first anniversary today. That means we've got 6 months to go!
>
> Katie

I read it twice. And smile twice. In six months the fireworks start. My mind wanders into holding a bank statement six months from now. How will all the zeros fit on the page? There's barely enough room for the brackets and the minus figures on my current statement. Perhaps they have wider statements for multi-millionaires. It's not something I need to worry about today but I'll Google it later anyway.

I've got the daily update from *SiliconValleyNews* reminding me the Oat House Pitch & Present is tomorrow, and two more emails - each from a different set of lawyers – and each chasing me for a different amount of money.

The first is from 'accounts' at Squiffy Myers telling me my indebtedness to them is nearly thirty thousand pounds which they tell me is 'considerable' in both its size and the length of time it's been overdue. They make it sound like quite an achievement, before threatening me that I have 72 hours in which to settle it after which they're going to pass details to their collection department. They've also kindly attached another invoice for £2750 and an updated statement.

I could do without this pressure right now. I desperately need their support and I'm frustrated the partner I'm dealing with isn't holding them off for me as I was promised.

I have nothing to tell them that they don't already know - so I delete the mail.

The other lawyer who's on my case is Lesley Becky from Enfield Family Law and handling my divorce. She too has sent me a bill and she too has asked me to settle it.

If the choice is giving money to her or Marie, I'm delighted to get her invoice. If I had any money, she could have it, with my love.

I fire off a quick reply:-

"Hi Lesley. Thanks for the email. Can you let me know if Marie's agreed to my final terms yet?

As you know, I can't settle this bill just yet but I'm expecting funds to come in soon.

Best

Barry"

Lesley will probably take 'expecting funds' to mean I've got a pay-cheque coming in shortly. It's actually millions. 'Soon', is six months or so.

I open my case in an attempt to prepare for my next four days.

There are four pairs of underpants, two pairs of socks and three shirts. The other personal effects are a toothbrush and a disposable razor. No toothpaste, no foam. I'll get those locally. From the way my shirt's stuck to my skin, I decide to add antiperspirant to the list.

The rest of the space is taken up with my laptop, fifty presentations – each a printout of a PowerPoint presentation - and fifty Non-Disclosure Agreements, each of which I'm hoping to take home signed.

There's also my trusted notepad in which I intend to list everyone who'll be contributing to my fortune.

I walk into the bathroom, which has no bath. It too is straight out of a movie. The smell of mildew is pungent. Everything's yellow, interrupted only by the greyish green stains. As I pull open the flimsy stinking shower curtain and pull the lever, a few drops of water trickle out. As I splatter them over my face, I vow to return here in a few months and have this room sealed in posterity as a shrine to where Barry Goodman stayed, just before he became famous.

By the time I've washed myself as best I can, a wave of exhaustion washes over me. I realise although it's gone 10pm here, my body clock thinks it's 6am. Tomorrow's a big day – possibly the biggest in my life. I pull back a nylon sheet and find sleep in an instant.

CHAPTER 6

As Marie awoke, it took her a few seconds to get her bearings. She was in unfamiliar surroundings until the screaming jets of a nearby aircraft reminded her she was near the airport.

She took another couple of seconds to consider who might be lying next to her. On her scale of hope, Richard Gere was the best. In her worst, it was Barry.

She stretched her arm to the side and realised it was actually no one, but the warmth of the mattress suggested it was a freshly vacated space.

She looked around the room. The flimsy curtains were drawn, but were ineffective against the bright sun just as the windows were against the sound of the departing aircraft.

She sat up and noticed the empty wine glasses on the table and remnants of her clothing strewn next to it.

She felt her head lower with the shame inside her.

This wasn't the love and attention she was hoping for. The only long-term in this relationship was the long-term car park onto which the hotel window looked out.

MiserableSpouses wasn't panning out as she'd hoped. She felt the last drop of self-respect she had, draining from her.

From the sound of the shower, she knew Greg or Gregory - or whatever his name was - was still here, and washing himself to remove any trace of her smell before he returned to his wife.

Greg was young. At only twenty-nine, he was very young to be on a dating site for married people. Most were in their mid-thirties before they were so disillusioned, but Greg was fast and furious in everything from his job as a city banker to his disenchantment with marriage – and not least of all his action in bed.

With Barry several thousand miles away, a stay-over was easy for Marie, after all she and Barry lived almost separate lives.

For Greg, a stay over was easy because his wife had come to accept the occasional nights he had to spend in his office talking to his Far Eastern clients.

She had no idea they lived mostly in Bracknell.

As he came out of the bathroom, he looked dressed and ready to go, when he noticed Marie awake.

"Mary, you are the sexiest minx I know" he said with a cheeky smile and a wink.

"It's Marie" she snapped. She really wasn't in the mood for this. She felt cheap, sleezy, slightly hung-over and a little sore.

Seeing him dressed and obviously eager to leave, she regretted being taken in by Greg's smooth-talk, handsome looks, and the box of wine he just happened to have in the boot of his car.

She discounted the possibility of Greg turning in to her dream relationship.

"Gotta go. I'll text you" he said with another wink, as he walked out the door with his jacket over his shoulder and a half used packet of condoms in his pocket.

Marie sat up. None of this would have been necessary if Barry had been the man he was supposed to be, or as successful as he'd promised her he'd be when they'd met twenty-five years ago.

The hopes and dreams they'd shared as newlyweds were now a distant flat memory, like a bottle of champagne after a quarter of a century without a cork.

Her son, the most important thing in her life, was no longer there to console her. She felt she'd lost him over a year ago to Jenna, his girlfriend in Nottingham with whom he now lived.

Now wasn't the time to mope. She needed to stay positive and strong for no other reason than to make sure she could fight Barry for what little he had. She threw back the bed sheets and made her way to the bathroom, where the towels were strewn over the floor and the mirror was steamed-up. She drew a sad face in the condensation.

"He's still out there" she whispered to herself, as she decided to give the man of her dreams another opportunity to find her on the dating site.

CHAPTER 7

Luke was up and out early again, ever hopeful that today would be the day he'd find his big opportunity. Uber driving was proving to be more tiring, less rewarding – and thanks to the aggressive cyclists – more of a danger than he'd imagined.

What started as a temporary fix to pay his rent was proving to be not so temporary, and not such a fix. He was still two months behind on it.

All he needed was someone to recognise his worth and give him the break he deserved. He knew it was just a matter of time, but hoped it would be sooner rather than later.

By noon, he'd had two airport runs, sandwiched between several local trips.

As always, he'd tried hard to engage in conversation with them all, and as always, no one had shown any interest in him.

He'd just picked his latest passenger from Cryptexion, the chip producer, and was ferrying him to the Santana Row Shopping Mall.

As shopping malls went, Santana Row topped them all. The shops were high-end and from the appearance of his passenger, Luke knew this man was the exact audience they catered for.

Luke scanned through his best opening lines and went for the one he felt was most appropriate.

"You're probably wondering how a guy like me's driving for Uber."

He looked in his rear-view mirror. His passenger showed no signs of wondering about anything; his eyes fixed firmly on his phone.

"Not really" he replied, without looking up.

"Well I'll tell you why" Luke continued, "You've probably noticed, I dress very similar to you..." his passenger hadn't. "Well, I used to run a couple of businesses. Big businesses. And I thought I'd retire to California and find my next venture..."

Nothing from the back

"...but I can't sit and do nothing, and what better way to meet people than drive them around?"

Still nothing. His passenger had yet to get in an Uber in the Valley without hearing a similar speech.

"So tell me, what is it you do?"

The passenger was caught off-guard. It wasn't a statement, but a question, and he felt obliged to answer.

"I run Cryptexion" he replied, still looking at his phone.

"Off to buy anything special?" Luke asked.

"Eh?"

"I mean at the mall. What are you shopping for?" He asked.

His passenger regretted engaging and now realised he'd have to continue.

He sighed "Window shopping for a pool party on the weekend" he said in a single monotonous tone, which sounded more like a thought spoken aloud.

"That's good. I'm having my own this weekend" said Luke, who had no pool and no friends to invite. "A guy like you's probably always on the lookout for talent and someone who can head up a division or bring something to market. I'll give you my card."

Luke leant over and opened his glove box, causing the car to swerve violently, narrowly missing a cyclist on his right. His passenger, horrified, spun to look behind, in time to see the bike wobble several times before the cyclist regained control. He couldn't quite make out what he was shouting, but whatever it was, he totally agreed with him.

Luke paid no attention as he shuffled through a stack of business cards before selecting one and turning his whole torso around to hand it to his passenger, taking his eyes off the road, and his hands off the wheel.

The passenger grabbed it quickly, and Luke returned to facing the front.

As he scanned the card, he was thankful they were almost at their destination.

'Luke Palatino. Divisional Head & Market Opener Extraordinaire.'

He didn't bother reading the contact details. He would never need them, and besides he had a dozen similar cards thrust on him almost daily.

He feigned interest before putting it in his pocket and as he left the taxi, grateful to be alive, he told Luke he'd be in touch if anything arose.

He walked away from the drop-point, and he put the card in a nearby bin.

Luke ranked his passenger four stars on his Uber App, and as he went to drive off, looked up, noticing the other shoppers milling around. Many of them were well-dressed executives, just like him. This was clearly a mecca for keyboard kings – exactly the kind of people he needed to mix with to find an opportunity.

These weren't the dreamers he'd been used to meeting. Amongst them he could see successful techies too, easily identified as their hoodies had expensive labels and gaping rips instead of the perfectly intact discounted hoodies he saw elsewhere.

He considered – apart from his lack of money - he too wouldn't look out of place wondering around Santana Row, and perhaps this was a better place to network than the low-grade geek-infested places he'd been used to. It also smelled nicer and most importantly it wasn't on his list of places he had to avoid.

Santana Row was unlike any other shopping mall with the noticeable difference that very little money actually changed hands there. Being in Silicon Valley, many of it's visitors lacked the social skills to interact with others, so the eclectic mix of upscale retailers were used as nothing more than showrooms, with customers preferring to place their orders online.

It mattered little to them that the orders they placed on their phones and tablets whilst sitting in the parking lot, were often with the very retailers they'd just left, and often for the very merchandise they could have just walked away with. This was the techie heartland so the thought of transacting without the conduit of a website or app was something only their parents generation did.

Unfortunately, the phone reception around Santana Row was weak. Many of those who placed their order online from the parking lot would give up in frustration and drive off in search of a stronger signal.

Luke turned his Uber App to 'unavailable' and pulled into the parking lot, finding a bay just as a Tesla pulled out of it. The driver looked young, bearded and frustrated. He rushed back to where he'd just dropped his passenger, and Luke watched as he disappeared into a small shop on the edge of the mall, called Octajour, which proudly described itself as 'purveyor of exclusive beachwear'.

Having considered how it would look if he suddenly appeared standing next to the very person he'd just dropped off, he decided not to follow. Instead, he decided to explore the Mall, networking with his targets in the streets.

After spending twenty minutes or so wandering round, Luke came to the conclusion he needed to focus on a single outlet. Bumping into someone in a store was acceptable. Bumping into someone in a vast outdoor space was clumsy and bordering on weird.

Of all the shops to visit, Octajour was perfect, especially as the pool-party season was just starting, and any keyboard-king would only be seen in their brand of shorts.

Octajour swimming shorts were neither high fashion nor better quality than any others but they were bright in colour and had the all-important Octajour label on the back, front and side to ensure everyone knew the wearer was able to pay $389 for them.

Along with the shorts, the price included a mesh bag, an Octajour booklet and a bucket load of kudos.

Before entering, he perused the window, and was struck by the display of swimming shorts on the mannequins. He noticed the teeny-tiny kiddy shorts in exactly the same design as full-grown versions displayed next to them.

It bewildered him why any father would buy his son matching shorts, especially for $389, and looked around the mall to see if perhaps there were any dads holding hands with young kids, wearing matching chinos and jackets.

Once inside the store, Luke was overwhelmed by the array of fluorescent colours and patterns. He wondered how many customers left with a headache or the onset of a migraine.

He purveyed the merchandise, curious to know how they warranted their vast price. Perhaps they were lighter, quicker to dry and had improved buoyancy. It certainly wasn't because they looked better - because they clearly didn't.

Frankly, whatever qualities they may have had were wasted as many Octajour shorts never actually got wet. Their owners proudly wore them to parade around - rather than in - their Olympic-sized pools, built only because their architect had to fill their four-acre garden with something other than tennis courts. No one told them techies don't swim, and were unlikely to until someone developed a floating phone or inflatable laptop.

He blinked twice to adjust to the harsh brightness and his eyes settled on the salesgirl. He couldn't help but notice how gorgeous she was.

CHAPTER 8

Marie sat in front of the screen. She'd been on her own for less than 24 hours during which she'd had twenty-eight messages and a disastrous meeting with someone she hoped never to hear from again.

With Barry away, she noticed the knot in her stomach had eased.

She wondered how she would fill the four days she'd taken off from work with no regard to the thirty or so women she'd left bereft of a nail manicure, and no doubt distraught. Some of them would go elsewhere, but most of them would cancel their social arrangements until Marie's service had been fully resumed.

She took a deep breath and logged back into the dating site. She trawled the list of profiles within twenty miles in the hope MrPerfect would be amongst them. Instead, she found BigCock, MuffMuncher and TheCumDoctor. Standing out in the list of profanities was the relatively Makemehappy69. He sounded far less of a player. He described himself as handsome, solvent and looking to take his woman somewhere special.

She crafted her message to him with care and humour, hoping to show herself to be both intelligent and great company.

She included details of how she loved to travel, finishing with an invitation for him to tell her where he'd like them to spend their first date.

She was disappointed to see the reply arrive just a few seconds later.

"A Travelodge ;-)"

She rolled her eyes, deleted the message and blocked his profile.

Just then, an alert popped up at the bottom of screen. It was an email from Atkins & Atkins, the good Samaritans in the form of highly paid divorce lawyers, who would help rid her of Barry.

Anything that helped propel the case quicker was gratefully welcomed so responding to Atkins & Atkins was always top priority. As usual, the email had a bill attached, and a request for payment.

With every payment she made them, she felt a sense of uplift.

The email detailed Barry's latest offer, being for Marie to take half his assets on the basis she had no further share of any businesses or ideas he had - either in the past or future.

Seeing as the man was a buffoon who, in a quarter of a century of marriage, had gone through dozens of ideas, all of them generating nothing but debts, any share of any business was worthless.

He had as much ability in bringing an idea to life as he did his own grandmother, and a knack of thinking of an idea at the point just prior to someone else launching it.

He was less like a good businessman and more like a bad clairvoyant.

The only asset they had was their house, and as she consistently earned more than he did, she had every intention of taking more than half of its value.

Nevertheless, he always considered his ideas to be worth a fortune, and if she really wanted to punish him, she would insist on having half of them going forward. The only value in them was the pain she could inflict on him by holding on to them – which made them priceless.

There was no decision to be made.

> Hi Derek. Tell him I wont settle for less than 80% of the house AND I still want ½ of all his ventures. I don't think they'll ever come to anything but I know it will piss him off.
>
> I'll settle the invoice in a couple of weeks.
>
> Thanks x

She returned her attention to *MiserableSpouses* to find within the few short minutes she'd spent elsewhere, another seven virtual kisses, winks and virtual flowers had arrived.

CHAPTER 9

Luke had spent almost an hour at the Octajour store, touching and groping a variety of shorts whilst his eyes flit back and forth between the door to see who came in and the girl behind the counter. She really was gorgeous.

Since his arrival, no one else had entered the store. He wondered if it was perhaps too early for keyboard kings to be out, and that his passenger had been a fluke. He also wondered if the sales-girl was single. Most of all he wondered if she had any headache tablets.

Conscious he looked like some sort of shoplifter - or pervert, he decided it might be a good time to leave. He would return later in the hope there would be more people around.

As he walked past the toweling bathrobes, he wondered what possible excuse he could have to loiter around again tomorrow, when suddenly he had a brainwave.

He picked up another pair of shorts and checked the price tag. $389. If he bought them now and returned them within the next couple of days, both transactions would cancel each other out on his credit card, provided of course, he had enough available on his pre-paid credit.

That would not only give him a valid reason to return, but also demonstrate to the gorgeous girl behind the counter that he was both successful and shared an appreciation for $389 swimming shorts.

Next time he'd come back later in the day and no doubt bump into a keyboard king, and hopefully have the opportunity to talk to her.

He placed the fluorescent shorts on the counter and removed his wallet from his back pocket.

"Nice choice Sir. They're my favourites" said Janice as she brushed his hand with hers. "Will you be paying by cash or card?" she asked, sounding as cute as she looked; her blue eyes dazzling.

Luke, uncharacteristically lost for words, removed his Mastercard from his wallet and smiled as he gave it to her.

"Oh. I see these are triple-x sir, I'm guessing you're more of a large" she said, standing back and eyeing Luke's waist, whilst holding the shorts up. They were clearly large enough for someone twice his size.

Luke felt an idiot. He couldn't believe he hadn't even bothered picking a pair that were credible.

"They're for a friend. A gift. I'm not gay ... he's my cousin" he spewed.

"Aww, that's ok" she said "feel free to return them if they're wrong" she continued as she placed the shorts in a laminated carrier, and popped in a mesh bag and booklet before sealing the top and sticking a bow on it.

Grateful that his card wasn't declined, Luke smiled and left the store.

He'd be back tomorrow, hopefully with more success, and certainly with sunglasses to avoid another headache.

CHAPTER 10

I finally get up at 5:10am. I woke every couple of hours through the night, each time thinking it was morning, and each time depressed to find it wasn't. I considered getting up at 1am, which was 9am London time.

I no longer notice the smell in the room, but that's probably because I'm desensitised to it, and worse, I probably now smell the same.

I'm washed and dressed in a few minutes, and I've managed to brush my teeth with just water. I haven't bothered to shave as I've yet to see anyone around here that does.

I switch the TV on and wait for the fat rounded screen to burst into life. As with everything old, it takes an age. I'm just grateful it's in colour.

As I flick through the channels, I find only ad breaks. Finally, I'm on an actual programme. It's *Fox News.*

They're at San Francisco Airport showing the arrival of Mickey Roughton yesterday.

I would have been somewhere waiting in line for passport entry when this was being filmed. They would have had to keep the cameras rolling another hour and a half to see me coming through, without the entourage, or the sunglasses – but with an umbrella.

The interviewer's talking directly to the camera as he rattles out the long list of hit movies that Mickey's produced. I'm mesmerized by his bright white teeth.

As the camera pans out, we see he's in a makeshift pop-up studio at the airport, with Mickey seated next to him. He starts on his long list of inane questions.

"So why are you here Mickey?"

Mickey starts spouting what I know to be a long list of bullshit as he tells Chuck Jenkins how delighted he is to be in one of his favourite cities in the world, and how he couldn't wait to visit.

Not knowing where to stop, he even tells Chuck how he's considered moving here because he finds it so difficult to leave.

Chuck's lapping it up, nodding in between sentences and occasionally averting his gaze to the camera and flashing his teeth.

Mickey's unstoppable.

"This place and the wonderful, warm people here are the inspiration behind my latest movie, '*Silicon Robots*'.

He tells us how he's here to record countless interviews to promote it, and possibly look for a beach house to buy before the launch in two weeks.

Chuck's either taking no notice or being too polite to point out there's no beach in San Jose.

"It would be an injustice to premiere it anywhere else in the world, which is why I insisted we launch the film where it's set, in San Jose"

As he's shuttled off, the anchor turns to camera to tell us to look out for an exclusive interview with Mickey Roughton and the films lead star Boogie Trent being broadcast next week. I know how much Mickey hates Boogie.

The interview comes to a close as Chuck tells Mickey how much he admires him, and then gives us a final flash of his teeth before handing back to the studio. As he does so, the camera pans to follow Mickey as he leaves his chair and moves to another seat just yards away for another interview, with a female equivalent of Chuck. She too has bright teeth, a fake tan – and is no doubt telling her viewers how exclusive this interview is.

Back in the studio, the anchor thanks Chuck as though they're best mates, and with all the excitement he can muster, he continues to spout about the upcoming premier. It's at the Hackworth IMAX in San Jose, and all the great and the good of the online world will be there by special invite. There follows a brief clip where Boogie Trent's in a VW campervan being chased by an Aston Martin which can't seem to catch it. There's gunshots and explosions in the background but my mind's elsewhere so I turn the TV off. I'm too excited thinking about how the premier will change my life.

With nothing else to do, I return to the yellow bathroom to splash some water under my armpits. I dry my hands on my hair as I pat it down before heading out the door and leave for the first venue on my list. It's not yet 5:30am.

At 5:32am I return to collect my notepad and a pile of Non-Disclosure Agreements.

Not surprisingly, the famed Starbucks is totally empty when I arrive at 5:40am. It's already been open over an hour, long enough to fill the air with the smell of fresh coffee. I order a croissant and an Americano with an extra-shot although my body's telling me it's time for a sandwich and soup.

I'm hoping that all I've read about this place is right. It's where techies come to swap big ideas and argue over coding.

I'm expecting to see groups of bearded geeks, fired up with coffee, arguing over which language is the best to write code; SQL, ruby-on-rails or good old-fashioned PHP.

I'm hoping the one thing they'll all agree upon is that my idea's the future of communications.

I need as many of them as possible to take my idea, run with it, and most importantly, get it funded, managed and launched.

Unfortunately, the only people here at this time are the two staff and me.

I still feel a little light-headed and I'm questioning why I've bothered bringing five NDAs. I may have been a little over-ambitious. I also realise I've forgotten to bring my umbrella, for which I'm thankful.

I talk with "Lamona" assuming she's wearing her own name-badge.

"Hello Lamona, what time's it get busy here?" I say trying to sound formal and British.

"Say what?"

She had no problem understanding my order for coffee and croissant, but now she's looking at me like I'm talking rubbish.

"I'm wondering what time folk turn up" I said, giving in to local colloquialisms.

"We get kinda busy nearer seven. You talk funny. Where's you from?"

"London."

"Does everyone talk so funny and look so grey there?"

I don't reply so she thinks I have trouble understanding her.

"Honey" she says, this time slowly – "The kids come in around ten am. That's when we get kinda busy."

Shit. I'd assumed they'd be in here earlier. Perhaps they're up late coding and getting pissed and stoned. Perhaps they're up all night and this is the last stop before they go to sleep. Either way, I've got to hang around for over four hours.

I sit and nurse my croissant and coffee whilst I read yesterday's *Mercury News*. It's been well thumbed and missing several pages, but the lead story's about Mickey Roughton's impending visit to the valley and his movie *'Silicon Robots'*. It goes on to say they're adding an additional 300 seats to bring the capacity at the Hackworth IMAX to 600 guests. They're also adding marquees and hospitality tents around it, but it's still going to be one hell of a squeeze in there.

Because of all the celebs likely to be there, both the pre-show and post-show will be broadcast live on TV. I wonder whether viewers will see me in the background.

My attention returns to the coffee shop as the door bursts open and a small huddle of bearded looking youths in hoodies march in. They've all got headphones on and they're all looking down at their phones. Quite how they're navigating themselves is a mystery. Seeing as it's a little after 6am, this group look like they're from the not-yet-been-to-bed camp.

In what looks like a well-rehearsed, highly choreographed movement, they approach the counter, arriving seemingly in height order. There's no need for dialogue with Lamona. They've ordered online.

One by one, they point their phone at the terminal by the register as they pay for their beverage.

I wait as they wait, and when four mugs are placed on the counter, I follow them to where they sit.

Round one. I'm on. I check my watch. It's another timestamp I'll need to remember when I come to pen my autobiography.

"Hey guys" I say, dispensing with the whole exaggerated British accent.

No response. Even if they can't hear me, I was hoping they might have noticed someone in their peripheral vision. They're in a frenzy as they each rip a multitude of sugar sachets open, filling their mugs with the contents, three at a time.

I move position to block some of the light coming in from the window and try again.

"Guys!"

All four look up.

"Barry Goodman. Good to meet you" I say, extending my hand.

"Hey dude!" say's one, far too loudly, suggesting he's still not hearing me.

I gesture for them to remove their headphones, knowing this might look more confrontational than I intend.

They take their headphones off in unison. I can hear it's not music they're listening to, it's a podcast, and they're all listening to the same one.

"Hey man. Get yourself a coffee" says one of them to me as he takes my hand and places a screwed up dollar bill into it.

"No no ... I'm not a whino" I say, "I'm Barry. From London."

He takes his dollar back and looks at me puzzled.

I continue. "I've got a project that may interest you."

"Thanks Dude but we're cool" the spokesman said, about to return to his headphones.

"It won't take long, and it could change your life" I say, as I find myself repeating an advert on TV that hooked me into wasting hours of my life trying to reclaim PPI insurance I'd never had – even though I had enough bloody loans.
It works, and the spokesman shrugs, shakes his head and signals for the others to humour me.

I spend the next fifteen minutes fighting a battle to keep their attention from their phones as I explain why I've come to San Jose and how I'm looking for coders to help create the software needed to bring the revolution I have in communications.
To ensure I'm not wasting my time, I pre-qualify them by checking their credentials and what it is they actually do.
I don't want to waste time pitching to what could be a barbershop quartet, although looking at them, I know it's unlikely.
I learn the four of them are the lead coders in a team of 40, and that they work for an outfit called Linkosys, a software house that produces gambling software. It's not really something my idea has synergy with, but they're coders, they're geeky and they're better connected than me.
It's my first pitch so I'm a little clumsy. I know I'll get fluent with time.
I explain the need for them to sign a Non-Disclosure Agreement before I can divulge the idea, so I can prove it's mine if they try to steal it.
"Sure Dude" he replies, with seemingly little understanding of what I'm talking about, but I'm so grateful to be making headway, I don't bother explaining it again.
I produce two stapled pages of legalese jargon which says something along the lines that project's called Ronald, I'm the originator, they're the recipient, and lots of bits in between, most of which, I'm not sure I understand. Their eyes glaze over. A couple of them return their attention to their phones.

To bring them back to Project Ronald, I knock a coffee over, making it look like a clumsy accident. They all grab their phones to protect them from the growing pool of sticky steamy liquid, which I dab at with a pack of napkins from the next table. I'd lifted my paperwork to avoid the spillage, and they don't seem the slightest bit suspicious.
I need to get it signed and move on as quickly as possible. I've learned from experience that NDAs are worthless if they can prove they've already had the idea before I've told them, but these guys don't seem sharp enough to realise they may have an out. I doubt they can remember what they were doing ten minutes ago, let

alone their ability to convince a court they'd been working on a project like mine months before they signed my paperwork.

Nevertheless, I stress the need for them to let me know within a month if they've been working on something similar.

I've got confidence in my lawyers and for the amount I've paid them, I expect this to be bulletproof.

At the foot of page two are two boxes, one for the Originator to sign – which I assume to me- and one for the Recipient. There's also a dotted line by each for the date.

On the original the lawyers emailed to me, there was also a box for a witness to sign, but I deleted it before printing them off as I didn't see the necessity for it, and besides it would have run onto three pages.

I go back to the counter to borrow a pen as none of us have one. I've forgotten mine and they haven't used one since high school. We scribble our names and dates. Although there are four of them, I allow them all to sign the same document so I don't exhaust my supply too quickly. I suspect NDAs are two-a-penny in Silicon Valley, and the spokesman doesn't even bother reading it before signaling for everyone to sign on the dotted line.

I'm conscious not to tell them all the facts nor all the applications; after all, I don't want to ruin my masterplan.

I move onto the business of telling them what my idea actually is. I open my laptop and talk them through the PowerPoint, asking them to excuse the images as this is only the first draft. I don't tell them this is the best I could do and it's taken me almost a month to get it to even this level.

One of them points and laughs at the yellow starbust on page one. It hurts a little as I'd always considered this to be the highlight.

Slowly, I watch the reaction of the pack as they go from mild disinterest to full engagement.

By the end of it, they're cooing and whistling.

They love it.

"Dude, that's cool. I'd use it!"

"I'd love to code that" says another.

They turn to each other.

"Ruby or PHP?"

"Gotta be Ruby."

"No man. PHP."

They're so enthused, the whole mood lightens and we progress to an introduction.

As they go round the table, they tell me their names.

I note them all in my pad.

Jim, Josh, Jake, Jez.

They go on to tell me they've been looking for something to replace their core focus of gambling to make their parents proud, and they're in no doubt my project is it. They also can't wait to show it to their funder too, who in their own words "will throw shit loads of cash at it".

It's inappropriate to hug them, but that's exactly what I want to do.

As we say our goodbyes, I extend my hand, but they seem to have little idea what to do with it. For an awkward moment, Jim lets it hang there before slapping his against it. It's a sort of horizontal high-five, which is repeated with each of the others.

Lamona was right. The place slowly filled with geeks, and the aroma of fresh coffee was soon clouded by the odour of stale beer, pot and sweat.

By the time I leave Starbucks, it's 10:55 and I'm frazzled.

I've had five coffees, the last two of which were decaffeinated. As I make my fourth trip to the toilet, I recap how this morning's gone so far.

I've got all five Non-Disclosures signed; twelve email addresses and Facebook pages scribbled in my notepad, and a warm glowing feeling. All of them loved it, all of them want to work with me to bring my idea to life, and none of them have considered in order to progress, it might be necessary to have my contact details - which I've given to none of them.

It's also not on my presentation, which I've given each group a copy of.

I notice the time and realise I've spent far too long here. The caffeine's fueling a sense of panic as I wonder if I'm going to get to my second venue in time.

The Oat House Pitch & Present is the main event for me and it starts in five minutes.

I've still got to get back to the Self-Starter Inn to re-load my Non-Disclosures and printouts of my presentation.

I've not really got the time, but I can't help briefly checking my emails.

Lesley at Enfield Family Law informs me Marie wants 80% of the house equity. She also wants half of all my ideas.

Shit. I'm part way through my master plan and if I don't get her to agree to another deal, I'm going to have to give her half of everything.

I'll have to think of another way.

CHAPTER 11

Marie had spent much of the last day swapping messages with Goodtolove.
His profile was honest and intelligent, peppered with poetry. By the time she'd logged off, the meeting had been arranged. Unfortunately, it had not gone well.
The photo he'd sent her was apparently from a time when he was younger, more handsome, with considerably more hair on his head – and presumably less on his back.
The flat in the city was actually his office in Stepney, and 'a date' was not the way she'd care to remember it.
From start to finish she'd been with him for fifty minutes which included 7 minutes of fumbling sex – during which his shirt and socks stayed on - and 20 minutes of him telling her about how much he loved his wife, and how she wouldn't 'put out' anymore, but she'd divorce him if she ever caught him having an affair.
Marie considered his wife sounded like she might be better company than him.
In the remaining time he took several calls, and even checked his emails - presumably some of which were from other meets he'd lined up on *miserableSpouses*.
Within minutes of meeting, Marie knew this wasn't a relationship with a destination.
Once again, Marie left disappointed. She was disappointed with Goodtolove, disappointed with herself and mostly disappointed with Barry. As with everything that hadn't gone right in her life, it was all his fault.

As she sat on the tube returning to the suburbs, she wondered how her life had come to the sad sorry state it was in, and how different it should have turned out.
At nineteen, her life had been full of promise. She was about to finish college where she'd been an outstanding fashion student, had a fantastic social life, and received no shortage of approaches from eligible men.
And then Barry had shown up.
Barry had no real qualifications and appeared to have no hope.
Even then he was over-weight and unappealing, but he did have his own Ford Cortina (with stereo cassette player) - and a bucket-load of ambition. She was unaware of his pungent aroma, which he'd masked by his over-bearing use of Brut aftershave.
Marie had pitied him enough to ignore the sniggering from her friends and the warning from her parents, and had accepted his invitation to go out with him.

The first date was disastrous. He was boring, self-absorbed and took food from her plate after he'd finished his own. Despite his pathetic dreams of one day being rich, he had no idea how he was going to achieve it, or even what line of work he hoped to have.

The evening went from bad to worse. Barry had lost his wallet, had his car towed away and chipped his tooth on a popcorn kernel.

Marie had paid for the bus fare home and hoped that would be the last time she'd have to spend time with him.

The following day, after reflecting on the evening, a renewed sense of pity overwhelmed her and when he called to see her again, she found it hard to refuse him. She told her friends it was only so she could collect the coat she'd left in the back of his car before it had been towed.

The next date, she sat opposite him appalled by his table manners, and watched as he splashed curry over his shirt. She'd sat back in her seat when he'd spoken so as not to be spat upon.

She wondered if someone like Barry could ever find himself a wife.

As each date went by, her pity grew – and the more it grew, the more she let Barry do to her.

Barry had never had a proper girlfriend before. Certainly not for more than one date, and certainly not one that returned his calls.

It was just a matter of weeks between their first date and his marriage proposal , which of course she declined.

The thought of marrying him made her shiver, but she didn't mind spending time in bed with him, certainly until she could find a boyfriend she wanted to be with.

When the pregnancy test came back positive she was sick every day for two months.

She'd compromised when she dated him, and now she was compromising in marriage. She wouldn't compromise in divorce.

As the tube trundled home, Marie decided on two points of action.

She would put off meeting someone until she was properly divorced and she would ensure Barry suffered as much as possible until then. That would mean taking all the money in the house, leaving him with all the debts, and most of all taking half of every idea he had. She knew that would be worth the least – but hurt him the most.

She vowed to delete her profile as soon as she got home.

CHAPTER 12

It's 11:25am when I arrive at The Oat House Meeting Hall.

I'm pissed that I'm late, and I'm cursing the idiot of a cab driver who spoke no English and couldn't find it. I've managed to find the only driver in Silicon Valley that doesn't use Waze.

Now we're here, I realise we've driven past it at least three times. I could have been here ten minutes ago - and for $15 less.

It's nothing like I expect. It looks run down and redundant. I wonder if these monthly meetings are now it's sole purpose.

It's a wooden building that looks not unlike a massive scout hut, probably a couple of houses wide and twice as deep.

It's out of place in what seems to be a quiet residential street, within earshot of the busy Bayshore Freeway.

As I look over the chipped wood and tired paintwork of the exterior, I question what I was expecting. Given the build-up and the importance of this place, it should be a marble temple.

There are several geeks sitting on the steps outside tapping on laptops and a small queue of eight or ten people at the entrance, which I join.

I'm armed with all forty-five remaining Non-Disclosure Agreements, my laptop and my trusted pad.

I've given up with the umbrella.

I pay my $20 entrance fee, and write just my name instead of my email address in the contact column on the entrance form. As I move into the main hall, I see dozens of seats laid out in front of a small stage with a podium, a bar area and a couple of tables on which an urn of hot water sits beside a catering tub of coffee and a stack of styrene cups. Having counted three Starbucks on the same block, I assume this isn't their main attraction.

To the left is a charging hub, which is currently where most of the attention is focused. There are cables all over the floor, exposed plug sockets and charging cables bunched up like spaghetti. It's a health and safety nightmare.

Looking around, I can see there are two distinctive types of visitors here. About two-thirds of them are geeks, sporting beards, hoodies and beanie hats and clutching at

laptops. The other third are dressed casually in smart jeans or chinos and formal shirts, looking less stressed.
It's the latter group that gets attention from everyone. These are the investors, or representatives of funds.
Surprisingly, my own jeans and jacket combo appears to confuse no one. Nor does my age. I'm clearly the oldest in the room, by at least a decade, but everyone has the decency to ignore it – apart from one of the suits who tells me parents traditionally wait outside. And the person serving the coffees who asked me if I'm here to pick up Pete, whoever he may be.
Someone who's neither from the geek nor the chinos camp moves up to the podium and bangs it.

The gabble in the hall reduces and everyone turns to face him.
"Morning Guys. Most of you know the score, but I'm here to welcome any newcomers and explain how we work here at the Pitch & Present".
He goes on to explain that those that are here to find something new will be seated on the right. These will include funders of all levels, software houses looking for new projects and those that run the event. Those that have something they want to present will sit next to them, each in turn, and have two minutes to give their elevator pitch, before they take a seat to the left of the hall.
As he continues with his instruction against a background of keyboard tapping, I'm trying hard to work out when I should sit, where, and with whom.

It sounds like how I imagine a speed-dating event to be, but there's no second date unless they're the one's who ask for it.
The scenario brings back some unpleasant memories, and trips home alone.
He goes on to tell us we'll each get a list of who's present and gives a final word about confidentiality, instructing those who have NDAs with them to hand them to him. Before the proceeds start, he will insure everyone signs them.
As I pull out my own stack of paperwork, I realise I don't have enough for everyone in the hall. I can't print more, and I'm reluctant to let anyone see my idea without agreeing to the Non-Disclosure.
I'm comforted knowing everyone in the hall will assume they've signed NDAs on everything, even if they haven't and besides, I'll get a full list of all attendees anyway.

There's a frenzy of activity as we hand in our Non-Disclosure paperwork and a line forms for us all to sign each others. Again, I manage to avoid giving my email address or contact details.

By the time the suits, the jeans and the chinos have taken their seats on the right, it's twelve-thirty.

Once again, I'm in another line, but this time I have no idea where I'm supposed to be going.

I'm pointed, rather aggressively, in the direction of an empty seat, which I stumble towards. It's next to an Asian looking guy in a blue suit and open shirt. He seems rather disappointed when I sit with him, and when I spend a couple of minutes going through my idea, he shows little interest. I build to the finale but there's no reaction. I briefly wonder if he speaks English. Then he says "Okay. Thanks" and ushers me away. I'm prompted where to move to, and watch the man's face drop as I sit down.

By pitch number four I'm confident in my delivery, but less confident anyone's interested.

I've sat next to a dozen or so people, and not one of them has reacted. I discretely check my armpits. Nothing particularly offensive there.

I'm wondering whether I should perhaps hold my order for a Ferrari.

After all the pitching's complete, there's a ten minute break as everyone re-positions themselves to the correct side of the hall.

I stand in line for coffee, expecting to be hijacked by a crowd of funders eager to impress me, now they've had time to digest my pitch.

I'm disappointed to get to the front and have to order yet another coffee I neither need nor want.

I take a seat again, and am relieved to be approached by a chap in chinos.

"Hey it's Barry with the comms idea, right?"

"Yep"

"I'm Bob Harper, Silifunders." Like I should recognise the name.

"Silly Funders?"

"Sili." He says it slower, exaggerating how the inflection goes up before the funders bit. "Used to be called The Silicon Valley Project Investment Group Funding Corps."

When everything in the valley revolves around simple domain names, this one's a corker and I can see why they've shortened it.

He goes on.

"Love the comms project. I think we might be able to help."

He sits himself next to me, and hands me a card and a glossy brochure which I don't need to open to know it's full of cheesy pics of Bob and his mates sitting around a board table waving pencils in the air.

As he's giving me his spiel on the long list of very impressive companies in which they're either lead or secondary investors, another pair of chinos approaches.

"Don't mean to interrupt guys" he says interrupting.

Behind him there's two more chinos and behind them, a couple of suits.

I can only assume everyone I've presented to has been playing their cards close to their chest to ensure not to alert others to their enthusiasm.

As I feel the warm glow spread through me, I can't help feeling sorry for the other pitchers, many of who are sipping coffee on their own. Some are making themselves look busy on their laptops, but out of choice, they'd have them closed.

I'm temporarily distracted as I consider whether perhaps I should order a Ferrari after all – and whether I'd actually fit in it.

Within fifteen minutes, I'm surrounded by twenty or so guys (and one very attractive girl) firing off questions about my communication system.

I notice the Asian chap's amongst them, except this time he's bursting with enthusiasm.

I've heard the questions a thousand times in my mind. I'm no longer talking to Bob directly, I'm addressing them all. Bob looks pissed.

I impress myself with my ability to deliver the answers exactly as I rehearsed them, although through my excitement, I'm delivering them at hundred miles an hour.

My laptop's open and I've now got the opportunity to go through all the finer details of the concept that couldn't be squeezed into the two minutes I had with each of them, and doesn't appear on the brief presentations I'm handing out.

One of the guys, a skinny looking man in milk-bottle glasses and scraggy hair tells me he loves me. I learn his name is Harry Harris, and I vaguely recognise him as someone whose photo I've seen before.

He asks me if I'd like to go cycling with him and explore the bay area. I decline, but take his card.

If I exclude his invite, I'm experiencing my ultimate dream – and exactly what I need for my plan to work. I wonder who'll get to play the part of me in Mickey's movie.

I tell them how I came up with the idea, how I visualise it being used and how it will spread virally. I miss out on a couple of details, one of which they'll work out for themselves and the other which they'll work out with their lawyers.

They may have started cold and aloof, but once they'd seen the competition, they realise they need to sell to me. And they do, hard.

I have an array of funders trying to convince me of their expertise in Seed funding, Incubation funding, Second round funding and IPOs. They're throwing acronyms at me left, right and centre. I make a mental note to look up the one's I catch, and try to impress them with a few of my own.

"FYI, I think you'll agree this has a fantastic USP. LOL"

There's a brief silence whilst they look at each other puzzled, before they continue pitching me.

I have heads of software houses wanting to collaborate with me.

I have entrepreneurs who have been involved at an early stage – and subsequently made fortunes with - Skype, Cisco systems, Netflix – and of course, my old favourite, Facebook. I consider telling them that Facebook was my idea and whoever they invested in was the bastard who stole it from me. Fortunately, I think better of it.

By two-thirty I feel exhausted but exhilarated at the same time, due in the main to the huge intake of caffeine I've had.

I've got a pile of business cards, a mountain of glossy corporate brochures, and assurances that I'm going to be contacted by each and every one of the names on them. I wonder how they think they're going to do that as none of them have my details.

Elated, I turn to leave, and notice – not for the first time - the attractive looking female - a true rarity at today's event.

She's got flowers in her long strawberry hair and she's wearing a cute denim skirt from which her spindly legs hang before they disappear into her fluorescent pink pixie boots. She's hanging around the coffee machine and appears to be waiting for someone although no-one's given her any attention. Not even other geeks are hitting on her. I'm not sure whether it's through pity or a wave of parental concern, but I approach her and ask how her day's been.

I learn she's called Nancy and has travelled here from a small-town in South California where she lives with her parents and two dogs. She loves nothing more than baking, wearing bright colours and making daisy chains (she didn't mention the daisy chains, but it looked rather apparent).

As I ask her idea, I fear it may be a mistake, and when she tells me, I'm no longer surprised she's had no interest. Out of politeness I act overwhelmed by the brilliance of it and wish her well, although it's unlikely the world's ready for an app on which cupcakes can be ordered, even if you do get to select your sprinkles from a dropdown list.

She's aware of the hoards I'm carrying and can see I'm struggling.

She hesitates, then offers me her empty hessian bag – decorated with flowers and squiggly lines. I tell her how sorry I am she's not been able to fill it with brochures like I have and she astounds me by telling me she's already raised over twenty million dollars but she's spent the lot in a matter of months. She tells me she needs to fundraise again, just like she has twice before.

She's just arranged dinner with an investor she's met who's promised her another ten million.

I have no idea whether she's high or deluded, but I appreciate the offer of the bag.

I fill it with my morning's spoils. I also take her details and promise to return her bag.

I take one last look around and try to guess at how many of these investors are going to be throwing their millions at me, and how much that works out for each minute I've spent here. The number's simply too great to calculate.

I can't wait to tell Katie about my success, but by the time I get to email her it's past midnight in London and she'll probably be asleep.

> Hi Katie
>
> Today went well. I've got a bucketload of coders that want to code it, and funders who want to fund it. The masterplan's going down a storm. Should be a breeze.
>
> B

I realise I haven't eaten since the croissant in Starbucks, and get the Uber to drop me a block before the Self-Starter Inn, at Denny's.

Considering it's mid-afternoon the place is surprisingly busy.

I walk through the parking lot, which I now notice has a large area designated for handicapped parking and another one, closer to the entrance, designated for handicapped scooters.

I feel positively trim, and order the Bourbon Bacon Burger with fries and a coke.

It arrives in several stages, each bigger than the preceding.

As I eat, I move several plates to one-side to create enough space for me to open-up the laptop to prepare my profile on the *illictencounters* dating site.

As it locks onto the free wifi, a couple of emails come in.

Thankfully, they're mostly spam – I don't need reminding how small my penis is, and I've got no interest in taking a short-term loan. Actually I have, but they probably wouldn't give it to me anyway.

I've also got the daily email from *SiliconValleyNews*, which I scan. Nothing major today, although they're promising feedback tomorrow for todays meeting at the Oat House.

I return to the original task I came here for, and start typing, ensuring I wipe the grease from the keyboard every couple of minutes.

CHAPTER 13

Mike is 47, handsome, and looking for love. He's a lawyer, he's got no kids and he also happens to be entirely fictitious. His profile's a masterpiece.

He lives in North London and has a penchant for well-dressed women who are – he hopes – in the same position as him and looking for something that will develop into a long-term relationship. His username is "possiblypermanent".

In my mind he's the female version of Marie, but I don't think a long list of negatives will get the desired response he needs.

He differs only from Marie in that he's not stupid enough to leave his laptop open without deleting the history of sites visited. I wonder if his fictitious wife will find his login details out as easily as I did Marie's.

I hadn't considered the possibility when I started, but I'm actually quite excited when a message pops up from a woman who wants to chat with me. Or Mike. I'm even more surprised when I realise how desperate she must be as it's gone 3am in London. I ignore it; I have too many distractions in my head as it is.

In my praise, he does sounds like every woman's dream.

I open my notepad and find her profile name, which I'd hurriedly scribbled down a couple of days ago.

I craft my message to lookingforlove1234 with care, before I return to the more important issue of making my fortune.

Feeling bloated and tired, I make my way back to the Self-Starter Inn to decant the contents of my hessian flowery bag.

Now they're folded, thumbed and signed, the Non-Disclosure Agreements take up a great deal more room than when I first brought them. I flatten them all out and the pile's probably two inches high. I check each one to see who's signed it, and scribble the names and contact details in my notebook.

I have nothing to put them in, and the messenger bag I've been given has a loose handle, which is in danger of ripping off under the weight of all the brochures and business cards.

Looking around, I spot a dirty yellow folder lying on my bedside table. It's courtesy of the Self-Starter Inn and full of local attractions and things to do.

It's an attempt to make it appear like a hotel rather than the dump that it is.

I suspect anyone who stays here is desperate for an excuse to leave the place, so the leaflets are well thumbed.

The folder is the perfect size in which to put my signed Non-Disclosure Agreements, so I empty the bumf from it, and slide my own paperwork in its place.

Now I just have to work out how to get everything back home.

I tut out loud as I realise I haven't considered the amount of stuff I'd need to take back with me, and consider perhaps I should have brought a full size suit-case rather than the carry-on.

It's clearly not going to fit, so I eye my clothes to see what I'm prepared to leave here in sacrifice.

I then remember Mickey's words just before he got off the flight.

"... let me know if there's anything you need before I return to London on Wednesday..."

I fumble for my phone and send him a text, smiling as I do as I realise how it's an obvious part of the masterplan I nearly overlooked.

> Hi Mickey, I've got some papers I need to get back to London, but no room in my case. Would you mind taking them bak 4 me? B

It's only 9pm, but as I recount the day, I'm overwhelmed with how well it's gone. I doubt I'll sleep, so once I'm in bed, I click on the TV.

I don't recall watching anything before I slept.

CHAPTER 14

Janice hadn't slept well. The migraine hadn't lifted until the early hours and she'd spent the rest of the night wondering how much longer she'd have to sell over-priced swimming shorts.

She was hoping to have left Octajour by now and be well on the way to implementing her master plan, but knew patience was key to its success.

It was certainly far from being the liberating or grounding experience her lawyer had assured her it would be. Until the divorce settlement was finalised with Tod, Janice would be unsure whether taking a low-paying brain-numbing job was really the best way to maximise her payout.

She sat at her breakfast bar with her coffee, grateful her nanny had sorted the twins and got them to school.

Just as she did every morning, Janice opened her notepad and flicked through the pages, one for each of the colleagues she'd worked alongside at the bank. By each name was a list of their likes, dislikes, favourite drinks, preferred drugs, and how much money they'd made as a result of her hard work. There was also a section for the names of their wives and mistresses and finally a list of the banking rules they'd ignored and laws they'd broken.

The daily ritual kept the flame of revenge burning.

She flipped to the back page and run her finger down the long list of tech companies – most of them huge successes - she had personally recommended to her colleagues. A total of thirty-six names that had made the banks billions and her team millions, none more than Tod who held what were rightfully her spoils too.

She put the notepad down and took out the box file.

She thumbed through its contents.

Congratulations On Your Wedding Day cards.

Congratulations On Your Twins cards

Sorry to See You're Leaving cards

... and a stack of letters thanking her for her application, congratulating her on her perfect track record and apologising for not having any vacancies.

Each ended with 'hope the twins are well' which was their way of saying we know who you are, but our hands are tied.

Six months later and here she was. A mere shop-assistant in a store serving the very crowd she was once a part of. Her paycheck simply paid for treats for the kids and fuel for the Jeep - and kept her busy from going mad.

At thirty-five, Janice was striking. Her long flowing blond hair, finished with a French plait, looked neat. It used to look immaculate.
Her blue eyes were bright. They used to be piercing.
Her svelte figure was a little more curvaceous now.
She felt her batteries draining.
She was aware of the need to start on her plan before they completely died.
It wasn't for the lack of trying, but the right opportunity was still to present itself.
It wasn't just any opportunity either. What Janice needed was a very specific set of circumstances.
Even when she could afford to, she never understood why people shopped in Octajour. She'd never taken advantage of her 40% staff discount. Her twin boys were well stocked in similar looking shorts, albeit without the mesh bag and booklet, bought from Walmart for $14.99.
Her basic pay was paltry, but her commissions were amongst the highest in the company and a testimonial of her ability to convince successful techies they looked good in shorts in which they didn't.
Most of her customers were regulars. Techies who'd made money but only ever spent it on fast-food, weed, beer and gaming consoles. Most of them placed their orders online – usually just minutes after visiting the store. Janice knew the zipcodes of the wealthiest neighborhoods, mainly because she lived amongst them.
Why they'd be attracted to her store was a mystery, but once they were in, Janice felt it her responsibility to educate them on how to spend their money and look cool.
It wasn't an easy task. Most lacked social skills and were incapable of conversing with her. Their competence in coding was balanced perfectly with their *in*competence with women. A simple smile, a compliment on their taste in dayglo yellow, a brief touch on their hand, and they'd run back to their cars desperate to tap in their order.

CHAPTER 15

I must be settling into the time zone better because I only woke up once at 4:00am, and it's now 7:35.

I switch my phone on and straight away it beeps with a text. It's from Mickey.

> Sure I can take your papers back ;-) ;-) ;-)
>
> I'm going back to London at 5 tonight. Let me know where you're staying and I'll send a car to pick up your stuff. M ;-) ;-)

Perfect. Enough with the winks though.

> Thanks Mickey. I'm at the self starter inn on north st, by sonora ave. My flights tomorrow so I'll call you in a day or 2. Really appreciate it.

My thoughts turn to Marie and how I can't let her have any part of this business going forward. Why she even wants to staggers me. More than anyone, she's aware of my long list of failures and piles of debt. There's no way she can know how different the outcome will be this time.

I decide Mike, my alter ego, needs to work on her a little more.

I logon to *MiserableSpouses* and am relieved to find Mike's profile, possiblypermanent has a message from hers, lookingforlove1234.

I consider putting off reading it until I've had breakfast, but the temptation's too great.

> Hi. Thanks for the message. I see you sent it at 3:30 in the morning! Are you an early riser lol. Maybe you've got a paper-round lol. Or maybe you're just going to bed?
>
> Anyway, like you, I'm also getting divorced and also looking for something a little more permanent. I think we're a rarity on this site lol. I'm Marie, a 39 year old nail-beautician but I used to be a fashion-designer and then a flight attendant. I actually only logged to cancel my membership (long-story. If we ever meet I'll tell you why).
>
> Just so you know, I'm divorcing my husband. He's an idiot (I'm not being rude. Everyone thinks he is), who's also totally incompetent and has ruined my life. Anyway you sound lovely. Probably better to contact me using my email address as I probably won't login here again. Hope to hear from you x
>
> Mariefornails@hotmail.com
>
> M x

She's a little ambitious knocking off a full seven years from her age, but I know Marie and it doesn't surprise me. I can't believe she thinks studying fashion at college makes her a fashion designer, and she's never been a flight attendant. She doesn't even like flying.

I can see what time she last logged in so she'll know I've just read her message. I know she'll be logging in regularly now to see the last time possiblypermanent was online. Now she's seen me – or Mike - I'll have to reply quickly to show I'm keen.

It's difficult to pretend I know nothing about her, but I think I pull off a masterpiece when I reply to Marie about how Mike's wife is unloving, uncaring, and seriously ill with a mystery debilitating illness - and as a final thought I also add she's a complete alcoholic.

I want Marie to live in hope that it's just a matter of time before he has no-one to answer to.

I'm on a roll as I tell her how intolerable Mike's life is, and how he's now living in a spare-room in the marital home and desperate to move out. I don't want to portray him to be as broke as I am, so I add something about how he stays in one of the many spare bedrooms in the detached house (with carriage drive) simply to look after his youngest daughter who still lives there, whilst her mother spends most of her day in bed. Finally, Mike tells her he's expecting to be totally free in a matter of months, which coincidentally is when his youngest goes off to Uni.

I realise it sounds a bit harsh so I add something about how he's been trying to work at the marriage, and get help and support for his wife, but knows it's just a matter of time.

I throw a little hint in about how he wants a clean break from her and that's why he's given her the house, but then when I reread it, I wonder why he'd bestow his house on a woman who's likely to be dead.

I rewrite it a couple of times until Mike explains to her he needs to move on and the only way he can do that is severing all links with his wife – deceased or otherwise. He's decided the only link he'll ever have with her is the children.

His final bit of advice to Marie is to have a clean break from her own husband.

As we continue in our messaging, I'll expand on that, and make it Mike's mantra. Hopefully Marie will take guidance from how clever Mike is, and under his gentle persuasion, maybe she'll go for a clean break from me.

I hit the send button and am instantly aware of a phone ringing.

I had no idea I even have a phone in the room and follow the noise to behind the TV. It too is dusty and dirty, even by my standards. I pick it up but hold it away from my ear.

It's the kid in the lobby telling me a driver's arrived to collect a package from me. She takes the opportunity to tell me if she suspects it's drugs, she has a duty to contact law enforcement.

I shoot down the stairs, with my stack of papers in the yellow folder from my yellow room, together with a girlie hessian bag full of brochures, thankful the dump I'm in only has two storeys.

Before I hand them to the driver, I flick through the papers and wave them under the nose of the girl sitting on the front desk. Apart from an aroma of lavender from the hessian bag, she gets the whiff of the same musk that fills my room.

Pleased that my documents are now safely en route to their destination, my thought turns to food, so it's back to Denny's.

Considering this is my third visit in three days, none of the staff seem to acknowledge me or welcome me back. I seat myself at the same table I've sat at every visit, where the same waitress who served me each time introduces herself again, gives me the same speech about how she relies on tips and hopes I'm having a nice day.

I order a French Toast Slam which comes with bacon and eggs. With a totally confused body-clock, the combination satisfies both my lust for dinner and the time for breakfast.

I want to tell her I am indeed having a nice day. In fact if it's anything like yesterday, it's going to be fantastic.

With all my chores out of the way, my paperwork winging its way home and my purpose for coming achieved, I wonder how to spend the rest of the day. I didn't plan to have any free time, and now I've got a whole afternoon to fill.

I return to the Inn and shuffle through the local attraction leaflets I'd removed from the folder I used for my Non-Disclosure Agreements.

After discarding those which hold zero interest for me, including Rose Gardens, Churches, Zoos and the San Jose Museum of Quilts & Textiles, I'm left with just two. One's a leaflet on the Tech Museum of Innovation and the other's what looks like an outdoor shopping mall. Neither of these are particularly appealing, but the photos in the Tech Museum are mainly of kids with cheesy smiles.

I can't think of anything worse. By a process of elimination I end picking the one remaining leaflet for Santana Row, which also happens to be the nearest, being less then five miles away.

My app tells me it's quicker to walk the five miles than wait for the bus. It's quicker still by Uber, which arrives barely before I've ordered it.

CHAPTER 16

Silicon Valley is a mecca for the outrageous, the colourful and the downright insane. Even the relatively bland employees of banks and investment houses are still abnormal by other bank standards.

Many of them have risen to their positions through hard work, determination and a will to succeed, others by sheer luck – but the one common link they all share is their good fortune to be in Silicon Valley at exactly the right time to witness – and profit – from the explosion of the tech industry.

The salaries and bonuses are out of kilter with the entire banking world, let alone any other profession. These are sporting superstars who have no kit to change into and no matches to attend, but they play their game daily. And the banks money is the ball they play with.

Up until just a few years ago, they were happy investing millions, hoping to reap the bank tens of millions in return. With the exponential growth of the technology companies, the rewards became even greater and the millions soon became billions.

As the rewards grew, so did the appetite for bigger investments. Suddenly no one was interested in investing millions to make tens of millions. It had to be tens or hundreds of millions to make billions.

With the bigger tech companies – many of them less than a decade old – fetching valuations of hundreds of billions, the stakes increased even further.

Soon enough investments of under twenty million were considered nothing more than mere punts.

The chances of an investment working out might still be slim – but those that do more than, make-up for those that don't.

As well as the traditional banks and funders, a host of investment houses had sprung up, owned by major tech companies who have generated such vast sums of cash, they've become the biggest investors of all.

Then there are the investors that have sold their own tech businesses to larger companies, only to find themselves with huge amounts of cash and nothing to do, except turn it into more.

Bob Harper was one such person. He was one of Silicon Valley's heroes. He had formed Silifunders after selling his company Skopeez, the online tracking service he was famed for starting in his garage as a teenager.

His was a wonderful rags-to-riches story complicated only by the fact none of it was true.

He'd actually started the business from his parents pool-house when he was twenty, and his father's loan of two million was never mentioned in any article. Nor were his mates, Archie Stern whose idea Skopeez was, nor Sam Mesner who coded it. Skopeez became the success it was solely down to the two friends who received no recognition and less than a half-percent each.

When the business was sold to LustCorp for $1.8billion, they each received nine million dollars, with which they were content; Bob got over a billion and a half- and wasn't.

When Bob sold the company he was thirty-four and bored, so did the only thing billionaires can do; invest in others in the hope of making more.

He had neither the know-how nor capability to create anything new, but he was adept at recognising new ideas he could exploit as his own.

Being a billionaire was the only criteria he needed to start his own investment fund so when he launched The Silicon Valley Project Investment Group Funding Corp, there was no shortage of money to follow him.

For the first three months Bob and his investors sat around the boardroom table arguing over what to call themselves. Finally, they agreed on Silifunders.

Bob was then tasked with finding ideas to fund, which he insisted on doing alone.

He was a stalwart at the Oat House every month. On the days in-between he hosted an endless stream of geeks and techies who pitched their latest ideas to him from across his desk. Many had been on the fundraising circuit for months or even years, tweaking, changing or replacing their ideas until they could find one that attracted the interest of investors like Bob.

Despite the several hundred PowerPoints and animated videos he'd seen, Bob was rarely enthused by anything new. He'd seen a thousand ideas for social networking sites catering for just about every genre from pets to cell-mates, from sportsmen to dead people. He'd been bored by robotic parrots, dogs and cats, motorised skateboards, virtual reality headsets (for games and porn), and wearable technology covering everything from bracelets to full body armour.

He'd downloaded so many cutting-edge Apps, his phone was infected with every type of virus known, and even unknown.

He had all but given up on finding anything to excite him, but this recent visit to the Oat House had changed that.

Within a few minutes of meeting Barry, Bob realised he was wrong to have pre-judged the rotund, sweaty unpleasant looking man in elasticated jeans.
His idea was brilliant, but he was clearly incapable of managing it himself.
Bob wondered if perhaps he could keep the idea, and lose the creator but having signed a Non-Disclosure Agreement, Bob knew his reputation rested on him honoring it. In his time, Bob had lost track of the number of Non-Disclosure Agreements he'd signed, but he guessed it was in the high hundreds or possibly even thousands.
He'd also noticed the glaring omission in the presentation – Barry hadn't included GPS, which would add functionality and dramatically increase take-up. Including it would certainly slow down the coding, but would reap far greater rewards.
Any investor was happy to sign such agreements as a sign of trust and fidelity. Breaking the terms and stealing someone else's idea would ensure he would never be trusted again.
But perhaps with Barry it would be different. There was unlikely to be any bank in the valley that would entrust their funds to this disaster in wait.
As Bob left the Oat House his mind was racing. As soon as the phone signal was strong enough, he called his Head of Legal, Mike Kapinsky.
Mike was playing Call of Duty on his massive monitor at his over-sized highly polished oak desk. As the call came through, he lurched forward to pause it and knocked his full coffee cup over. The contents poured over his desk like a wave.
"Hey Bob."
"Hey Mike, you busy?"
"I'm pouring over a deal" he said, as he picked up two sodden bits of paper to see if they could be reunited. "What can I do for you?"
"Mike, I've got a question for you" he said, wondering how best to couch it.
"Um.. Mike, let's say, a friend of mine sees an idea – which I … sorry, which *he* loves – and wants to run with, but doesn't want to work with the guy – or girl – whose idea it is."

Mike was now standing, dabbing at his trousers where the sticky liquid from the desk had been pouring.
"Damn!... I mean that's a *damn* good question Bob. Well, as long as you, or your friend haven't signed anything, you, or your friend, can just do it yourself" he said.
"Ok … but let's just say my friend signed an NDA. I'm not saying he did… but just *say* he did, can he just do it then?"

Mike's mind was elsewhere, as he desperately tried to focus.

"Bob, you know you can't."

"How about if I come up with something they've not thought of and make it even better?"

"I assume you mean your friend?"

"Ah ...yes ... my friend came up with it."

"Well tell your friend he ... or she ... still can't do it if they've signed an NDA unless they, you ... or whoever it is, can show they had the idea before they signed."

"I have no idea what you're talking about" said Bob and hung up.

As he got in his car, Bob scrolled through his contacts and called Peachy, his head of software development. He explained the idea as though it was his own, making no mention that he'd just been presented with it by someone else, but trying to incorporate all the features he'd been told about and the GPS feature he hadn't.

"Fantastic idea!" Peachy said with genuine enthusiasm. Peachy was always enthusiastic when he was stoned.

"Well Peachy, I'm pleased you like it but – and I don't want to put words in your mouth - but if I gave you this idea six months ago, what would you have done?"

"Well, assuming you'd signed-off the budget, I'd have a team of coders working on it."

"Good, so now if I tell you I did actually mention it to you six months ago, what would you be saying now?"

"Er... that I'm sorry it's taken me so long to get it started?"

"That'll do. Apology accepted. Get on with it!"

The line went dead.

Peachy looked at his phone wondering what Bob had been talking about. If he'd really had the idea six months ago, why was he only now choosing to tell him? Maybe he had told him six months ago. Maybe time had warped. He picked his joint out of the ashtray and studied it.

Whatever it was, Peachy opened his laptop and started work on Bob's comms idea.

When Bob returned to his office, he emptied his slim leather briefcase ontc the desk and shuffled through the contents for Barry's business card. The sooner he could email him with the news Silifunders were already developing a similar project, the sooner he could forget him.

Amongst the business cards, leaflets and stapled presentations, there was nothing from Barry. He wondered whether he'd actually mislaid it, or whether Barry had even given him one.
He decided he'd just have to wait to hear from Barry.

* * *

Across the street, in a glass tower called simply 'The Glass Tower' Harry Harris was in his office, playing with a remote-control car.
"It's brilliant. I love it!" he chuckled to the techies in front of him as he rolled his head from left to right.
"Look up" said the techie with the blue hoodie, "and it'll slow down ... look down and it will speed up."
"I love it. I love it." exclaimed Harry, "So I steer it by turning my head, and change speed by looking up or down?"
"Yep" said the red hoodie.
"We should do something together. I love you guys. I love this car. Can I keep it over the weekend?"
"Sure."
"By the way, do any of you cycle?"
The techies left and Harry continued playing for another ten minutes before his PA came in and reminded him to take his medication.
Without it, Harry was a very different animal.
At thirty-one, Harry had quite possibly spent more hours in front of a computer screen than anyone in the world. Ever.

From when he first got access to his Dad's Tandy 4000 computer, aged just three, Harry was addicted. By the time he was ten, he could code, create basic games and calculate his father's tax return. He never slept more than four hours a night, and had no interests other than generating code.
No one wondered why Harry wore the thickest glasses and suffered from ADHD.
No one knew if he was straight or gay, or whether he'd ever been in a relationship with anything that didn't have a screen and keyboard.
Computers were his life.

Through his constant coding, problem solving and determination to make things work, Harry created some of the best-known softwares used on all IBM machines, and then Microsoft.

Money didn't motivate Harry, so the several billion he got when he sold his company did nothing for him other than attract a great deal of propositions through the mail – some of them for investments, but mostly just begging letters.

If anything, Harry had become more intense and more withdrawn. He never went out, and no one called for him.

Then, in 2009, that all changed with his new medication.

Suddenly, the new Harry had arrived. He was engaged with life and he loved it. He loved everyone. He loved everything. His enthusiasm was boundless.

He ran twelve miles a day, cycled the fifteen miles to his office, and always greeted everyone he passed.

His skinny frame, bedraggled dark hair, large framed milk-bottle glasses and friendly wave became known throughout Silicon Valley. Here comes Happy Harry Harris.

Happy Harry joined GCC – the Geeks Cycling Club and befriended other techies on two wheels but his most serious relationship still required an electrical supply and WiFi signal.

Shortly after he'd sold his second software company, Happy Harry started his investment house - the main purpose of which was to relieve his boredom and give other techies an opportunity to explore – rather than exploit – new ideas.

He had no intention of making more money, which was a shame because everything Harry touched turned into a golden opportunity.

He gave money to designers, engineers, techies and geeks, all in the hope they could then carry on doing what they loved doing, without the pressures of worrying about overheads for rent, beer or pot.

His over-excitement and enthusiasm for everyone and everything meant he was indiscriminate with his money, often giving it to those that had been turned down by every other investment house in the region. Most of the investments he made were to no-hopers, just like he had been when he was their age.

One by one, everyone he backed created global brands, enhancing his billions and making Happy Harry 'the world's shrewdest investor' according to Forbes.

When Harry had got back from the Oat House Pitch & Present, he relayed, in excited detail to his PA, all of the presentations he'd seen and loved.

With animated passion he listed the array of toppings available for cupcakes, before moving onto the idea he was most excited about from the loveable character, Barry. He was exactly the type of guy that no one else would invest in, making him an ideal candidate for Harry's investment.

How much funding Barry wanted was something Harry neither knew nor cared about.

He asked his PA to contact him to find out, and when she told him there was nothing in his backpack other than a pair of cycling shorts and a couple of coding magazines, he looked genuinely upset.

"That's a shame" he said. "See if you can find him and tell him I'd love to work with him. You can also tell him we'll add GPS to make it even better."

As his PA's main focus was ensuring she administered his medication at the correct time, finding a needle in a haystack was something she had neither the appetite, nor the capability to do.

"Sure" she said.

* * *

Two blocks away, on the fourth floor of a similar glass tower, but with bronzed mirror, was GalactInvest. Since 2005, the large boardroom table had hosted the heads of some of the world's leading internet and tech brands during their early years of investment.

GalactInvest was acclaimed for being a canny investor, and Tod Damar, its Vice President of Funding was the man credited as the reason.

Tod had moved to San Jose in the early internet gold rush at the turn of the century, after several years of working his way up the banking ladder in New York.

He was acclaimed for his skill in sifting through the myriad of opportunities that arrived in his department and identifying winning opportunities before they'd got off the drawing board. His record of success was unparalleled, his bonuses, unbeaten. He was quick to made sure everyone knew it, and dined out on the many stories of how he'd advised no-hopers on what to do to turn their idea into a reality.

Out of the staff of twenty or so in the funding department, he was the only one who had no skills at all, having relied solely on his assistant Janice to advise him. He'd never intended to get her pregnant and certainly not to marry her, but now they were divorcing, he hoped he could maintain his reputation without actually knowing how to recognise the right deals.

He'd not only managed to convince everyone he knew what he was talking about, he'd also coined his own phrases on how he did it.

Tod's Firebox was the collective term for all his deals, with each one referred to as a Firework. He would explain how he found the firework - or idea - married up the right team, and invested in it.

"It's a no brainer," he would say, "find the firework, put a match to it, light the blue touch paper – and stand back"

He never explained it was only thanks to Janice he never got burned, or mentioned only she knew how to strike the match.

He spent as much time as possible overseeing his firework displays and pushing Janice to find the next one. During his downtime, he indulged in his two loves: shopping and women, often combining them both by lavishing generous gifts on women he wanted to bed. Marriage cramped his style.

Since he'd forced Janice to leave the bank so he could pursue other women, the bonuses were smaller and less frequent. He grew ever more doubtful whether an idea presented to him was a rocket or a damp squib.

Determined he could manage without her, Tod made every effort to see as many new ideas as possible and view as many pitches as he could, preferably from attractive women – a rarity in the Valley.

At the recent Oat House Pitch & Present, he'd lavished attention on a striking woman with an idea for a cup-cake app. He had no idea whether it was viable but she'd already burned through twenty million dollars, meaning he could take comfort that others have obviously seen her fit for investment. Besides, she had a fantastic bust and had accepted his invitation for dinner. The cheque was almost hers.

As he'd turned to leave, he'd noticed a small crowd of investors surrounding someone. From the colour and appearance of the man in the centre, he assumed it was because he'd been taken ill, and by the looks of it, a heart attack.

As he approached the throng, he noticed the man was actually alive and well, and excitedly explaining his idea.

Not wanting to be left out, Tod joined the crowd and accepted a hand-cut of the retro-styled PowerPoint presentation.

After a brief introduction, he found himself moving to the front of the party to be directly in front of Barry. As he caught the aroma, he realised why the gap had appeared, and found himself shuffling to the rear again.
In the few minutes Tod stood there, he wondered whether the idea was genuinely good or whether the crowd was simply there to witness the freak show.
With the fervor in which the presentations were being taken, he assumed perhaps this was an idea with legs. Tod was clueless whether it packed gunpowder or not, but if everyone else wanted it, he'd make sure he got it.
One thing he was sure of though, this man could never be in Tod's firework set. He was doomed to fizzle for a short-burst before extinguishing himself, leaving a cloud of disappointment.
Being unsure of how good the idea was, he decided to take the presentation and return to the office to see what the board thought of it.
If they hated it, he'd tell them he did too, but was merely using it to demonstrate the low caliber of ideas at the Oat House pitching event. If they loved it, he'd agree wholeheartedly and bask in the glory of his ability to find fantastic opportunities.

At eleven am sharp, Tod walked into the boardroom. The full complement of directors was there, hungry to hear of Tod's opportunities, which they'd all noticed were somewhat lighter since Janice had left.
Tod wasted no time in telling them about Project Ronald taking care not to show any enthusiasm in case the idea was a pup.
By the time he'd got to slide three, the board were cooing and whooping.
"Tod's back!" shouted the head of compliance.
Tod threw a wink towards the table and finished his presentation with a little more humour and a slight swagger in his step, before launching in to how he had been the first at the Oat House to recognise the brilliance of the idea.
The board then spent the next fifteen minutes talking in the usual riddle rubbish they did every meeting, which they all pretended to understand, but actually didn't. There were helicopter views, blue-sky thoughts, lots of reaching out and singing from the same hymn sheets before they settled on the business of discussing how they were actually going to proceed with Project Ronald.
"We need to fast-track this," said Tod, full of gusto now he knew he'd found a winner, "there's only a limited window so let's fire-up the chariots on this."
"Have you signed an Non-Disclosure?"

"Yes" he said, "but we need to ditch the founder. He's not someone we want to take to the party going forward."

"How about we buy him out? Make him an offer he can't refuse to give us full ownership?"

"Is that something that fits in with us holistically?"

"Can we have that conversation off-line please?"

"Has anyone recognised the elephant in the room vis-à-vis the lack of GPS?"

After much deliberation, they decided they should make Barry an offer for him to leave the scene and give them control of the idea. From Tod's description, he sounded like he could be seen off for a mere few thousand, but for the sake of fairness, they wanted to give him more – although nothing like the true worth of his idea.

They finally settled at two million dollars, but agreed if he pushed them, they'd be prepared to double it.

It was after all a game-changing idea.

As the excitement tailed, Tod cleared his throat.

"And now, I'd like to show you something you're going to love even more."

Quiet filled the room with the only sounds being as the chairs were pulled closer to the table as everyone sat bolt upright. Surely nothing could be more exciting than Project Ronald.

"We're talking cupcakes ... "

The room erupted to the sound of laughter.

After laughing with his board and convincing them he'd thrown the idea in merely for entertainment purposes, Tod quickly returned to the brilliance of Project Ronald and the attention changed back to the matter in hand.

They concluded that the head of legal would prepare a formal offer to send Barry. All that was needed were his contact details.

Tod emptied his pockets and poured an assortment of business cards out in front of him. He quickly retrieved one with a phone number scrawled across it in lipstick and another from a massage joint.

Of the few remaining, it was clear none of them were Barry's.

Everyone's eyes were on Tod as his eyes lit up with the solution.

He remembered the Oat House had a register which all visitors were required to sign and signaled for his PA to contact them for a copy.

Later that day, when the email with the scanned list arrived, Tod saw the only name against which there was no email address was Barry's.

He did however note Nancy's details were there, which he scribbled in his pad before deleting the email. He'd have to think of another way of contacting Barry.

Meanwhile, the GPMT (GalactInvest Project Management Team) had taken the presentation to marry with the correct team to ensure the project would work. They also calculated the additional time they'd need to add the GPS module and then calculated the investment they'd need to make, confident Barry was no longer a part of the plan going forward.

* * *

Four blocks away, in a converted warehouse was Linkosys, the gambling software company. Jim, Josh, Jake and Jez sat in their recliners around the pool table, which was slightly too high for them to see over, so they each lay almost horizontal.

They'd finally decided on the programming language and now they've got to allocate the work to their coding team, which they'll need to build - quickly.

To do it properly, they know they need funding but they're coders, not businessman and they have no idea how much to ask for. As usual, their interest lies in producing the clever coding required to bring the project to life. They have no concern for the viability or worth of the project, but they want recognition of their brilliance – which is why they've decided they can enhance the idea further simply by adding GPS.

Fortunately, they have a great relationship with their funder, based on their track record of producing fantastic gambling software that's given them a share-value of several hundred million. Not that they've ever seen a penny of it. But then, they're not in it for the money. They're quite happy in their rented accommodation living off pizza and beer, top brand headphones, early morning Starbucks, and basking in the kudos of their coding skills. If they happen to have shares worth a couple of hundred million each, that's a bonus, but other than their Teslas and Playstations, they can think of nothing they need to spend it on, although if the auto-pilot self-driving software isn't released soon they'll have to actually learn to drive rather than just leaving the cars plugged in all day.

Jez throws out a figure. "How about five million?"

"We haven't raised that little for years. Let's ask for twenty" said Josh.

"Is anyone going to take this seriously if we ask for less than forty?" said Jim.

"Let's ask for a billion" said Jake.

They laugh for a bit, throw a few more numbers around, then settle on seventy-three. It sounds like a number that has a plan behind it, big enough to show it's a serious opportunity, but small enough not to topple the business if it all goes wrong.

"How about the fat old guy?" asked Josh.

"We don't need him" replied Jez.

"But didn't we sign a contract or something?"

"Yeah, so what?"

"Ah ok. I thought we had to give him something that's all."

"I think we just signed a document to say we'd promise to work on it or something. He talked in a funny accent and I was still concentrating on the podcast so I'm not really sure.

They put a call in to Alan Androposa, the man who'll have to write the cheque, to tell him the good news; they've finally got a spin-off opportunity.

That day, across the entire Silicon Valley, there are sixty or so meetings convened solely for the intention of discussing Project Ronald, it's many benefits and how it's going to change the world.

Fifty eight of them have recognised the opportunity's even stronger with the addition of GPS.

There are two main focuses.

How quickly they can prove they were already working on the idea so they can report back to Barry and tell him his NDA is worthless, and where the hell they put his contact details.

They have just four weeks to do both.

CHAPTER 17

Wednesday 4th June started like any other day for Luke, Ubering techies around the Valley. Ninety percent of his business was ferrying a group of people that all looked and smelled the same to him.

It was rare for him to meet captains of industry like the man he'd delivered to Santana Row the day before, and even rarer to strike up a conversation as he competed with mobile phones, laptops, headphones and a general disinterest.

That didn't stop him trying. It was through his efforts that he'd first heard of the Oat House.

The two geeks sitting in the back were headed to Infoquark, another of the funders in the valley, specialising in seed investment for new and revolutionary ideas. Their level of investment was relatively low – typically under thirty million, and their long list of failures was balanced by a few of the biggest tech names in which they'd been an early investor. The small number of successes had made them countless billions, fuelling even more seed investments in an ever-increasing list of bizarre ideas.

"Hey guys. Working on anything interesting?"

Unusually, Luke struck lucky.

"Dude, we're working on somethin' awesome" replied an excited geek.

"Cool. I might be able to help. You know I'm only driving to fill my time between projects. I'm very successful in my own rite – you're just lucky you caught me whilst I'm available."

Neither of the geeks looked up. Undeterred, Luke continued.

"Guys, I'm actually a deal-maker. I can help get your idea off the ground. I could even come in to Infoquark with you ... make sure you get the right deal ... you know, bringing some experience to the boardroom. Looks like you kids could do with some."

It was unusual to find an Uber driver without a similar pitch.

"That's cool dude, but we're fine. We met a guy in Starbucks with a cool idea so we're going to IFQ to see if they'll fund us to do it."

"Take my card anyway" Luke said as he leant over to his glovebox and pulled a box of cards out. He steered with his knees as he flipped through the cards, selecting the correct one before handing it over his shoulder to the geeks behind.

'Luke Palatino. Deal Negotiator Extraordinaire'

The geek scanned it and slid it into his back pocket.

Luke dropped them outside the imposing glass building with Lion statues either side of the revolving door, and decided to head over to Santana Row and return the purchase he'd made the day before.

Being lunchtime, he considered the store may be busier, and even if it wasn't he'd get a chance to chat to the woman he couldn't get out of his mind.

As he pulled into the parking lot and saw there were no empty spaces, he knew his hunch was right. He slowed to see if anyone was leaving, and noticed a young guy in a convertible throw his tablet on the back seat as he screeched out.

Janice didn't look up as the door opened and Luke walked in, but continued frantically writing in a notepad.

He stood for a moment as his eyes adjusted then watched her, paying particular attention to her ringless finger. She was even more gorgeous than he'd remembered. He moved towards her, conscious of how shy he suddenly felt. Shy was one word no-one had ever used to describe Luke. He wished he had a card for such a situation. Luke Palatino, Lover Extraordinaire.

"Hey!"

Janice looked up, closing her notepad as she did.

"Oh hi. How's your cousin who's not gay?" she asked with a smile.

"Ha" he said as he wondered what clever retort he could muster. None as it turned out. "Well, ummm ... turns out, he's fine and would you believe, he's lost a whole lotta weight. He's not a triple-x anymore."

"Wow. That's fantastic. What size do you wanna change them for?"

That smooth voice. He could listen to it all day.

"Well, actually I don't. I er ... I bought him ... I bought him pyjamas instead"

"You sure love buying your cousin intimate gifts, eh?"

He felt his face flush as he realised what a pratt he was making of himself.

"Look, I'll level with you" he said. "When I got home, I realised he can't even swim. If it's ok with you, I'll just take a refund."

Janice smiled as she took the bag. It was still sealed with her neat bow, which she peeled off before fumbling inside the tag for the barcode.

Luke considered what to say next. It wasn't like him to have to think about it – ordinarily he'd be throwing out lines playing with his catch.

It must have hurt when you fell from heaven,

Do you have a name or can I just call you mine?

Fortunately, he plumped for the mundane.

"So how long you been working here for?" he finally asked.
"Too long. Way too long."
"I know the feeling" he mused. "Ever feel like just throwing it in and taking a new career?" he asked in a voice a full octave lower than he expected it to be.
"Well actually, this is my new career. I was in banking" she said, wondering why this guys voice kept changing in tone.
"Really?" Luke was taken aback. "That's quite a change."
"I know. It's only been temporary while my divorce is being sorted, but I'm just waiting for the right investment opportunity to come along and I'll be off."
Janice knew from her banking days, the most unlikely sources are sitting on goldmine ideas, so she was happy to engage in conversation with anyone - particularly those that could converse coherently, which excluded most of her techie customers.
"Hey, don't tell me about time slippin' away. I've been looking for a new opportunity since I got here four years ago."
"Really? Turns out everyone's looking for an opportunity around here. You don't look like a techie" She said, eyeing his neatly creased Chinos.
"Thank God for that! No, I'm actually searching for a techie with an idea who needs a rainmaker to make it happen. You know, pitching, funding, putting a team together, marketing – I'm the man. Hey, here's my card" he said, pulling as he slid his hand in his back pocket, shuffled through a selection and deposited one on the counter.
"Luke Palatino, Rain Maker, Funding, Marketing, Team Assembler Extraordinaire."
"Wow, that's quite some title" she mocked, as she handed him the refund receipt, inadvertently brushing his hand as she did so. Luke felt it through his entire body.
"Small world" she said. "Maybe we can help each other."

Luke wasn't used to such enthusiasm to help him and wasn't about to let the opportunity pass, especially from someone as attractive as Janice, no matter how casual the interest was.
"I would have thought lots of opportunities pass through these doors" Luke said, after all, that was his sole purpose of being there in the first place.
"They do" she said, "but it's difficult getting a conversation going with half the drips that come in here, and besides they all have funding. I want the ones that don't."
"So how can we help each other?" Luke asked, as several possibilities flashed through his mind, most of them unrelated to anything she was likely to offer.

Janice turned her notepad towards Luke, showing the long list of names she'd written.

"Everyone on this list is a friend of mine from my days in banking" she said as she presented her notepad to Luke, displaying the long list of names that had refused her the opportunity of working back in banking. She ran her beautifully manicured hand down the list before continuing. "If I'm excited about something, they'll back me." She sounded convincing.

She studied Luke a little closer.

He looked good, although possibly a little tired and worn, and she deduced he'd probably seen success earlier in his life, and since lost it.

He sounded good too, but clearly lacked the sharpness or intelligence to make it in the Valley. He also lacked the hoodie, t-shirt and headphones around his neck. No one would take someone in chinos seriously.

If only he had an idea, he'd be the sort of person Janice needed for her plan to work.

They chatted through what each was looking for and swapped numbers.

It was vague and informal, and frankly not considered to be the hottest lead by Janice. Luke was beside himself with excitement.

CHAPTER 18

From the moment the driver pulls into the drop-off zone at Santana Row, I wonder why the hell I've come to a Shopping Mall, and whether I would have been better off looking at quilts and textiles after all. At least I wouldn't feel so under-dressed there. I have no money, no-one to buy anything for, and I'm not the least bit hungry. I decide to find somewhere I can linger over a coffee and people-watch.

I take a walk in search of a Starbucks. The well-manicured faux sidewalk reminds me of when I visited Disney twenty or so years ago. I remember it being the trip-of-a-lifetime, which is exactly what it turned out to be as I'm going to spend the rest of my life paying it off.

As I walk amongst the well dressed beautiful people, I consider how many of them are living off the fat of an internet idea and whether there's a single creative genius like me amongst them.

I recognise the classic dress of the men in chinos, amongst the slinky women in their heels. There's also a few ripped hoodies.

I think about how, soon enough, everyone here will be using my messaging system, and how I'm not going to be able to walk through here without people pointing me out and calling my name.

"Barry?" I hear in my perfect imagination.

"Barry!" again, but I know now I'm not imagining it. I swing round to see it's actually a guy I met at the Oat House yesterday. I consider how he spotted me, then realise I'm wearing exactly the same clothes I did when we first met. He's wearing lighter chinos and a blue shirt instead of the white I remembered him in. I recall little else other than he was one of the many who were interested in working on Project Ronald, and he seemed to be asking everyone's opinion on whether they thought my idea was a good one.

He catches up with me and shakes my hand enthusiastically.

"It is Barry, right? We met yesterday. Tod Damar, GalactInvest?"

"Hi Tod. I remember. Nice to see you again" I reply, only vaguely remembering him.

"Barry, I'm pleased I bumped into you."

We're standing in the middle of the plaza, and people are having to walk around us to avoid the perfectly manicured lawn, which I surmise is probably plastic grass.

Tod's excitedly telling me how he's skilled at spotting a winning opportunity, and if he let's me hand mine to him he's going to turn me into a rocket from the sparkler that I am. He talks about blue-touch papers, pyrotechnics and flames of colour – until frankly I have no clue what he's talking about, other than it sounds dangerous. As he animates explosions with his flaying arms, I notice his gold Rolex sliding up and down his forearm. Not understanding a word he's saying, my mind wanders to whether he's in danger of over-winding his watch.

Finally, he mentions money, and my attention's back.

"Sign it over and we'll write you a cheque for a million dollars. Today."

I want to ask him to keep his arm still so I can check his Rolex and log the time I was offered a million dollars. There's a voice inside me screaming for me to reach over, hug him, take the money, and disappear into the sunset. I feel my mouth dry and my hands sweat.

An image pops into my mind of my small suitcase being full to the brim of cash.

He's looking at me, waiting for a reaction, and I wonder if dribbling is amongst the possibilities he's considered.

The last thing I want now is to agree a deal with anyone, as that's not part of my plan. I briefly consider whether at this moment, being a creative genius might be a setback.

Inside, I'm screaming for the deal, but I'm sensible enough to hold him off, and it kills me to.

As I open my mouth to speak, I hear the words leaving my mouth, and wonder if I'm more surprised at my response than he is.

"Tod, I appreciate the offer, but I'm not looking to exit just yet. I appreciate it."

I force a smile but I appear to have less control over my cheeks than I'd hoped, and I feel them quiver.

"Barry, don't make a decision you'll come to regret for the rest of your life. I can tell you a million dollars buys a great deal of happiness." He moves closer to me and winks "... and a whole lot o' women."

I hadn't planned to squander my riches on prostitutes.

I say nothing – so he continues. "How about we have a coffee together, and see if I can come up with a figure that'll change your mind?"

I now realise a million was just his opening shot. If I draw this out over a coffee, perhaps a muffin too, I could get two, three – who knows - maybe even four million dollars. I'm trying to convert it to sterling in my mind when I hear my voice again. I almost dread hearing what I'm going to say.

"Tod, I'd love to, but I'm here to buy some gifts to take back and I really don't have the time right now. I'll be sure to email you later though."

"Can I take your contact details? I'd like to send you our offer"
"I don't have one" I say. He looks at me as though I've just told him I kill puppies for fun.
I feel my left leg shaking and I have visions of collapsing, but manage not to. I hold out my hand, moist with sweat. As he takes it, his bright white-toothed smile turns to feint grimace.
For an instant, I imagine an entire row of suitcases brimming with cash and wonder if taking a few million today is a better option than the multi-millions I'll get when I pull my plan off. I push the thought aside, wondering if a creative genius can still lack common sense. I've got to go with what I believe in, no matter how painful it feels.
The exchange comes to an awkward end, and after a farewell and a promise to speak by email later, I walk off with much purpose but no idea of where I'm actually going. I see the sign for a Starbucks, and I head towards it, but realise I've just told Tod I don't have time for a coffee and if he sees me headed there he's going to think I'm some sort of simpleton. I turn round to see him wiping his hand with a hanky so before he looks up, I aim for the nearest store.
I walk straight into someone who's just walking out. As I brace myself for him to tell me what a clumsy git I am, I'm pleasantly surprised to hear him apologise and wish me a good day. I watch as he regains his balance and strides off, almost skipping with happiness.

I smile and as I push the door to enter the store, I peruse what they actually sell. The bright colours and fluorescents dazzle me momentarily as I realise.
Bloody swimming shorts.
I'm just looking at the mannequins wondering why anyone would buy a tiny little pair of shorts to match their own, when a head pops up from behind the counter. A rather attractive head.
"Hey, can I help?"
"No, I'm just here to ... look" I say, still blinking rapidly.
"Take your time. I'm guessing you're a triple-x" she says, holding up a pair of fluorescent pink shorts as she removes them from a laminated bag as though she's already prepared them for me.
"Where are you from? Australia?"
"Yes" I say, feeling playful, but she appears totally disinterested.
"Cool. Well, if you need any help, just holler."

I have no recollection of ever buying swim-shorts. I have one pair, rarely used, and several years old. Quite how long someone can spend shopping for swim-shorts is a mystery.

Another mystery is why anyone would want high-viz shorts. You'd either have to be swimming at night or need to cross a highway to get to the beach to justify them.

I move back towards the door. I assume Tod's now gone so it's safe to leave, but then I consider I have a free morning tomorrow and perhaps I'll take advantage of the Self-Starter's pool. I select a pair of dayglo orange shorts, being the least-offensive, check the size and take them to the counter.

"Great choice sir. Cash or card?" she says, as she picks them up and folds them in a way that's strangely erotic.

"Charge please" I say.

"Sure. That's three-eighty-nine."

My first thought is how a pair of shorts for under four dollars is remarkably good value, then I look around to reassess where I am and the décor of the place.

A feeling of unpleasantness washes over me as I realise there's no decimal point in the price, and this rather ordinary pair of shorts is going to cost almost the same as my flight over here.

I put my wallet back in my pocket and wonder how I'm going to save face, and realise whatever I say, I'm not going to.

"I'm sorry" I say, feebly. "I've changed my mind."

"Hey honey, don't worry. They're a lot of money. You know Walmart sell a similar pair for fifteen bucks".

I'm relieved and slightly insulted at the same time. Do I really look like I can't afford them? Despite knowing the answer, I ignore it, choosing not to tell her I turned down an offer of millions of dollars just moments ago.

"It's not that" I say, preparing to dig a hole I don't need to. "but I'm only here until tomorrow anyway, and I'm not going to get a chance to use them."

If I were her I'd ask why the hell I bothered picking them up at all, but she's far too sweet to humiliate me further. Nevertheless, I continue digging my hole.

"... but I'm coming back in 3 weeks for a movie premiere - and I still won't have time to use them then."

"Hey, really" she says, losing patience. "It's fine. You can come as often as you like without feeling obliged to swim"

Now I've started, I can't stop.

"I'm only here for the Oat House Pitch & Present and ... " Her eyes suddenly widen as she cuts me off.

"Wow. What's the chance of that? You don't look like a geek either. Come to think of it, you're definitely not an investor. Are you here with your kid?"

Seeing the opportunity to regain some of my lost humility, I find myself telling her everything about Project Ronald, but only after briefly mentioning an Non-Disclosure Agreement I'll need her to sign, which she agrees to and asks me to mail. I know she's only a shop assistant, but everyone around here's only a degree or twos' separation from a techie. For all I know, she's related to Bill Gates.

As I'm telling her, I wonder why. Is it my endless need for more praise and recognition– or is it because this woman's gorgeous and lavishing attention on me I've not had since ... well ever.

Whatever it is, I find myself spilling out far more than I intended, but hold short of giving her the full story. I even give her a printout of my presentation, which I had left over and stuffed in my jacket pocket.

Unsurprisingly, she also seems incredibly excited by it, and not the least bit put off by its slight dank appearance.

"What's your name honey?"

"Barry" I say as she scans it, using only the very tips of her nails to avoid skin contact with the paper.

"Barry, there are several flaws, and I'm not just talking about the yellow starbursts - but those aside, do you have a team to make this happen?"

"No. I'm looking for that too"

For some reason, that seems to interest her even more.

"You gotta have a team. No-one's going to back an idea without someone to make it happen" she said, although she makes it sound more of a positive than a negative.

She looks deep in thought, and then composing herself, goes on to tell me that Silicon Valley is like nowhere else on the planet, and if I don't understand it, I'll be eaten alive.

Apparently, my idea is flawed because I don't understand how the system works in the Valley. She teases me that, with her help she might be able to iron out some of the flaws, but no guarantees.

"Barry" she says, "forget the flaws for a minute, there are two things you have to know about the Valley." She's talking much quicker now and she seems to have entered some kind of hypnotic zone. "Firstly, in an industry where the currency's measured in billions, millions is nothing but small change."

She waits for me to digest, before she continues.

"And secondly, it, doesn't matter whether you think an idea can work or not. It ALWAYS works if enough money's thrown at it - so the important thing for any investor is to make sure they own it before anyone else. They can be ruthless in making sure they do. So what I'm trying to say, is, however much cash you think you need, always ask for more. Much, much more."

I wonder if she realises how good that is to hear.

"Thing is Barry, I think I can help you with your idea."

There's something about this woman that makes me believe she actually knows what she's talking about. It might be her sheer beauty, her understanding of the system in Silicon Valley, or perhaps it's just the context of having this conversation in a swimming shorts shop. Whatever it is, I'll go along with her.

Although she's identified flaws in my plan, which should concern me, I remind myself her expertise is possibly limited to the field of selling brightly coloured swimming-shorts, rather than launching multi-billion tech ideas.

By the time I'd left the store, despite having more interested parties than I'd ever dreamt possible, and having already turned down million, I'd agreed to let the shop-assistant help me.

I leave the store, delighted to return to normal sunlight, and check to make sure Tod from GalactInvest isn't stalking me. I decide to head back to the Inn to see if they even have a pool, and whether even four dollars would have been wasted.

CHAPTER 19

Janice had a spring in her step as she followed the exact route Barry had just taken around the store, spraying her air-freshener as she did, grateful he'd not tried a pair on.

She'd been through months of looking and waiting for the right opportunity, and in a single day she'd found both an idea and the right person to front it.

She'd not for a single second considered Barry for any future role in it.

Overall, his list of short-comings was so long, he was as useless to her as a discount at an Octajour store – but she was in no doubt, his idea was perfect. And if there's one thing that Janice knew, it was how to recognise a brilliant idea.

Fate had been shining on her that day though, and as she delved deep into her handbag, she found the card she was looking for.

> 'Luke Palatino, Rain Maker, Funding, Marketing, Team Assembler Extraordinaire'

As she passed in front of the mirror, she noticed herself standing slightly taller, her chest pushed forward, as she felt the energy surging through her veins.

She could feel it. She was about to make a fortune and take revenge on the banking world too.

She could finally move on with her masterplan.

* * *

Luke could hardly believe his luck when he got the call from Janice.

In the space of just a couple of hours, he'd got a partner, possibly even a girlfriend – and certainly a prospect. It more than compensated for the death-threat he'd received from a cyclist on his way home and having his car spat at by another.

During the call, she'd spilled out Barry's idea with such enthusiasm, he was gripped by the brilliance of it, even though he didn't quite understand what it was supposed to do – or what his role was.

Putting that aside, he assured her he was just the man to make it happen. He'd explained how – in his earlier career – he'd run large teams of sales people, from his large offices, making himself large amounts of money in the process. He omitted the fact that most of his activities had been dishonest and that he'd spent time in prison as result.

He also didn't tell her he was currently driving for Uber and that he was banned from taking credit – or that he couldn't even pay the rent on the dump he lived in.
Luke felt he'd impressed her suitably, as she'd asked him to pop back later to join her for a coffee and give her the opportunity to explain how they would work together.
Having explained his diary was full, he assured her he'd postpone his next meeting to accommodate, he just had to deliver an urgent package to the airport and he'd be right there. He hoped his passengers didn't mind him talking on the phone, or being referred to as packages.

Janice had already made a dozen or more calls before she'd called Luke.
Among them was a call to her bank manager to discuss the possibility of remortgaging the house, which was now registered solely in her name and debt free. According to the valuation she'd had for the divorce, it was worth over a million dollars. She was delighted to hear they would lend half a million against it.
Next she'd called another business banker and arranged for a new business account to be opened in preparation for her new tech project. She explained she was expecting several million dollars to be paid into it over the coming weeks.
The manager had shown no reaction but agreed to post documentation for her to sign. This was, after all, Silicon Valley.
She'd then called Francois, the manager of Octajour's bigger branch in San Francisco to inform him she'd be out for the afternoon and needed cover. As usual when speaking with him, she spoke slowly, accentuating each syllable so he could understand. She could have spoken to him fluently in his native French, but chose not to. French was one of five languages Janice spoke.

Francois had listened as Janice explained the reason she had to leave. It was the standard excuse he'd heard dozens of times before. As a fellow sufferer of the same interminable headaches from working in an Octajour store, he fully sympathised.
He wished Janice luck with her doctor's appointment and as he put the phone down, he accepted takings would be considerably down without Janice there.
Finally, she called some of the bankers on her list that had made excuses why they couldn't employ her.
Each call had started as a strained conversation until each had realised she was no longer asking for a job, but was offering them an investment opportunity.

Men who had been so reluctant to speak with her before suddenly dropped their voice a full octave and listened intently to what she had to say.
For Janice to describe an investment opportunity as 'game-changing' it had to be outstanding.
All of them knew of her reputation. All would have jumped at the opportunity to employ her - if Tod hadn't threatened them.
When each heard she was investing around half a million dollars of her own money, it drove them to a frenzy. If it's good enough for Janice, they thought, it's a golden opportunity for them. All she had to do was tell them how much she needed, and show them what it was – after all there were still processes to be followed.

By the time she'd called Luke, she had ten bankers desperate to invest in her venture and nine dinner dates. It would have been the full ten but Gary Saunders was gay and far more interested in what her ex was up to.

Candy and baby came to her mind.

CHAPTER 20

As Luke whisked the two beards in the back of his car to San Jose airport, he couldn't stop himself from relaying how his day had gone. The embellishments were small but significant.

The lights were all red, the traffic was heavy, and as neither of them wore headphones, he had their full attention.

During the hour's ride, his two captives in the back seat learned how Luke had bumped into Janice in an upscale store - although no mention that she'd served him - she was in banking, she was stunning, she'd come onto him, and she had a big deal for him to head up.

As he stopped at a set of red lights, once again, he leant over to his glove box and removed a box of cards. He emptied the pile and took two from the bottom, and handed one to each of his passengers.

'Luke Palatino. Ubering - but don't need to.'

As they each read it, he insisted it was for no reason other than they could tell their friends and family who they'd been driven by, as in a short time he was likely to be a well known name. On this occasion, he didn't ask where his passengers were headed or what they did. Nothing could impress Luke anymore.

He was also quick to point out that they were amongst the last passengers he was ever likely to be ferrying around. His future was riding in the back – not the front – of a chauffeured limo.

As they crawled along the freeway, Luke went on to tell them everything he could remember Janice telling him about Project Ronald, which he'd listened to with great enthusiasm and little understanding, but could repeat almost parrot fashion.

Just as Janice had said to him, he relayed to his riders how they should prepare to delete their messaging and email apps as they'd soon be redundant.

By the time they got to the airport, his passengers knew everything about Janice, Luke - and the project. They also knew he took a Large in swimming shorts and that his cousin isn't gay.

They got out of his car at the General Aviation drop-off and gave him a feedback of feedback. As they wondered through the exclusive terminal, they talked about what they'd just heard. By the time they'd been escorted onto their private jet, they understood the scale of the opportunity.

On the flight to Seattle they discussed what resources they'd need to put in place to make it happen.

* * *

By the time Luke got back to Octajour, the stand-in had arrived so Janice was already waiting outside. They both walked together.

Luke was excited to know what his role was and whether it involved hot steamy sex with Janice. When he noticed her legs, he became more focused on the latter.

"Luke, I'm going to help you make a great deal of money" she said, as she hooked her arm with his and steered him towards Starbucks.

As they entered the store, she directed Luke to sit in the comfy seats in the back and asked him what he wanted.

He wanted an iced tea, but in an attempt to impress her, he asked for a venti, half-whole milk, one quarter 1%, one quarter non-fat.

When she returned, she was holding two lattes, which she placed on the table and moved her chair closer to Luke.

She sat on it, flicked her hair behind her ear, and stretched her long legs to the side of his, and winked as she moved in closer.

Somewhere on the two-minute walk between Octajour and Starbucks, this woman had turned into a powerhouse.

"Luke, I have a lot of funders with a lot of money who will back a project with two essential ingredients. A great idea and a good leader."

Luke smiled, his hands clenched in the hope she didn't notice the trembling.

He wondered whether he had a business card for such an occasion, but thought perhaps on this occasion, he should stop the pretense and leave the talking to her.

She patted him on the leg. He edged forward in his seat.

"They desperately want to invest their piles of money, and Project Ronald's perfect."

"I think it's brilliant" he said, hoping she wouldn't ask him to explain why.

"Well, that's great, because the guy who came up with this idea is what they term in my circles as ... " she stopped to think of the phrase "... a retard"

"Oh!"

"Yes. Luke, no-one – and I mean no-one – will want to invest in him. He lacks the presence, the appearance and the credibility to negotiate terms with any banker."

"I see."

"He looks like he's about to have a cardiac arrest, and he sweats when he talks."

"That's awkward" he said, hoping she wouldn't notice the beads of sweat he could feel on his forehead.

"It is Luke. It's awkward, because somewhere along the line he's stumbled over a brilliant idea, and he doesn't realise it, but the biggest obstacle between him and success is ... well, it's him." She touched Luke's hand. Luke felt his face redden.

"Where do I come in?" he asked, surprised at the slight quiver in his voice.

"Well, Luke, I'm pleased you see there's an opportunity. I think you can make this happen. I see you as a rain-maker, am I right?"

"Janice, that's exactly what I am!" Luke sat back up. Bolt upright. "Look" he said producing a business card from his back pocket "I've even put it on my card"

he said as he thrust it in her hand, as though validating her.

"That's great Luke, I knew I was right about you. So if I give you a brilliant idea and a great deal of money, am I right in saying you're the right man to deliver it?"

"Of course I am. You can count on it" he said, with total confidence, but no idea.

"I knew you were the right guy from the moment I saw you, that's why I'm going to invest everything I have into you Luke. I'm going to mortgage my house and put my children's home on the line because I know you're going to make us a fortune" she said, as she watched the colour drain from his face.

Luke shuffled on his chair and put his sweaty hands under his legs.

Janice sensed the time was right to discuss how they would split the shares.

"How much can you invest in it?" she asked

"Well ..." Luke looked up as though he was calculating in his head. Finally, after much thought, he replied. "Actually, most of my cash is tied up at the moment, so if I'm honest, I'm not going to be in a position to liquidate any of my assets in the short term."

"Anything?" she asked.

"Well, let's say nothing currently."

"That makes things awkward" Janice said, leaving the problem hanging in the air for an uncomfortable amount of time.

"I have an idea" she said excitedly. "If I'm putting up say half a million dollars, how about I hold all the shares until you're in a position to match it?"

If the opportunity was as good as Janice said, Luke desperately wanted to have shares in the business from day one, but accepted he wasn't in a great position to bargain - and certainly wouldn't have the same percentage of the business as her.
"How about this" he said, "I hold twenty-five percent of the shares for the moment, and I don't put any money up"
"Ten percent" She replied, instantly.
"Fifteen"
"Ok, you get fifteen percent of the shares, and of course you'll be on a salary of say a hundred thousand – or whatever you think appropriate. I know it's not a lot of money to someone like you, but hey, it's a startup."
Janice was delighted. She'd allowed for double that. She had to negotiate hard so as not to give her plan away, and the last thing she wanted was for Luke to feel the slightest bit suspicious.
Luke basked in his fine negotiating skills and hoped he was masking his excitement well. He'd not considered there might be be a proper salary too, but considered a hundred thousand was very appropriate indeed. It was all sounding a bit too good to be true, so he wondered if there might perhaps be a flaw.
"What about the retard?" asked Luke.
"Well, he'll have a few shares for the idea and his assurance to stay away from it" replied Janice. "Leave him to me."

Luke put his feet up on the other chair at the table and placed his hands behind his head as he leant back on them. He took a brief moment to assess his position. Here he was in Silicon Valley, about to start on a hundred grand a year job and have stock in a tech company, of which he was the CEO. It was exactly what he'd dreamt of, apart from the minor detail of not knowing what the company he was heading actually did.
His mind flit from moving out of his dump in Tenderloin to driving a new Lexus – or perhaps even a Merc, before Janice continued with more details.
Although Luke would have fifteen percent, Janice explained each of them would have to give a percentage of their shares to the funders in exchange for the investment they received.
Luke was neither interested nor cared. He'd be willing to surrender however many shares he'd cleverly negotiated, firstly because he was more interested in getting a secure salary, but chiefly because he had no understanding in what the venture actually was. Having any shares at all was a bonus, and having a hundred grand

income was going to be very welcome. If she was putting in half a million and aiming to raise more, the likelihood was he'd be earning money for the foreseeable future.

As Janice continued, interrupted only to order more lattes, she explained what each of their responsibilities was and how they would go about them.

She would look after the fundraising and accompany him to the banks he needed to present to. He would forecast the expenses and prepare a cashflow which needed to include the cost for everything from securing offices, recruiting a Chief Technical Officer, Chief Marketing Officer, Chief Operating Officer, Chief Financial Officer and HR personnel to manage the myriad of staff they'd all need. Luke would be the Chief Executive Officer.

Once he'd worked out how much the business was going to need, she'd know precisely how much money she needed from the banks. What Janice didn't explain was she was already in no doubt of the size that figure needed to be in order to get the banks salivating even more.

As soon as the necessary funds had been raised, and her own half million dollars invested, Luke would then be responsible for managing the board and delivering the business plan.

Luke had hoped at some stage in the afternoon she would have explained the idea and business model to him. Looking at the long list of work he had in front of him, he wondered if it was perhaps a little inappropriate to ask for a reminder. He didn't want her to lose confidence in him and he certainly didn't want to show his ignorance. He'd blagged his way through everything he'd done so far in his career, and had no doubt he could do the same with this.

From the way Luke had compiled his list, it was obvious to Janice he had little understanding of how to go about his tasks, nor how he would bring the idea to life. Frankly, for her plan to work, it was immaterial but he would need to know how to assemble the team and at the very least make it look like an exciting venture. She reminded herself that once he'd ditched the chinos for jeans and his crisp shirt for a hoodie, he'd look the part and worthy for banks to back. She tried to think of a way of helping him without making it obvious.

"How about I give you the short presentation the retard left with me earlier?" she said as she leant over her bag and pulled out the print-out Barry had left on her counter.

She sensed Luke eyeing her cleavage as she did so, and smiled sweetly as she handed the document to him.

Luke felt his face redden and returned her smile as he unfolded the papers and looked over the first page.

"I like the starbursts" he said, before folding it again and sliding it in his inside pocket. He wouldn't embarrass himself by trying to understand it now, he'd look at it later and hope by the time they next met, he would be able to discuss it with intelligence and understanding.

Before they parted, Janice reminded him of the need to move quickly. She made it clear she'd already set up meetings with the banks to arrange funding and was going to need to know how much they needed before her first appointment. Luke assured her he'd have something for her within a week.

"No good Luke" said Janice. "I need the figures quicker. We've got our first bank presentation in two days.

CHAPTER 21

As the plane touched the runway two-hours later in Seattle, the two bearded techies raised their champagne glasses to toast the Uber driver who'd given them the idea of the century. They'd already toasted each other on their brilliance for improving his idea by adding a GPS function.

They took out the business cards he'd handed each of them which they vowed to frame for posterity.

'Luke Palatino. Ubering - but don't need to' was to be entombed in glass alongside the business cards of the company board, which included some of the biggest and best known names in the world.

As the screaming jets quietened, they each switched on their mobile phones.

The stretched limo pulled up alongside where the Citation jet had come to a halt and the beards handed the driver their bags and continued on their phones.

The taller one was shouting to be heard over the departing aircraft in the background.

"...Yes, that's what I said. *Everyone* in the boardroom please. We'll be there in about thirty minutes. I want the comms team, head of coding – and can you ask Larry to be there too."

The shorter one sounded no calmer.

"...just tell them something urgent's come up and I have to postpone it until next week. Find out when they're booked to be back in Tokyo.

Also, can you check with the Disclosures team to see if anything came in marked Project ..." he searched his memory for the name "... Donald?"

CHAPTER 22

Back at the Self-Starter, I login to *MiserableSpouses* and see that true to her word, Marie did in fact delete her profile, so she wouldn't have seen my reply. I have to send it to her email address – but first I need to set up an account she doesn't know. Sending it from *barriegoodman68@gmail.com* is something only an idiot would do.

I waste ten minutes setting up a hotmail address, during which time every name I try is unavailable. Finally I settle on *mikewantsmuchmore@hotmail.com.*

Without thinking, I use my new email address to send the Non-Disclosure Agreement to Janice, reminding her she promised to sign it when I met with her in the store earlier. I also attach the presentations on how the concept works, although I'm missing some print-outs and suspect I may have left them in her store.

I get an email straight back asking who Mike is, and what is it he wants more of?

To cover my embarrassment, I write a feeble reply telling her this is my brother-in-laws email address, and I'm only using it as I didn't think my overseas email address would work in the US.

After I send it, I cringe at how ridiculous that sounds. I worry she thinks I might appear stupid.

I turn my attention back to Marie. She's probably sitting there waiting for fictitious Mike's email. The creative genius is fully unleashed on her.

> Hi Marie
>
> So good to hear from you. I often have to be up in the middle of the night to look after my sick wife, that's why I sent my last mail at 3:30am.
>
> I'm hoping she'll be in rehab around the same time my youngest goes to Uni – then it's freedom for me!
>
> I feel bad for my wife. I used to love and care for her so much, even though she never returned it. Now I'm looking for someone who will.
>
> Until then, I know life will be tough, rattling around in this big old detached house with just three of the six bedrooms (all en suite) being used (we sleep separately).
>
> I love it that you're a beautician. I'm a stuffy old lawyer, working mainly on divorce cases so I know what I've got ahead of me (but at least I'll save money. I know most people stretch out their divorce longer than they need to and could save themselves a fortune if they just cut ties sooner!).

So where are you on your divorce? Anything I can do to help? I always give my clients the same advice: Get out as quick as you can and break ALL ties, especially those that you think are worthless.

Mike x

PS Do you have a pic?

I have no idea why I asked for a pic. I have no desire to look at her any more than I have to, but I suppose it adds to the authenticity.
It's 10am in the UK so she probably thinks I'm sending it whilst at work.

Within a couple of minutes I'm delighted to see both Marie and Janice have replied.
The picture Marie's sent me is from a summer we spent in Bournemouth four years ago. She's managed to edit me out, although my hand's still visible, resting on her shoulder.
She must have worked hard to sort her way through hundreds of photos to find one she obviously thinks shows her at her best.
Judging by the speed at which she replied, she's obviously kept this picture on her desktop and I'm guessing I'm not the first she's sent it to.
In her message, she tells me how bad she feels about my wife, and she hopes I didn't drive her to it (lol). She goes on to tell me her lawyer's slow, expensive and unsympathetic. Like mine.
She hates her husband and she agrees about the suggestion to break all ties, but can't help herself from holding out for a share of his business for no other reason than to piss him off. He's a loser who's never managed to support her, or her kid – who she goes to great lengths to explain no longer lives with her. He's a fat, sweaty, sad looking idiot of a dreamer. No mention of being a creative genius. And by the way, can I send a photo.
I decide to deal with it when it's 3am. If nothing else, she'll think I'm consistent.
Janice's email is rather sweeter, although I'd be more appreciative if she too had sent a photo.
She's agreed to the Non-Disclosure Agreement, but can't print it out until she's at home. As she knows I need a hard signed copy, she's offered to meet me tomorrow.
She also tells me, although she's no techie, she's never heard of an email address that only works in one country.

It's only early evening, but I'm bored, broke and tired. I'm also hungry. I decide to stay in my room and watch TV. I'm hoping I can get a pizza delivered as I can't be bothered to go back to Denny's.

The phone buzzes and I'm surprised to see it's a text from Mickey.

> planes delayed.
>
> Got yor stuff with me
>
> Give me yor lawyers and Ill get something over for the movie rights
>
> I can get anyone to play you – but whos going to play me? ha ha

I love his impatience, but we've a lot to do between now and any movie.

> Thanks mickey
>
> I'll call u when im back and we'll discuss

I go to bed forgetting to check if there's a pool here.

CHAPTER 23

Luke had returned home from his meeting with Janice and pored over the presentation she'd given him.

He knew how to text, he received emails, and on a couple of occasions he'd even tried whatsapp - but no matter how simple the diagrams, he didn't understand what Project Ronald actually did to simplify them, nor how it worked nor why everyone would be using it in the future.

He wondered how problematic it might be if a company CEO had little to no idea about what it was they actually did. It was doubtful the CEO of Boeing was actually an aircraft engineer, or the CEO of Kellog's was a corn farmer.

Eventually, he concluded his role just required him to put the right people in place and make sure they got on with whatever they thought they needed to get on with to make whatever needed to happen, happen. He would focus on steering the business, which at this point was limited to preparing the costings and presenting them to Janice.

He opened his laptop, which was now several years old and lacked all but the basic software. It was refreshing to use it for something constructive at last. For the past couple of years it's purpose had been limited to porn, for which it was frustratingly slow.

Now, this out-of-date, fit-for-nothing laptop was about to be used to produce a multi-million dollar business plan.

Not understanding how it works was actually the least of his problems. He now had to work out how many people he'd need to employ and how big the office would need to be in order to house them. He'd then have to come up with a budget for each department. Without a starting point, and no idea of the end game, he had no idea of where to start. The very best he could do was take a wild stab at it.

He opened Excel 98, and created a new worksheet listing all the key staff he would need in a column on the left and monthly costs as headings going across. Periodically, he stopped and stared into mid-air seeking inspiration as he wondered what to do next. He then added columns for rent, rates, software, computers, marketing and a dozen or more other overheads he remembered needing from when he ran his previous businesses.

After spending forty minutes listing everything, he wondered how much cost to allocate to each, and what other columns he'd forgotten.

Conscious his spreadsheet had to show a depth of understanding he didn't have, he knew no amount of formatting, heading columns in bold or colouring rows, was going to compensate for leaving out vital costings or showing incompetence in how much expense he'd allocated and where.

He sat back and perused his work. There was no question, the overall look of the spreadsheet was impressive. There were italics, there were boxes around where the totals were, and there were certainly lots of rows. Unfortunately, the only figure he'd inserted was his own salary of a hundred thousand dollars.

He slammed down the lid of his laptop in frustration and sprung out of his chair. He walked a few short steps in his tiny flat, removed a bottle of bourbon from a cupboard, and took a swig.

He took another couple and returned to where he'd been sitting, with the bottle. He opened the laptop and deleted the spreadsheet he'd just spent hours producing. He put his head in his hands and stared at his now empty screen.

No one would describe Luke as a man of patience, and he certainly wasn't renowned for fact-checking or detail, so any attempt of putting together a spreadsheet of this magnitude was futile. He had to find a cheats way of doing it – and as he had his first presentation to a bank in a couple of days, it had to be quick.

He opened his web-browser and typed in the search box 'Facebook Financial Accounts', and from the myriad of responses, he found the accounts they'd filed for the previous year. Several websites made them available for their investors but few had them in an excel format, which was how he wanted them.

After scrolling through several pages, he finally found what he was looking for. He downloaded the file and deleted all the content with the exception of the sheet referring to overheads, and set about changing the figures – initially reducing them by fifty percent, then by seventy percent, and finally by ninety percent but they were still far too high. He reduced them again, and again until finally it looked more palatable to him. He then added his own salary to the total.

After a little dressing and tweaking, he had his total overheads. He sat back proudly and admired his work.

It was almost 6am and, he concluded, not worth going to bed. With nothing in his apartment other than bourbon, he decided to visit Dunkin' Donuts for a coffee and something sweet before heading over to Janice.

He had several thoughts on his mind. How would he break the news to her that they needed three million dollars; would she have any chance of raising that much; how quickly can he start drawing a salary; what was she like in bed.
Tired and weary from his night's work, but excitedly confident, he drove to where Janice lived in Willow Glen, some fifty miles and a world away from Tenderloin.
Willow Glen was probably the nicest area of San Jose, and where most of the players in Silicon Valley had their city home when they weren't on their vast country estates somewhere upstate.

The rush-hour was well under way and the traffic was heavy, but Luke still arrived fifteen minutes ahead of schedule.
He surveyed the townhouse from outside and guessed it was worth a million dollars or so - smaller than the house he once owned in Florida, but significantly larger than the dump he rented in Tenderloin.
As she opened the door, Luke was taken aback.
She wore a simple grey dress that accentuated both her stunning figure and her bright blue eyes. She accessorised with burgundy earrings, matching shoes and a choker.
Luke was immediately aware that as well as not sleeping, he'd also not changed and was wearing the same chinos and shirt as he'd met her in the day before. Both were creased and he was unshaven.
There was also a feint waft of alcohol in the air which he realised might be coming from him.
Any hope of hitting on Janice today evaporated, but if he could impress her enough with his efforts on the business plan, perhaps it would merely be postponed rather than written off altogether.
She escorted him into the front room where a large dining table sat covered in children's toys and scattered paperwork.

Luke opened his laptop and wiped the screen with his sleeve.
"I've been up all night making sure I got this right" he said "you're going to be impressed with the figures."
He opened the file and started talking her through the list of expenses, grateful he'd had the foresight to delete any logos or reference to Facebook.
As she scanned the document, several rows caught her interest.
"What's the FB subsidiary heading and all those countries for?" she asked.

"Ah. I'm pleased you pointed that out" he replied as he rubbed his stubbly chin thinking of a response. "Well ... er ... it's actually the ... would you mind if I had a coffee?"

Janice apologised for not offering her guest a drink and left to get one, leaving Luke staring at the screen. Again.

She waited for several minutes before returning with two steaming mugs of strong coffee with which to mask the unpleasant odour.

"Ok, so where were we?" he said, as he sipped from the mug and focused his attention on the screen.

"FB" She said. "I assume it's Foreign Branch, and I think it's brilliant you've thought of including them so early on."

Janice was delighted to be able to cover for his incompetence and even more confident Luke was exactly the right guy to ensure her plan worked.

"Thank you Janice, yes, I thought we should get a foot in each of those markets from day one" he said, proudly.

"So what's the bottom line?" she asked. "How much do we need to get the tech up and running and get through the first year?"

Luke scrolled down to the bottom of the sheet.

"I'm afraid we're going to need three million." he said, gritting his teeth, wondering if he should have reduced them further.

"No good" Janice said.

"Well I could probably get them down to ... "

"No! I mean we need more. Much more."

She folded the lid of Luke's laptop and turned towards him as she explained the golden principles of fund-raising in the Valley, repeating the mantra she'd explained to Barry just the day before.

"Where the currency's measured in billions, millions is nothing more than small change, and secondly an idea ALWAYS works if there's enough money thrown at it, so you have to show you're asking for enough."

Luke showed no expression. The coffee was either decaffeinated or he was more tired than he'd thought, but he had to repeat the words he was hearing several times in his mind before he understood them.

"Luke, bump the numbers up to show we need thirty *or forty* million"

"Really? You can raise that kinda money?"

"I can't raise *less* than that kinda money."

"So if I put a plan together to show we need thirty million, we'll get thirty million in the bank?" he asked, in the hope of clarifying what sounded too good to be true.

"Of course. Leave that bit to me. And I said *between* thirty and forty"

"Ok ... well, how about I sit here and adjust the figures right now? It'll only take me a couple of minutes" he replied.

"I was thinking perhaps you could work from home today and maybe have a shower and change" she said, patting his leg. "... and perhaps you can sort yourself out a hoodie and a pair of jeans. I think it would make you look much younger" she winked. "I have to leave now or I'll be late opening the store, and now's not the time to get fired." She rose, in the hope he would follow her lead so she could escort him out and get on with her day.

CHAPTER 24

I'm delighted to awaken when it's actually morning. It's the first time I've slept through the night.

As I reach over to pick up my phone from the bedside table where it sits on charge, the pizza box falls off the bed, scattering crusts across the floor.

It's 8:06am. I must have been exhausted.

I've got to be at the airport around 2pm for my flight back to London, so I figure I'll pop in and see Janice on my way there.

I have no idea why I feel the need to see her, but there's something about her that makes me feel I can trust her.

Packing for the return journey takes a fraction of the time it took to come here, and after standing under a trickling shower, I've got a full hour before I have to leave for the swimwear shop in Santana Row.

I open my laptop and check my emails on both accounts, mindful I need to reply to Marie's email, but it's too early.

Today's emails include one from The Oat House telling me what a success their event was this week, with one opportunity being hailed as outstanding. They emphasise that due to confidentiality and Non-Disclosure Agreements, they can't divulge any more details other than it's in the Communications Sector and it's come from someone without technical expertise – or indeed any expertise - which they say, goes to prove no one should assume they're not capable of game-changing ideas.

There's another from Virgin Atlantic, asking me to check-in for my flight and the usual *SiliconValleyNews* digest, which I don't bother reading.

My focus is on the last one, from Katie. I open it, although I've got all I need to know from the subject line.

Subject: Need money!

Hi Barry

Hope it's still going well and everything's going to plan.

Just need you to know I'm doing all I can, but we need money desperately.

As always, I'm fighting your corner but can't guarantee I'll succeed.

Anything you can do?

Katie

I know Katie's doing all she can. If she's had to email me about money, I know it's because she's tried every other delaying tactic first.

Other than Mickey, she's the only person who knows of my plans and she's certainly aware of my finances. Things must be desperate, and she's the only one who knows how catastrophic the timing is. If between us we can't hold them off, we're in danger of losing everything.

I now have precisely 180 days left. I desperately need her help to get me through them.

If I'm going to make the fortune I plan to, I need to make sure everything's wrapped up by then.

Worried I'd be reaching the limit on my credit card, I decide to save my last Uber journey for the trip to the Airport.

I revert to transport that takes cash. I take two buses and walk for fifteen minutes to Santana Row so not only am I sweating profusely by the time I get there, but I'm faintly aware of a squelching sound as I walk.

Of all the journeys to take by public transport, the one where I'm taking luggage is the least sensible.

As I enter the store, blinking several times, I can make out there are two people standing behind the counter, and consider maybe the older one with dark glasses is a short-sighted customer before I realise it's another Octajour sales-assistant.

I catch the tail end of a conversation between them, hearing Janice being told "... and that's why you should wear sunglasses too" before I catch Janice's eye.

As she steps out from behind the counter, she looks me up and down. I do the same back but realise it makes me look like a sexual predator.

I offer her a sweaty hand, which she takes and then, by the pout that follows, regrets.

I tell her I'm on my way to the airport, and happened to be passing by.

It's mildly credible if I'm walking to the airport, but if I'm using any other means, it's clear I've broken my journey at great inconvenience to visit a shop selling swimming shorts.

I ask her, now that I'm here, whether she'd care to join me for a coffee to see how we can work together on my project and she whisks me by the arm and leads me out of the shop.

She shouts back at her fellow assistant that she has to sort out some personal issues.

It's not clear if the woman's even watching as her glasses are so dark.

We leave the store and walk towards the Starbucks I was aiming for when I bumped into Tod from GalactInvest yesterday.

We make polite conversation and she tells me to grab one of the comfy chairs whilst she orders the coffees.

I quite fancy a hot-chocolate but in an attempt to impress her, I order a low-fat version.

"It's great you're doing something about your weight" she says.

She approaches the counter to order and I make myself look like a busy executive by burying my head in my phone. What looks like me sliding emails up and down is actually one of my lower-scoring sessions on Angry Birds.

As she approaches, she looks serious. She puts the coffees on the table and moves a chair to face me, then sits on it, stretching her long legs to the side of mine.

I'm halfway through pouring the third sugar before I consider I may have killed the illusion.

"Barry, I'm so glad you came by. I've been thinking about your idea a great deal and well ... I'm not sure if I can help yet."

She touches my leg and continues "Let me start by saying, there are several flaws in the way you presented it to me, are you aware of those Barry?" I open my mouth to answer, but don't need to as she's in a flow. "Because I'd love to work with you, but I'm not sure you're ready yet."

She rubs her hand along my leg. I wonder if this woman is actually coming on to me and whether she expects me to do the same to her. I, of course, don't.

I open my mouth to speak again, but this time, I have the opportunity, but my mind's gone blank.

She watches my mouth pensively waiting for a sound, but hearing nothing, she continues.

"Barry," every time she says my name, I think she get's a little thrill inside "I have a partner who might be able to help us. He's a big player with good track and the banks love him – and he just happens to be available now, so if you'd like me to, I'll see if I can get him to work on it."

She makes it sound like Bill Gates is going to run my project.

"... but you'll only end up with a percent or two."

Bill would be more generous.

With the techs I met in Starbucks, and all those I met at the Oat House, I figure there are sixty or seventy other interested parties possibly doing the same thing, but right

now, I'm happy to go along with her and see where it takes me. There's something about her that tells me this could unfold rather differently to how I'd planned it.
"And Barry, I think that's a good thing. You'd have to do nothing, and who knows – in a year or two you could be sitting on millions. If things go according to plan, I can safely guarantee you a million at the very least."

It's the second time in two days I've been offered a million dollars, and I'm surprised at how blasé I'm becoming. I sense this is just her opening shot too and consider whether I should negotiate a little to see just how high she'll go, but having never won a game of poker, I decide not to. Besides, I'd rather not know in case I'm tempted. I have to keep my eye on the end game.
Her phone rings, and she reaches in her bag to switch it off. I briefly forget the big prize as her fragrance wafts over me.
I impress myself that I've found a voice.
"Janice" I leave a gap to show my brilliance and to consider whether I've actually got anything to say. Eventually, it just pours out "I agree. Your partner sounds fantastic, and taking a small percentage for doing nothing sounds great to me. Can I just ask you for the signed NDA, and then let me know how you want to move forward and I'll show it to my lawyers back home."
Wow. I sit back, basking in my brilliance. I can't believe I've thrown in the bit about my lawyers looking at it. She probably thinks I've got a whole team looking out for me. The truth is no-one – with the exception of Katie and Mickey – knows what I'm up to, or what to look out for.
"Oh. I nearly forgot. Here it is" She returns to her bag, giving me another waft, and then hands me the signed NDA which I don't bother checking.
Her bag buzzes as the phone she silenced now vibrates. I'm disappointed she chooses to ignore it.
I'm overwhelmed by her looks, her hand on my leg, her wink and her overall manner, and I'm desperate for her to answer her phone so I can smell her again.
"Barry, how about I email you once I've made sure my partner's signed up and the funding can be arranged. I know you don't think emails travel long distance but I'm pretty sure it's worth a try."
I cringe, and nod at the same time.
I tell her if I don't hear, perhaps I can meet her again when I return in three weeks.
She leans over and kisses my sweaty forehead.
"Sure honey. I'd like that."

I watch her as she gets to the door and blows me a kiss as she walks out.

I stay sitting, in the hope she thinks I have important messages to attend to.

CHAPTER 25

Luke drove slowly on his journey back to his flat in Tenderloin. He was worried about being stopped in case he was still drunk from the night before, and his mind was flooded with thoughts of fast cars, big houses and white sandy beaches, and a return to the life he once had in Florida before he'd been arrested and imprisoned for fraud.

This was different. This was no fraud, and he was using legitimate funds from legitimate banks to fund a legitimate business. He hoped.

He wished he'd remembered to ask Janice how long it would take for the funds to arrive. He hoped it would be weeks, not months before he'd be drawing a fat salary and heading a team. In hindsight, he wondered if a hundred grand was a bit low for the head of a multi-million dollar tech company. He would tell her he wanted more - perhaps a quarter of a million. It wasn't as if they were going to be short of money – and after all, she'd been quite clear when she'd said 'a salary of say a hundred thousand – or whatever you think appropriate'.

Perhaps he should get a bonus too – maybe another quarter of a million. He'd also want his car and rent to be covered by the business, and of course, travel and any other perks necessary for the life-style he intended to live.

By the time he'd got home and showered he felt the lost night's sleep catching up with him. He had a shower and lay on the couch, considering perhaps whether it might be simpler if he just drew a half million in salary, and drifted off to sleep.

It was almost 2pm by the time he woke. His first thought was to speak to Janice. He wanted to tell her he'd now re-considered his position and decided his responsibility and expertise commanded an eighty-three thousand dollar monthly remuneration, which he felt sounded less than the million dollars a year to which it equated. She obviously needed him a great deal, and he wasn't about to give his expertise away for bargain rates.

In the back of his wardrobe he found some old blue jeans, which he put on with a faded t-shirt kept only to wear in bed on cold winter nights. Before he left the flat he spent a couple of minutes at his laptop, multiplying all of the expenses by twelve, including his salary. The forecasts now showed the business needed thirty-six million dollars in funding, of which one million, two hundred thousand was to cover his salary.

On the way to Janice he made two stops, one of them being Kmart to buy a hoodie.

When he arrived at the store, Luke was surprised to see the woman in sunglasses that was standing-in for Janice yesterday was back again today.

She explained Janice had left for personal reasons and wasn't expected back until later that afternoon and that perhaps he should leave the wilting bunch of flowers with her so Janice would see them on her return.

He was disappointed he didn't get the chance to impress her with his spontaneous visit and gift of flowers, which he'd planned the moment he'd left her this morning. They were the best the gas station had, but they still looked tired and saggy, especially against the bright colours of swim shorts.

As he left the store, he tried calling Janice. He tried again when he returned to his car, and once more when he got out of the parking lot.

Finally he sent her a text.

> Hi J
>
> Hear you've got personal problems. Hope everything's ok.
>
> I've reworked the figures
>
> When do we meet next – we need to discuss my salary
>
> L x

He hoped Janice was ok. The last thing he needed now was for her to postpone the project due to personal issues. Whatever happened, he still had to pay the rent until his salary started, so he switched his Uber App to "available" and within seconds his next job pinged up.

It was a pickup within twenty yards of where he was, requesting a ride to the airport.

He looked up to where the shops met the main road, and saw a large sweaty man with a small black suitcase standing there.

He opened his window as he pulled round.

"Are you Barry?"

As he got in the back, the car sunk on its suspension, and they drove off.

CHAPTER 26

I'm still amazed at how many Uber drivers there are around here. Today's a record, with one turning up within eight seconds of my request.

"Are you ok sir?" he asks with concern in his voice.
"I'm fine thanks."
"You sure? You look a little pale." I ignore him, but he continues. "Are you afraid of flying?" my driver asks me.
"Not at all. I'm looking forward to getting back to London" I reply.
"I've never been. Is it true everyone carries an umbrella there? Were you here on vacation?"
I slap my forehead as I realise mine's still leaning against the wardrobe in the Self-Starter.
"No. I was here on business."
"Cool. Anything interesting?"
"Well actually, I was at the Oat House Meeting Hall, if you've heard of it?"
"Heard of it?" He almost exploded with his enthusiasm. "It's my second home buddy! Take my card."
With that, he lunges out of sight for a brief moment, resurfacing with a box of what looks like business cards. He searches for one and hands it over to me.
'Luke Palatino – Oat House Introducer Extraordinaire'
I've no idea what it's supposed to mean, and just as I'm about to ask, he tells me he's only driving for Uber to fill his time until he finds his next project.
I wonder what sort of a reaction I'd get if I used that line when I was Ubering in London. Somehow it just wouldn't sound the same.
There was no stopping him.
"Actually, scrap that. I can't take on anything right now, I'm working on something massive" he gushed. "I'm on over a million a year and I've just raised nearly forty million" he said, as he screeches the car to the side of the road and asks me to return the business card he's just given me.
It's hard to believe anyone on a million dollars is doing airport runs for forty dollars on the side. He reads my mind.
"Sir, you're probably wondering why I'm in the front and you're in the back if I'm on that kinda money. Should be the other way round, eh?"
I choose not to answer in the hope he'll leave me alone.

"Just waiting on the cash to come in and it's goodbye Uber. You could well be my last passenger. Feels kinda special, eh?"

I'm rather insulted he thinks there's a possibility I could be driving him. I wonder whether I should tell him I'm probably nearer to my tens of millions than he is to his paltry million. I ponder on telling him I've actually turned two offers down for more than that in the past twenty-four hours alone. I decide not to as I can hear how much of an idiot he sounds and I don't particularly want to compete.

He's not the slightest bit concerned about whether I believe him or not as he launches into telling me about his venture, which, as I sit back and listen, sounds suspiciously like mine. He lacks much of the knowledge of what it can do and shows no understanding of how it works, but he seems to have grasped how clever it is and why everyone will use it.

As he continues, I'm in no doubt he's spilling everything he knows about Project Ronald, albeit somewhat confused.

He takes a full ten minutes to tell me the spin-off opportunities, which magnify his lack of understanding, and how our children will laugh when they hear how we used to communicate before it, which I agree with, having written exactly that line in my presentation. The final insult is watching him as he takes his hands off the wheel to draw a starburst with his index fingers.

I want to ask him how he knows. I certainly don't recognise him, but he clearly knows everything about it, and it's obviously not from the Oat House. I decide to tease more out of him.

"Wow. That's a brilliant idea. Who's the genius that came up with it? How's it work?"

"Well, if I'm honest, I have no idea but hey, that's not my concern. I'll recruit a team to sort it. And by the way, the guy who came up with it's no genius - he's actually retarded. I bet he's one of those artistics".

I stop myself from correcting him as the anger builds within me. If I'm going to get to the bottom of this I need to stay calm. I swallow hard before I speak.

"So how do you know about it if you haven't met him?" I ask.

"Who says I didn't meet him?" he says as he scrapes the kerb.

I backtrack, realising he hasn't told me.

"Oh. What's he like?"

"He's Australian. He's an old boy who obviously has no understanding of anything techie" he laughs as he adds, "Would you believe the shmuck can't even use email properly. He doesn't think emails can be sent from one country to another" He shakes his head in disbelief.

There's a gap in our conversation whilst I consider it's only Janice who thinks I can't use email, and she thought I was Australian.

"What a shmuck" I laugh with him "Where'd you meet him?"

"Well buddy, you were right the first time. You must have some kinda sixth sense, it's actually my girlfriend that met him. She's also my junior partner."

"Should you be telling me this? Didn't she sign an NDA?"

"What's that?"

I take out the crumpled paper Janice had handed me in Starbucks and which I'd stuffed inside my jacket less than an hour ago.

I recall the conversation in my head:

I have a partner...

The irony of the situation hits. I realise that there's only one idiot here, and he thinks he's going to be leading my project.

"Well, maybe you can help me on my project too" I say.

"Sure" he replies, as though he'll honour me by sharing his expert opinion and superior knowledge.

I tell him about my idea for an App that allows anyone to order cupcakes any time of the day, and have them shipped anywhere in the US within 24 hours.

It sounds no less pathetic than when I heard it pitched by Nancy in the Oat House. I still feel her pain. Now I also feel guilty for sharing her idea. I promise myself at least I'll return her messenger bag when I get back to London.

I go into the minutia of the idea, hoping to fill the time up until we get to the airport.

As we trundle along, I'm getting into the swing of how the app lists the ingredients, the types of toppings, even the paper it's wrapped in. Nancy didn't tell me any of this but I'm going with the flow.

Finally, as we turn off of the Bayshore Freeway towards the airport, I draw it to a close.

"... and you even get to choose the wording on the label."

The driver shakes his head.

"Buddy, I gotta tell you, I've heard better" he says with no attempt to hide his disappointment. Again, I feel for Nancy.

"Well, I thought so too, but my partner's been working on it for a while now. She's been baking cupcakes for months. It's just a matter of time before she quits her job at Octajour and goes at it full time."

"She works in Octajour?"

"Yep. She tells me she's found some mug to take on her other projects so she can focus on cupcakes."

He takes his eyes off the road to study me in the rear view mirror as we glide up to the drop off zone at the departure terminal.

"Really? You have Octajour in London?"

I clamber out, and as the car's still rising on its suspension, I deliver the punch.

"Sure we do, but Janice works here in the Santana Row store."

I quickly grab my suitcase and hot foot it into the terminal building.

CHAPTER 27

Janice returned to Octajour and thanked her assistant for standing-in for her.
Her eyes rolled when she pointed to the tired looking bunch of lifeless flowers. As she threw them into the bin, she noticed the card.
'To building a special relationship together' Luke x
Unwelcome though his advance was, she'd fully encouraged it. She was used to using her femininity to get her way, and used to the consequences that rose as a result. Luke was small time though. She could handle him, at least until she'd made her money and taken revenge, by which time she'd be moving to Florida.
She'd already been online and found several properties in Ponte Vedra Beach in the North East of the state.
Even if she only got ten million dollars, she could still buy one of the more beautiful houses and not have to worry about working again. She'd be disappointed if it was only ten million though.
She took her phone from her bag remembering the missed calls she'd had whilst she was with Barry. She read Luke's texts and saw the calls were from him.
As she waved off her stand-in assistant she was already on her phone going through her list of calls.
The first was to Ray at BFD TechBank, top of the list of investors she'd lined up to meet. He answered immediately.
"Hey babe" he said, slightly slurred. "You're not calling to cancel the meeting are you?"
"No Ray, I'll be there" she assured him. "I'll be with the guy I'm backing. I just wanted to let you know he's a bit, you know ... eccentric."
"They all are babe" he said.
"... and although he say's very little, he knows exactly what he's doing."
"Of course he does babe. You wouldn't be puttin' half a mill of your own in it otherwise, eh?"
"... and by the way Ray ... so I know we're not wasting each others time, what's the limit you can sanction without going to the credit team?"
"You know the score Jan, we don't play in the kiddies playground. It has to be at least thirty before we're interested, and I can sign-off up to forty without board approval."
"Good. We're in the right ball-park."
"Hey Jan, how about we take the afternoon off together tomorrow?"
"Ray, I'd love to, but tomorrow's no go. We'll sort something when we meet."

She ended the call and sent a text to Tod at GalactInvest. Since he'd left her, Janice had learned phoning was a waste of time.

Can we meet later this week. I need to chat.

It took just seconds for him to respond.

No. Send me an email

Fantastic, thought Janice. She knew within a couple of weeks he'd be begging to meet her.

Next, she called Jeff, her accountant.

He was part of her new team of professionals she'd had to find since she'd split from her husband and had to avoid using his.

Jeff was fantastic. He was full of clever advice, and most importantly, totally smitten by her so he'd do whatever she asked of him.

"Hi Darling, how are you?" he asked as he answered almost immediately.

After the formalities and another polite but firm refusal for a dinner date, Janice went on to explain the purpose of her call.

She needed a letter from him confirming her income was high enough to support a mortgage of the half a million dollars she intended to borrow from the bank.

She waited as she heard him tapping away at his keyboard.

"Janice, you know I'll do anything I can to help you, but according to your last return, you're making less than thirty grand as a shop assistant. I can't tell them you can afford it because ... well ... you can't."

"Jeff, write the letter and then let's have that dinner."

"Ok. When are you free?"

CHAPTER 28

The traffic police at the airport moved Luke on. Parking in the drop-off zone was permissible for three minutes maximum. Shouting and ranting after your passengers wasn't permissible for any amount of time.

Before he'd picked up his passenger, Luke was imagining his new life making a million dollars a year and heading up a company that did whatever it was it did, with Janice as his new girlfriend.

By pure chance, he'd now found out his dream girlfriend was actually nothing more than a scammer who'd tricked him into babysitting an idea that he never understood - probably because there was nothing to it – whilst she's been busy baking cupcakes and getting ready to launch her app.

Confused and angry, he drove out of the airport and pulled into the Dunkin' Donuts at the first turnoff to compose himself and ponder over a Reese's Square and coffee.

He took his phone out of the glovebox, and read the text from Janice.

> Hey L
>
> I didn't have personal problems. I just used that as an excuse to get out of the store today.
>
> I was with the idiot I told you about. Trying to get him out.
>
> Think I managed it
>
> Don't forget we're meeting with the bank tomorrow
>
> PS thanks for the flowers but don't get the wrong idea
>
> x

He considered whether he was dealing with some crazy nutcase.

She sounded convincing enough with everything she'd told him. She'd shown him a list of her banking contacts who were desperate to back the idea she'd given him.

She'd even told him she was putting her own cash in, and her house on the line.

Why had she never mentioned her cupcake business?

Once he'd played with his donut, which he no longer wanted, he sipped his coffee and fired off his reply.

> Hi Janice my CUPCKAE!
>
> I'll pick u up at 10 so we've got some time to go over figures and have a coffee and a CUPCAKE!!
>
> Perhaps you can bake them ;-)

He grinned at his brilliance. Perhaps she'd not realised who he was.
Luke Palatino can't be fooled.
He switched his Uber app to show he was available and drove off back towards the city, making a mental note to order business cards with his new slogan as he did so.

Back in Santana Row, Janice was puzzled by Luke's text.
What the hell was this guy going on about cupcakes for? Perhaps there were hidden connotations. She found nothing online to suggest it was a euphemism for anything sinister or sexual. Maybe he just had a thing about cupcakes.
Whatever it was, she decided it was something she could discuss with him later, but for now she questioned whether Luke was actually the right man to help her in her plan.
He didn't need to be a techie, he didn't need to be particularly clever, but he'd definitely need to be sane.

CHAPTER 29

Safe behind the Oversized Baggage desk, I bend over to regain my breath.

I assume the driver's now gone but I can see a few bewildered people are still standing by the entrance discussing their interpretation of what the nutter was screaming about.

Fortunately, no one's tied me to being the fat bastard who's cost him a million dollars, and no one knows why he'd like to stick a cupcake up anyone's ass.

I only truly relax once I've checked-in and gone through passport control.

I've got four hours before my flight leaves, but with nowhere else to go, the airport's the most comfortable option – and there's free WiFi too.

It gives me plenty of time to start work on putting the list of contacts into a database, which is the next stage of my masterplan.

I open an excel spreadsheet and type in every contact I've made, with the name of their company, contact details and a column for each area of expertise so I can tell whether they're a funder, techie, entrepreneur or a mix of all three. I also add one column in which to place a cross if they've signed an NDA.

I take all the information from my handwritten notebook, which I've been diligently updating throughout my trip.

By the time the flight's called, I've got a list of sixty-eight names, sixty-six of which have signed the Non-Disclosure Agreement.

I'm confident none of them have any details of where or how to find me, but I know the next time we're in contact it will be of my choosing, and none of them will be pleased to hear from me.

I see the queue forming to board, and as I join it, I work out how long until I start getting my money: 178 days.

CHAPTER 30

Luke's alarm clock had been screaming long enough for the neighbour to bang on the thin wall separating the apartments where he lived. As he stirred, he looked at the clock and saw it was almost 9am. It was no wonder he felt groggy having slept for less than three hours.

Since he arrived home last night he'd gone through every conceivable emotion starting with anger, briefly followed by depression, self-pity, frustration, back to anger for a bit, and then - as the enormity of the cupcake opportunity dawned on him – elation and excitement.

Overall, he'd thought lots and slept little.

He fumbled on his bed until he found the envelope he'd used to scribble his thoughts on sometime during the night.

He could barely make out what he'd written. It had been dark and his hand-writing was appalling at the best of times.

He'd made his notes frantically, listing all the opportunities for which he thought cupcakes could sell. The potential the mini cakes industry offered was simply staggering. The numbers were simply too large to fit on the envelope so he'd abbreviated with 'M' for millions – and 'B' for billions.

According to his figures and working on the basis there are some three-hundred million people in the US, each of them celebrating a birthday each year, the numbers were simply colossal.

Add to that all of the weddings, births, Mother's and Father's Day, Halloween and even funerals, Luke could see there were dozens of opportunities to order cupcakes for every man, woman and child in America.

If just two percent ordered cupcakes a couple of times a year, say six cupcakes per order, she'd be selling over seventy million a year.

If she sold them for say four-dollars each, she'd have a business with sales of around a quarter of a billion dollars a year. If she could roll the idea out globally, she'd have multi-billions in sales.

She may be sly and disingenuous, but there was no getting away from it, Janice was a genius. What's more, unlike Project Ronald, for which he still had no clue as to its workings, this was something Luke easily understood.

Luke didn't bother shaving, and in the same jeans and t-shirt he'd been wearing the day before – and through the night, he left for Janice's.
He needed to confront her immediately on her cupcake venture, and make sure she made him a part of it.

Luke's mind was fizzing. For the first time he was excited at the opportunity to be able to explain the workings of a business to the banks without worrying about being scrutinised.

Janice smiled sweetly as she opened the door to Luke, despite her concerns. She followed Luke's eyes as they rolled up and down her body as they had done each time they'd met.
"Come on in" she said. "Nice touch - wearing the same clothes for two days. Makes you look a whole lot more bankable" she added. "We've got ten minutes before we have to leave for the meeting."
Luke marched in and swung back to look at her.
His focus had moved from the bank meeting to confronting Janice, although he regretted he'd let his standards slip and not made himself more presentable. He wasn't going to let the brief derailment distract him.
"Cupcakes" Luke said "I get it. Let me in on it" he begged her.
"Pardon me? What are you talking about?" she said, her face screwed up.
"I know what you're doing, and I can help. I'd be great at it. Forget the million salary, I'll drop back to hundred grand, but make me a part of it."
Janice screwed her face up.
"What million salary? What's with the cupcakes?"
As she poured the coffee, Luke spewed everything he knew about her other venture, removing any reference to meeting the informant in his role as an Uber driver, or that he'd been screaming after him at the airport.
He went on to tell her how he'd had a sleepless night as he worked through the calculations and scrawled notes on the massive potential, and why he wanted to be a part of it.
Janice considered whether perhaps the crazed madman was the type to carry an axe.
"Luke, I have no idea what you're talking about. Where was it? Who was he? When?" she asked, shaking her head.

"He was... it was... I met him at San Fran airport yesterday afternoon. I went there straight after I dropped the flowers into your store" Luke replied, hoping he'd given no hint he was Ubering.

He quickly added "I had to drop my niece there" hoping to add credibility to the story.

Janice pondered for a moment. From the description he'd given her it sounded like Barry – and the timing was certainly right because Barry had left for the airport straight after they'd met yesterday. But the chances of them both being at the airport at exactly the same time, and the notion that they'd got into a discussion about her and a cupcake idea was just bizarre.

Whatever was behind it, she would no doubt find out later, meanwhile she had an important plan to follow and she couldn't afford to derail it – especially now, when she was hoping to meet the bank and get them to sign-off forty million.

She decided to calm Luke by telling him whatever he wanted to hear, and work out what had happened later. As she considered the best way to respond, she recognised a hint of opportunity.

"Luke ... " she said as she took his hand and led him to the couch "... first of all, I'm sorry I didn't tell you about my partner and our cupcake venture. As soon as I met you, I knew I wanted to work with you, and from the kind of guy you are, I figured cupcakes wouldn't excite you, but hi-tech would, which is why I cut you in on Project Ronald."

Luke relaxed. Perhaps he'd been a bit harsh. She'd recognised his worth, and she'd wanted to work with him all along. He could already imagine how his new business cards would look. 'Luke Palatino – Cupcake King Extraordinaire'

Thinking on her feet, Janice presented Luke with an opportunity she was creating as she went along.

By the time they left for the bank, Luke was calmer and thankful to be included in both projects - and to show his appreciation he'd agreed to reduce his share in Project Ronald to ten percent, and to work on it for three months or so until she was ready to launch her cupcake venture. She had assured him he could then find someone to replace him as CEO and join her in the new venture – and have 20% of it.

Luke was delighted. He'd achieved everything he set out to do, and he still had a vast income coming his way until the new venture started. He continued to the bank with

a renewed vigour, and a slight chaffing in his underpants from the two days he'd worn them.
Janice settled herself in Luke's Prius and gave him the bank's zipcode for him to key into the satnav.
Luke apologised for all the suction marks on his windscreen, and they setoff.
The journey took less than ten minutes during which time she'd steered the conversation away from cupcakes and back to Ronald several times, whilst she held her head out of the open window.
"You might want to brush your teeth" she said, handing him a mint.
Once again, she briefed Luke on what he had to do.
"Luke, remember, sit there looking as though you know exactly what you're doing, but say nothing. Leave the talking to me."

* * *

The BFD-TechBank building was twenty-three stories of glass and glitz and dominated the street from its corner position. Originally called the BFD-GoldBank, it had opened as an outpost in 1852 during the gold-rush and was now considered to be one of Silicon Valley's biggest funders. The bank may have been old, but the furniture was modern. The highly polished varnished desks, the shiny washrooms and the polished counters were all highly utilised by the cocaine-fuelled workforce.

The 'Blue Sky Room' was a small meeting room, adjacent to the more intimidating Board Room, but was similarly decorated with plaques and awards in recognition of their astute investments and vast wealth.
Luke and Janice were escorted in and sat there alone, accompanied by water, coffee and biscuits, whilst awaiting their host.
As the door swung open, a well-dressed youthful looking man with watery bloodshot eyes, walked in making a beeline for Janice.
"Jan babe, how are you? I see you're gorgeous as ever" he said as he lunged at her, lingering a little too long in a hug. He turned to Luke, extending one hand, and wiping his nose with his other.
"Hey buddy, I'm Ray Sharp" he said, staring at Janice and almost crushing Luke's hand.
"Luke Palatino" he replied, but Ray wasn't interested.

"Jan, you delicious beauty. How long's it been? How you enjoying the single life? Man I can't get over how great you look. What's the story?" he gushed, winking his eye, wiping his mouth and sliding his chair from the head of the table to be next to hers. The three of them were now sitting in a row on one side of the table, which meant Luke was only visible if he leaned either forwards or back.

"Well Ray, it's been a couple of years – but you look good on it."

Janice let the mutual admiration continue before moving on to the purpose of their visit.

"Luke here's a great guy with a great history and a fantastic opportunity. He presented it to me, and in a heartbeat I was in. As you know, I'm remortgaging the house and putting everything I have into it ... which is half a million" She sensed Ray's attention span was likely to be short, and he'd forget half of what she was saying.

Ray interrupted.

"Jan, I'm behind you" he said with a wink, "if you're all in, we are too. How much do you want doll?" he asked, staring at her cleavage and wiping his nose again

"Forty" she said staring directly into his eyes, seeing them fixed on her chest and wondering if he would remember this conversation later.

Luke didn't know where to look, or what to say. He sat there, hands on the table, with a smile fixed on his face. He looked simple, exactly as Janice had told Ray to expect when she'd called the day before. She'd been spot on.

"Ok babe. Sounds direct enough. If anyone knows how to pick the winners, it's you. It's a no brainer for us. What you offering?"

"Fifteen percent" came the instant reply.

"Come on babe, fifty" said Ray.

"Forty" said Luke, delighted to be part of the negotiation.

Janice kicked him, and Ray ignored him.

"I won't go above twenty" said Janice.

"Let's settle on twenty-five" said Ray extending his hand to show the deal was settled. "How about we sort the paperwork over dinner tonight?" He got up to leave. As he moved towards the door he looked back "You still in Willow Glen? Pick you up at 8?"

"Sure."

"Oh. Bye Jake, good to meet yer" he said without taking his eyes off of Janice.

"Thanks Ray, you too. It's actually Luke."

"Sure it is" he sniffed as he left the room.

Luke was impressed with the ease in which Janice managed to get the funding, and relieved he wasn't called upon to supply any details on what the project was or how it worked.

"I told you to keep quiet" said Janice. "You nearly screwed that up."

"Sorry" said Luke, sheepishly. "What happens now?"

"Well" said Janice, "They'll do a little due diligence, which will probably be little more than checking I'm putting my cash in like I said I would, then they'll issue a contract – similar to those I sent out a hundred times or more when I was in a bank. I already know the clauses I'm gonna get them to change. Then there'll be a few pages of terms, conditions etc. and finally he'll want our lawyer and theirs to sort out the nitty gritty."

"Sounds like it could take a while" said Luke, wondering how many more months of Ubering he still had ahead of him.

"Shouldn't. I'll get it signed and sorted in a few days. We'll have the money within a week or two."

"So have we got a lawyer?" said Luke, delighted at the thought of drawing his salary so soon.

"Honey, leave it to me, but trust me when I say there'll be no lawyers, no staged payouts and I'll also get most of the other terms wiped out. We'll have the cash before you know it, so you'd better start moving forward on finding the premises, recruiting your board, and implementing the plan – sharpish."

Luke went quiet as the enormity of what he'd just witnessed washed over him. He'd considered himself wealthy before but he'd never been as wealthy as he was about to become. He'd never run a company with forty million dollars in the bank – actually, forty and a half including Janice's money.

That made his ten percent share worth over four million dollars already, and he hadn't even started it.

He wondered who he could call to tell them his news. As he mulled over all his contacts, he realised none. They were either people who no longer wanted to hear from him, other Uber drivers or business card printers. On second thoughts, he was relieved to have no one to tell, mainly because he wouldn't know what to tell them.

Whilst Luke was pondering, Janice had been making her own calculations. With the shares the bank would take, the shares for Luke, Barry, and a couple of allowances she'd hold back for others, she'd be left with sixty percent of the company.

Her plan appeared to be progressing well. She'd managed to hold on to more shares than she'd expected, and under Luke's stewardship she was confident she was just two or three months from moving to Florida.

She had one more bank visit to arrange - and Luke wasn't needed this time.

Luke drove Janice home and assured her he'd be in touch within a day or two to let her know how he was progressing on putting the plan into action.

Janice changed, and returned to Octajour to complete an afternoon shift. On the way, she called GalactInvest where Tod, her soon to be ex-husband ran the investments . After a quick chat with his PA, the meeting was arranged for the next morning.

CHAPTER 31

We land at Heathrow fifteen minutes before schedule to a bright summers day. It makes no difference as no one's here to meet me.

I'd slept intermittently and now I feel groggy - and my back aches from being squashed in the under-sized seat for ten hours.

I decide to go home, send some emails, sleep this afternoon and see if I can get out tonight for some Ubering. I may be on the way to millions but my credit card's maxed out and I'm going to need a buffer for my next trip.

The thought of having to see Marie dampens my enthusiasm, and I hope she's out when I arrive home.

Without anyone to pick me up I've got the choice of a forty-five minute taxi ride or a 90-minute tube ride for a fraction of the cost.

I need to survive for the next 177 days, so I opt for the tube.

As I leave the terminal building and start the long series of walkways for the tube station, I switch my phone on.

The tube doesn't go underground for a few stops, so I hang onto my phone signal long enough to open my news app and login to various other sites, including fictitious Mike's hotmail account.

I've got another email from Marie who's wondering if I hadn't replied to her last email because I didn't like her photo.

I remember little else about the journey until an elderly man nudges me and I wake to find I'm at the end of the line, one stop past where I should have got off.

I arrive home delighted to find the house is empty, and after dumping my bag in my room, I make myself a coffee and some toast. I open my laptop ready to send the first in my series of emails. I've titled it Email No.1 in my drafts, which I'd prepared at the airport last night - or yesterday afternoon - or whatever time it was.

I text Mickey.

> Mickey. I'm back. Let me know when it suits for the NDAs

I check my other emails.

SiliconValleyNews.com features several stories about a project several funders and software houses appear to be working on simultaneously.

Unlike the Oat House email, there's no mention that it's a Comms project, but BFD-TechBank is already funding an undisclosed outfit with an undisclosed sum for the undisclosed project. The only thing they've bothered to disclose, is the project was introduced to them by a seasoned and trusted expert in recognising new trends. I can safely assume that's not the Uber driver that took me to the airport.

I have no idea who this is yet, but I'm pretty sure they're saying someone's already got funding on my project. As I've not agreed terms with anyone, it can only be the result of someone stealing my idea and presenting it as their own.

The speed at which they've ripped me off and managed to get funding has staggered even me, and I thought nothing in the Valley was capable of doing that anymore.

There's a small part of me that's angry and wants to bring whoever it is to justice immediately, but that's not the plan. Waiting it out will have far bigger rewards for me than acting now.

I click the link in the email and open the BFD-TechBank website, which impresses me with it's track record of investments. I'm reminded there's no way I'd have ever managed to get to meet that caliber of investor on my own.

I'm comforted to know although they've never met me, their investing in my project and it's just a matter of time before they hear of me.

I decide it's time to email Janice and put an end to whatever game she's playing. I'm not agreeing terms with anyone, and if I was, it certainly wouldn't be her and her cowboy partner.

I spend a couple of minutes pondering which email address to send from, remembering she thinks I don't understand how emails cross borders.

I therefore settle on my Mikewantsmuchmore's hotmail address.

I'm desperate to ask her if she's been quizzed by anyone about cupcakes, and I'm curious to know how it played out, but right now's not the time, and she can't be sure it I have anything to do with it.

I feel uneasy as, once again I visualise what a million dollars looks like, which is what she'd guaranteed me. I consider how desperately I need the money, and whether I'll come to regret rejecting it – especially knowing I'm unlikely to make more than forty pounds from Ubering tonight.

I turn off the spell-check to ensure any illusions she may have of how incompetent I am, aren't shattered.

> Subject Line: Hope this mail reaches america
>
> Hi Janice
>
> Sorry to tell u but I no longer want to work together with you because of the broken terms youve breeched on the non disklosure agreement. Your so called partner has been telling everyone he meets about my idea. You cant

work on my idea without me because you signed the agreement but I hope we can still be friends.

B Goodman

In a penthouse flat in the centre of San Jose, Ray was nursing his sore head with an orange juice, two paracetamol and a line of coke.

BFD-TechBank was seldom concerned when one it's employees took the morning off. It was rare to find a full compliment of staff in the office before 11am due to the volumes of drugs they'd ingested the night before.

As he pieced together the jigsaw of events from what he'd assumed had happened the night before, he grinned.

For as long as he'd known Janice, he'd wanted to bed her – before, during and after she was married.

Now he'd not only achieved that, he'd also managed to invest alongside her in a golden opportunity. It was a good nights work and one that both he and his bank could be justifiably proud. It was a shame she'd not hung around for breakfast although he wasn't entirely sure if she had and he just couldn't remember it.

Now he put his fuzzy mind to it, he wasn't particularly sure of anything that had taken place. He pondered on what his last coherent memories were.

There was definitely a great deal of flirting in the restaurant. He clearly remembered his hand on her leg and he remembered visiting the disabled toilets with her and ingesting his entire bag of coke, through his nose, mouth – and from the strange numbness and humming he heard, possibly his ear.

He assumed he'd managed to sweet-talk her back to his apartment and there'd followed a night of passion, hopefully some of it fulfilling his most deviant fantasies.

As he stood up, something fell out of his trouser pocket, causing him to smile.

Last night must have been fantastic. He wondered if she'd got home before she realised she'd left both her knickers and her stockings.

Ray had already run numerous investments for the bank, making them several billion - and himself tens of millions in return, but he could remember no investment that had been as low risk and likely to reap such huge rewards as this one. There had also been plenty of other investments where the sex was as plentiful, but this occasion stood-out as he'd not had to pay for it.

He picked up his phone to check the UK and Japanese stock movements whilst he'd been sleeping. As always there were plenty of emails from his overseas counterparts congratulating him on his stocks, which had only ever moved upwards.

One particular email caught his attention. It was from his PA 'Re: Project Ronald'.

Ray

Got your mail. It's all setup. When you get in, just sign it off and funds will transfer. Are you sure there's no need for lawyers on this one?

It's an unusual setup and the contract's missing 9 pages.

Dianne

PS – You were up late!

Ray scrolled down the email to see what he'd sent that had elicited the response.

Dianne

I'm authorising the attached shortened contract
so no need for lawyers.

We're lucky to get in on this and I don't want to
slow it down.

Please set up transfer for $40m to the account details I've written on the form.

Hope you can read it all.

See you tomorrow.

Ray

PS I'll be in late. Very late.

The email was sent at 4:08am.

He took a moment to congratulate himself on the speed in which he'd secured the opportunity and closed the deal.

He remembered neither changing the contract nor sending the email, but it wouldn't have been the first time he'd sent something whilst he was incapacitated. Few had ever gone wrong, and none had the accolade of having Janice as a co-investor, so this would certainly be considered low risk.

He wasn't in the mood to start reading it now, so whatever he'd sent was probably fine.

He hoped he'd see Janice again.

CHAPTER 33

The offices of Mickey Roughton Movie Productions Ltd lay in the heart of Mayfair in an imposing-looking Edwardian house, with marble flooring and wooden paneling. Within the lobby area, large framed posters of his blockbuster films adorned the walls, and his many trophies and awards filled the glass cabinets.
The lack of carpets made for poor acoustics, and it wasn't unusual for his booming voice to bounce around the walls and high ceilings as he berated anyone and everyone.

Today, Mickey was like an excited teenager.
Despite the frantic activity as the date of his latest blockbuster premiere approached, his attention was elsewhere.
Today was a milestone day. Mickey would be acting out a scene from a movie for which the story had yet to be completed, the script had yet to be written and he had yet to start producing.
Seated in his ornate bottle-green leather chair, he sat behind his vast oak desk, inlaid with matching green leather and opened his mail, arranging the contents neatly in piles. His movements were slow and exaggerated as he imagined the cameras zooming in for a close-up at key points. There were of course no cameras.
He turned and flipped open his vintage briefcase and removed a large pile of papers from the dirty yellow folder in which they were given to him, before carefully placing them to the side of another similar looking pile.
He sat back in his chair to view them from a different perspective. It was the same. The two piles were almost identical in size.
Sixty-seven signed, folded and subsequently unfolded Non-Disclosure Agreements were indistinguishable from the one appalling idea for a movie script.
It was unusual for Mickey to receive less than three appalling ideas daily. Once a year there might be something worth ripping off, but he'd never know if today's script was one of them as he had no intention of reading it.

He swapped them around, perused them, and swapped them back again.
His mind flitted between the choreography on his desk and how Barry would react to what was about to happen.

If what Barry had told him was right, this paperwork was a key part in how he would make more money in a year as a nobody than Mickey had made in a lifetime of being a world-renowned producer.

Barry had asked for his assistance, and who was Mickey to question it.

He clicked the intercom for his assistant.

"Stacey, can you come in please."

Watching Stacey walk into his office was something Mickey always paid attention to. He would call her only when he was ready for her, so he could sit back and admire as she made her entrance. Stacey had never once needed to wait for Mickey's attention.

She had a way of maneuvering her long legs - accentuated with spiked stiletto heels - through his door, that demanded any red-blooded man to stop what he was doing and take notice.

Her long dark hair, smooth complexion and rich olive skin, was complemented perfectly by her bright red lipstick.

She always wore a lacy bra and kept it visible through her sheer blouse - on occasions, one button too many would be undone. Mickey always considered it to be two buttons too little.

Despite her long list of shortcomings, Mickey loved having her around. Her job interview had lasted barely five minutes, but Mickey had made his mind up as soon as she'd entered the room.

She was looking for a fast-track into acting and he was looking for some eye candy.

In the two years she'd worked there, she was still to be offered a single part, reading or audition. Mickey had no intention of giving her up and ruining one of his daily pleasures.

He paid no attention to her skills and frankly cared little for her ability or suitability as his PA, which was fortunate for her as she was as useless as she was gorgeous.

Since the day she'd started her employment with him, thanks to her total lack of administrative skills, Mickey had missed several meetings, been late at many lunches, and failed to return dozens of calls.

He'd also forgotten birthdays and missed deadlines, not to mention the small matter of booking flights to San Diego instead of San Francisco, which she'd had to change. Twice.

He'd considered it a small price to pay to have her around, and only mildly infuriating.

Having only left Mickey's office a few minutes earlier to deliver his post, Stacey was surprised to be summoned back.

Her heels struck the wooden floor as each footstep of her journey echoed throughout the building. As always, Mickey knew of her impending arrival and positioned himself for the most advantageous view.

As she walked in, she noticed – unusually - Mickey's attention wasn't on her. She wondered if he was ok.

As he leaned back in his chair, his eyes fixed on his desk, he seemed to be concentrating on other matters.

"Stacey" he said without even looking up or eyeing her legs, "I'm going out for a short while. Whilst I'm gone can you tidy my desk please?"

This was highly irregular. In the whole time she'd worked for him, she'd only been asked to tidy Mickey's desk twice and on each occasion it resulted in the introduction of new systems to overcome the catastrophes she'd caused.

There were now stickers on both his out-tray and in-tray reading "PUT NEW THINGS HERE" and "POST LETTERS LEFT HERE".

By the piles on his desk were tent cards marked "TO KEEP" or "NOT TO KEEP".

His desk didn't even look particularly messy. The piles were as he'd always kept them, and aside from a dirty yellow folder in his waste bin, she could see no urgency in clearing it.

Mickey rose to leave and as he walked out, he took one last look at his desk, and without being to resist it, one look up and down Stacey's legs.

He checked his watch. He'd want the exact time logged for the film script. Perhaps he'd close this scene with a close-up of the mahogany grandfather clock in the corner of his office.

The spa he visited was in a luxury hotel just a stones-throw from his office, on Berkeley Square.

It was fair to say that all the masseuses there knew him well and despite his fame, refused to treat him. Those that didn't were warned of his wandering hands and unorthodox requests. Today though, Mickey behaved himself impeccably, offending no one and keeping his lower half covered by his towel. He even left a generous tip.

Within the hour, he was back in his office. As he walked in, he once again logged the time, and once again summoned Stacey back in. This time, he sounded angry.

The clacking of her heels was quicker and louder as she rushed in.

Mickey didn't look up. His eyes were fixed at the tidied but somewhat emptier desktop.

He spoke calmly, as though containing himself.

"Stacey, the pile on the left is perfect. I commend you. I'm delighted to see it's in the tray clearly telling you not to throw it away."

She smiled.

"Thank you" she said as she turned to walk out.

"But" he boomed "... where's the pile on the right?"

As she swung round, there was a brief pause as Stacey lifted both her hands in the air and checked each of them to remind herself of which was her left and which was her right.

"Mr Roughton, that's the pile to shred. We've not changed that since our last talk" she said confident he was testing her.

"Well, surely you saw that next to, or possibly within that pile was a stack of stapled A4 papers. What did you do with them?"

"They're always A4 stapled papers, and as you know, I always shred-them." She wondered whether was this too was a trick question.

"Thank you Stacey. That will be all."

Of the sixty-seven NDAs, neatly packed within the yellow folder that Mickey had carefully escorted back from San Jose, it appeared all that was left was the yellow folder. The contents were now nothing more than a pile of two-millimeter strips in a plastic bucket.

He flicked the intercom switch again.

He spoke calmly.

"Stacey. I just want to check. Everything on my desk that isn't still on it, has been shredded. Is that right?"

"Yes"

"Can you just check the shredder to see if anything's retrievable"

"Yes. Hold on ..."

Several seconds passed.

"Yes."

"Yes what? There *is* something retrievable??"

"Yes, it's all been shredded. Nothing's left."

"Ok. Thank you."

Mickey stood up and paced the room as he considered how he'd deliver the news to Barry and whether he'd still make his millions.

CHAPTER 34

Janice stood outside the main doors to the glass tower in which GalactInvest was housed. The flow of heeled women and suited men poured through the doors, eager to get to their work-stations. She looked up and reminisced of a happier time when she worked on the ninth floor, eight or so years ago.

Today, she was here for a very different reason. She was returning, not as a member of staff, and not as the wife of a director – but as the introducer of an investment opportunity.

Dressed in a smart trouser suit and killer heels, Janice looked every bit the powerhouse she used to be when she still worked there.

She threw her shoulders back, took in a deep breath and filed through the doors with the herds.

As she approached the internal barriers by the lifts, she realised she no longer had a pass, and made her way to the reception desk.

"Hello, I'm here to see Tod Damar" she said, hoping the woman wearing the headset would recognise her. She didn't.

"Sure ma'am. And you are?"

"Janice Damar" she replied, puffing her chest out, anticipating the reaction – but there was none.

A few years ago, everyone in the building knew her name. She'd been a legend, known not just for her ability to pick the rising stars of the tech world – but also for being the wife of the banks top performer, a title many had sought, but only Janice had achieved.

The receptionist handed Janice her pass, and smiled sweetly, without any acknowledgement that this woman and the VP of Funding shared the same surname.

"Top floor ma'am" she said as she gestured with her hands, "elevators are to the right."

"I know where they are honey" replied Janice as she spun round and marched towards the lifts.

The woman who greeted her on floor 9, was slender, attractive – and very likely to have had more than a professional relationship with Tod, just like every other attractive women he'd surrounded himself with. This was obviously his latest PA, no doubt blissfully unaware of how many Tod had had before or, or would have following her once she'd reached her best-before date.

"Hello Janice, I'm Candy, Tod's PA. Would you follow me please."

Janice knew the route to Tod's office blindfolded, which was quite literally the way she'd entered there on more than one occasion when she and Tod were at the start of their affair.

She followed Candy dutifully along the long wooden paneled corridor, at the end of which was the large wooden door to Tod's office.

As the door opened, it revealed the large executive suite. Tod was at the back, on the phone with his feet on the desk. He gestured her in with a waving hand, and with a similar gesture, dismissed Candy.

Janice sat down in the leather armchair facing Tod. He'd changed little in the nine months since he'd walked out on her. She'd seen him only twice since then when she'd dropped the twins at his house, each time on her insistence, hoping he'd be keen to develop a relationship with them. She was wrong. On both occasions, he'd simply left them in the garden, bringing them in only when his housekeeper had prepared their lunch.

He finished his call, leant back in his chair and placed both arms behind his head to support it.

"So is it true?" he asked. No hello. No warmth. Straight to business. "You've got funding from BFD?" he barked.

"Your boys are fine Tod, thanks for asking. You know, you really should see them, they're growing up and you're missing out."

"Yeh, sure. I'll arrange something."

"Anyway, how'd you find out about the funding?" she asked, delighted he knew and hoping she was hiding it well.

"Come on Jan. You think my ex-wife raising forty million bucks isn't going to get back to me?" He paused. "Why didn't you come to me?" He'd softened his tone to maximise the forlorn act, but Janice knew him too well. She'd read him perfectly. If she'd come to Tod for the money first, he would have definitely turned her down and told everyone else to turn her down too. Now he knew someone else was involved, the predator in him desperately wanted his seat at the feast. He couldn't bear to miss out on an opportunity. He could imagine how he'd be the laughing stock of the valley for missing out on an opportunity in which his ex-wife was involved.

Janice played it coy.

"You wouldn't even take my call when I wanted help in getting my old job back. Why would you want to invest in anything I'm connected with?" She too could act forlorn.

"And I hear you're putting the house on the line. Where are my kids going to live if you call it wrong?"

Janice raised her eyebrows and stared at him. He'd never questioned her before when it came to identifying an opportunity. He'd also never cared about where his kids were living.

Tod knew it was a silly thing to say.

"So how about I lessen the risk of you losing the house, and I back it too?"

Janice's heart skipped a beat. She'd expected him to want in, but she'd not expected him to be quite as desperate.

"I hadn't thought of that" she said. "I've got enough funding, let me think about it"

"How much equity did you give for the forty?" asked Tod.

"Twenty-five percent."

"I'll give you the same, but I want thirty."

"What makes you think I need more funding, and even if I did, why would I give you more than the others?" she asked, realising he'd lost neither his directness, nor his chutzpah.

"Because Jan, you'd rather the father of your kids made the money than some klutz at a bank you have no relationship with."

"I'll give you the same deal" she replied, trying to feign reluctance.

Tod was delighted to be making headway, but made sure it didn't show.

"I tell you what. I'll take twenty-seven percent, but I'll put in more. How about forty-four million?" He waited to see her reaction, but there was none. "And I'll have contracts drawn up today."

"It has to be on the same terms as BFD. All at once, and I get to amend the contract. That's the only deal."

"Ok."

Both sat for a moment, trying to read each other. Both were delighted with the outcome, both desperate not to show it.

Without taking his eyes from Janice, Tod pressed the intercom button and summoned his PA.

"By the way" he asked "what is it we're actually investing in?"

"Does it matter?" she replied.

"Not really. I'm going with your judgment and I know how good that is - but I am interested to know."

Janice removed a copy of the presentation from her bag and slid it across the desk to Tod, who instantly recognised the front page and the yellow starburst splashed across it. He knew the presentation well - only yesterday he'd signed off thirty million dollars for his project team to get on with it.

Tod picked up an elastic band from his desk and started playing with it nervously; desperately hoping his poker face would hide his reaction.

He had to look interested. His mind was racing.

Had Janice agreed a deal with Barry?

Should he tell her he's backing it, even though he's cut Barry out.

Does she realise there's a bigger opportunity if they add GPS?

Could she know he'd found Barry in Santana Row and made him an offer of a million dollars to hand the project over – or that he'd turned it down?

As he flicked through the pages, pretending to read them, his mind was all over the place.

There was definitely a conflict of interests here. By both of them working on the same project, they were actually competitors.

He raised the paper to his face as if studying the fine detail, even though the font was clearly large enough to be read from the opposite side of the room.

He knew he couldn't tell Janice he was working on it otherwise she'd tell Barry and between them they'd put a stop to GalactInvest working on their version of it. Even with their enhancement it was obvious it was his idea.

If word got out GalactInvest had signed an NDA and then pinched the idea, they'd never get another deal again.

Would it be safer for him to let her carry on in ignorant bliss, even if it meant her losing everything she had - including his children's home?

On the other hand, if he did invest with her, he'd reduce her risk, and also have the unique opportunity of backing the project twice – one with GPS and one without. If one party didn't win, surely the other one would. It was like having two bites of the cherry.

Either way, he'd be a hero and make the bank billions. It was actually a fantastic situation, as long as Janice never found out that they too were working on the same idea – after all, there could only ever be one winner.

"Are you ok Tod? You've been staring at that page an awfully long time."

"Sure. It's fantastic. Keep me posted" he said as he reappeared from behind the paper.

His PA re-joined them and Tod gestured for her to take notes as he outlined the details of the offer he'd just agreed so she could arrange the necessary paperwork. He explained Janice would be returning it - amended - and she should then print it off and place it on his desk for sign-off within the next twenty-four hours at which time the funds need to be ready for release.

After a few false pleasantries, Janice was back in the elevator, buzzing but still careful not to show it in case the camera in the lift was being monitored. It was something she'd seen them do many times when she worked there. If their visitor left punching the air and dancing around in the lift, they knew they'd been too generous, and asked for more equity in the final contract.

Janice pulled her phone from her bag to call Luke. She'd want him to adjust the cashflow to reflect the additional pile of cash they were about to receive, and to explain that she'd given away more of their shares - which they neither justified or needed, but which would benefit them greatly. She wouldn't explain quite how though. Not yet.

"Luke, it's good news and even better news."

"Cool. A little difficult to chat right now as I'm taking my cat to the vet."

"No worries, I'll be quick. We've just raised another forty four million and we only have to give away thirty percent."

"I er... that's great." He sounded uncomfortable and distracted. He swerved to avoid the oncoming truck into whose lane he'd wandered, sending his passenger sprawling across the back seat.

"Hey. Do you think you can concentrate on the road pal?"

"Who's that?" asked Janice

"The vet."

"What the fuck?" shouted his passenger.

"The cat's losing consciousness, I'll speak later."

He ended the call and apologised to his passenger, explaining his sister had a rare form of tourets syndrome, which meant she couldn't stop spouting numbers.

"Fucking weirdo. Just pull over here and let me out."

With the call over, Janice stood shaking her head. She had been wrong to assume, after the cupcake reaction, that nothing Luke did would ever surprise her again.

She checked her emails and saw one was from *mikewantsmuchmore*.

Her stomach turned as she read it.

Despite the poor wording, grammatical failings and misspellings, Barry's email made it clear he wasn't interested in working with her.

He'd finished his message by asking her to confirm receipt as he was still unsure whether his email would travel long distance.

Without Barry's agreement, she had no business and therefore no investment. All her planning, calculations and patience was all in vain. She felt the bile rising as she slumped in a bench near to where she'd been standing.

After reading the mail three times, Janice concluded the partner to which Barry referred was Luke, who had obviously told him everything about the idea, without realising who he was.

Perhaps that's why Barry had dreamt up the whole cupcake story – simply to throw Luke off track and create mistrust between him and her.

She regretted not being more open with Barry and wished she'd told him of her masterplan. He would have understood she was no risk to the project or a barrier to stop him from working with another party to bring it to life.

It was nothing short of a catastrophe, particularly as she'd just raised eighty four million dollars, which if she accepted would be blatant fraud. It wasn't the fraud that concerned her – many people would consider that central to her masterplan – but it could never be proven, and it was anything but blatant.

Her first thought was to email Barry straight back asking him if he was deluded. She'd guaranteed him a minimum of a million dollars. Someone like Barry had no hope of ever making that kind of money. Ever.

She considered herself generous to have even made the offer in the first place, and now he'd given her the ultimate insult by turning her down.

It wasn't as if he could do it himself, and he had neither the expertise nor the charisma to hire people capable of doing it with him. He'd also have no chance of getting anyone to fund him.

She considered her options. She needed Luke, but even if she ditched him, there was no guarantee Barry would want to work with her – he'd been stupid enough to turn down a million dollars already.

The only alternative was to carry-on without Barry's involvement or blessing, and hope she could complete her plan before he – or the banks - got wind of it.

By the time she'd got to her car, she'd decided the only course of action to take. Ignore the email and pretend it had never made the distance.

He'd be stupid enough to believe it.

As a silver-lining to the gloomy cloud, she would also benefit from not having to give Barry the three percent she'd accounted for, which would give her even more.

CHAPTER 35

Having now returned and set my plan in action, there's nothing more I need do until I return for the film Premiere with Mickey in a couple of weeks. That doesn't stop it from playing on my mind as I still find myself spending every waking moment thinking about it.

I have no distraction other than Ubering, which I need to do anyway to keep me afloat. It's ironic that the very man who think's he's working on the very same plan is doing the very same thing in San Jose. We're both mindlessly driving until the big money pours in. There are, of course, several differences. Unlike my counterpart, I'm a genius – having come up with the idea in the first place - and I'm not talking about it to every punter I pick up.

Despite it being summer, London is a miserable place when you're broke, and Ubering's a mindless means to a mindless end.

I repeatedly check the list of events in my mind to ensure I've left nothing out.

When I'm not thinking of what needs to be done, I'm replaying what I'm going to be spending my fortune on. I've re-written my wish list a dozen or more times and it's now surpassed fifty million pounds – which is a shame because I'm likely to be thirty or so million short this year. I'll have to wait a little longer until it's sold to Facebook to get the billions. I reluctantly accept I will have to postpone a few of my purchases until then.

I check the list. There are several cars; a Bentley, Ferrari, Rolls Royce – and I've decided to keep the Vauxhall Zafira SE for posterity. There are homes in the Caribbean, Tuscany and Cannes although I've never been to any of those places, and of course I'll want somewhere in Florida. Definitely not in San Jose though. Despite the notoriety I'll have there, it would just be too uncomfortable walking through Santana Row with everyone pointing at me when they realise who I am.

I almost forget to add a London home, which I decide will be in Hampstead.

I'm undecided on a boat as I get seasick, but I might just keep a Sunseeker in a marina somewhere. To be safe, I've added £3million to the list, which is what the blue one I saw on their website costs.

I've added to that my annual running costs of all homes, first class travel between them and running costs of the cars. I've gone to great lengths to get insurance quotes on a Ferrari, and have assumed the other cars will be similar. I don't need to allow for any running costs for the boat as I've got no intention of it ever leaving the marina.

I briefly considered a private jet, but Mickey doesn't seem to need one, and I quite enjoyed the first class experience I had. I may change my mind when the billions roll in.

I've also allowed for a personal disposable income of five-hundred thousand a year, which I've worked out, at current rates, will require ten million to be deposited somewhere with a 5% return.

I've put a million in for my son Danny, as I hope (and expect) he'll have a renewed respect for me once I've made a fortune, and it's only fair I look after him. I've put nothing in for my soon-to-be-ex-wife, but I'm going to send her a postcard from everywhere I visit.

I've often wondered where people deposit large amounts of money before they spend or invest it, and decide I'll personally go to see my bank manager, so I can wave the cheque in front of him, stick two fingers up - and then tell him I'm opening an account elsewhere.

I then consider perhaps the funds will come in through a transfer, depriving me of the opportunity. I'll have to settle on calling him and being abusive on the phone, like he is to me.

I find myself wondering back to what my bank statement will look like with such an enormous deposit, only this time I consider perhaps rather than extra wide paper, perhaps they use decimal figures for the millions and knock off the pence columns – after all why would I be interested in the pennies?

I look forward to finding out, meanwhile, in addition to my main list, I've created a sub-list of much smaller spends by comparison, but include such necessities as sunglasses and clothes, new phones and laptops, TVs, a Rolex and iWatch and a Sonos speaker system. I've not gone into detail on prices but have rounded the lot up to be £500,000. I could make it considerably more, but I think anything more than two pairs of Octajour shorts is just showing off.

I'm considering the virtues of a Louis Vitton luggage set, when the phone buzzes. It's a text from Mickey.

Barry. We need to talk.

I can't recall his exact words or how he broke it to me, but within an hour, his driver has delivered a plastic tub of shredded paper, suitable for no other purpose than lining the bottom of a Guinea Pig cage.

I open it, and immerse my shaking hands deep inside to feel the strips between my fingers. Mickey's pushed the boat out on his choice of shredders, and opted for the top of the range type that slices in two directions. I pull out a single shred and although I can read nothing, I'm in no doubt, apart from the increased debt, this is all that remains from my trip to San Jose.

I sit down and stare into space, wondering how things will work out. I don't know how long I've been motionless for, but my fizzing mind has covered just about every scenario. I consider the feasibility of printing a fresh pile of Agreements and starting again - hoping I can track down everyone I met and that they'll agree to sign it again, despite having now been told my idea. I think not. My final thought is whether I should contact the police and ask their forensic team if they can reassemble the thousands of tiny strips and squares, but it's not a call I can see going well.

I remind myself that currently, it's only Mickey and I that are aware of the situation. No one else yet knows there's nothing I can legally do to stop anyone cutting me out of Project Ronald.

Although Mickey's paid for the flights to his premiere, he's not mentioned the hotel and since our phone call I'm probably not ready to speak to him until I see him there.

I've still got every intention of going though. Shredding or no shredding, he's my friend, and I know he would never do anything to harm me, least of all intentionally ruin my one opportunity to make it rich.

I search online and wonder if I should perhaps stay somewhere other than the Self-Starter Inn this time. Maybe there's somewhere else as reasonably priced but has been updated since 1970, is less of a health hazard and has a TV that's younger than me.

As I scroll through all my options, the Self-Starter is still the least priced and although it's also still the lowest ranked - by a considerable margin, I reluctantly rebook it.

Mickey's arranged the flight for me to arrive on June 14th. The premiere's on the 15th and my return's booked for the 16th. Other than the main event I'll have no time to do anything other than visit Denny's.

I book for two nights. If I'm not at my credit limit already, this will certainly see to it.

I decide I need to let Katie know about the NDAs, after all, she helped put the plan together.

Subject: NDAs

Hi Katie

I don't know whether it's sensible to put this in writing, but the NDAs have all been destroyed in a freak accident.

Anyone who signed one can now work on the project and cut me out.

Within seconds of hitting the send button it I realise it's absolutely not sensible to put it in writing. I am totally exposed. If any of the parties that signed the NDA have any decency, it won't matter, but from my experience, decency is as abundant in Silicon Valley as typewriter spares.

I close my laptop, grab my keys and switch my Uber app to 'available'. With any luck I'll make sixty-pounds by the time I return home.

CHAPTER 36

Francois had been the regional manager for less than two years, responsible for the seven Octajour stores across Northern California. He'd left his leafy suburb in Paris for a much sought after promotion in the land of opportunity.

As when he worked for the Head Office in France, too much of his time had been spent dealing with the legal claims his staff had brought against the company. Working within the confines of scented stores, filled with bright fluorescent colours, was clearly detrimental to both health and eyesight, and on each occasion he'd been responsible for agreeing settlements with departing staff.

Now he could see Janice following the all too familiar pattern. It starts with time off due to headaches, then 'personal reasons' – presumably to meet with lawyers - and finally progresses to hospital appointments and a threatening legal letter.

Ultimately, Octajour would have to write another settlement cheque, which was the prime reason why their ten-dollar swim shorts were priced at $379.

As he prepared his monthly report, he included allowances for the settlement and reduced sales figures in their Santana Row store.

When the call came in from Janice, he was well prepared. He had read, re-read and practiced the script prepared by the company lawyers, and had the cheque book ready.

The conversation had started with the usual formalities, after which, the proceedings had been somewhat confusing.

"… I'm so sorry to have to do this Francois, you know how much I've loved working here in Santana Row, but …" Janice was mid-flow before the thick French accent of Francois cut in.

"I must point out, much as we've admired your work here, and we admire your skills as a salesman or saleswoman, delete as applicable, we have come to notice several issues that might affect any claim you might have" Francois said, delighted to have delivered the script so perfectly.

"Are you talking to me?" Janice asked.

"Janice, I can tell you now, we'll never settle for more than ten thousand."

By the end of the conversation, Janice had agreed to work until the end of September to see out their busiest season, and in return, Francois had promised to up the settlement to fifteen-thousand dollars.

Having only called to hand in her notice, she had no idea why she was being paid off, and didn't care anyway.
She felt it inappropriate to tell him she was moving - probably to Florida, and probably to a three million dollar home, nor that his piffling fifteen grand wouldn't even pay the first six months gardening costs.
With her plan well under way, it was now down to Luke to do his job for just a couple of months before she could leave for Florida.
As she hung up, her thoughts turned to Ray and whether he had made it to his desk at BFD-TechBank following their dinner last night.
She'd already had emails from his banks legal team, desperately trying to get her to change some of the 'highly irregular' terms on the contract she and Ray had agreed. Having worked in banking for so many years, Janice knew what she was asking was at the very edge of what any bank would find acceptable, but was confident Ray would support her.
Ray had to. The alternative would require him admitting he had no recollection of agreeing to the terms, which would have been understandable as he was unconscious on the floor of the disabled toilet at the time.
The poorly scribed signature at the foot of the contract had been his own though, which he'd signed moments before keeling over.

Janice replied sternly to the banks. This was the deal she had agreed with Ray, and that's why he'd wasted no time in signing it off and instructing the bank to prepare funds.
She wondered whether slipping a spare pair of knickers and a single stocking in Rays trouser pocket had had the desired effect, and whether he'd remembered anything at all from their dinner.
It had been a long night, most of which Ray had spent on his own, unconscious and at great inconvenience to an elderly war hero with one leg and a weak bladder. She'd returned to her table to finish her dessert and edit the contract on Ray's phone at her leisure. The couple at the neighbouring table had heard her nails tapping frantically against the tiny keyboard for two or three hours before she'd returned to check on Ray.
Ray had even remained spark-out when Janice - with the help of two waiters - had slumped him in the passenger seat of his Ferrari before she'd driven him home.
It had taken another hour to bring him round long enough for him to sign the document on his screen and stagger to his bed.

By now, he would have seen the email he'd sent to his bank with the instructions to pay the funding out.
The text she'd received from him, thanking her for last night and trying to arrange a 'repeat performance' suggested all was fine. It was just a matter of time before she had his banks money.

The same afternoon, Janice received the email from GalactInvest with the attachment they'd agreed. Tod had stuck to his word, for no other reason than his fear of missing out.
His PA, Candy, had dutifully followed what Janice had agreed with Tod, and attached their standard contract. It took Janice twenty minutes of butchering before it was sent back to the bank in its highly edited shortened version.
She hoped Tod would pay it no attention, and that the final draft would be signed off with the same ease she'd experienced with Ray's bank. She knew how GalactInvest worked, she knew their limits, and she knew Tods greed.
With her side of the work completed, and Luke likely to be recruiting his new board and premises and preparing to implement the business plan, she just needed to collect the funds.
She re-worked the numbers in her mind.
Half a million from a mortgage on her house – which her accountant had finally agreed to sort - forty million from BFD-TechBank and forty-four million from GalactInvest. A total of eighty-eight and a half million dollars.

She called Luke to see how he was getting on.
Surprisingly, he appeared to be making good progress. He'd met with various agencies who between them, had assembled a short-list of suitors for all board positions. Having not checked the list of the requirements he'd copied directly from Facebook accounts before he'd handed them out, he wondered what his requirements actually were.
Luke realised he hadn't accounted for recruitment fees in his expense forecast, so had updated his spreadsheet with their charges, together with more realistic (and significantly higher) salaries for his employees. He took the opportunity to increase his salary too.
He had then changed the costs for premises, which according to the recruiters advice, would need to have the minimum level of facilities expected from the type of

employees and management he was seeking. This was, after all, Silicon Valley, where the perks were as outrageous as the salaries.

His real-estate agent worked on finding suitable premises, and an army of shopfitters, builders and other specialists set about adapting them to accommodate his long list of requirements.

He went through the list of facilities with Janice on the phone.

Three snooker tables (full size) with all accessories

A Go Kart Track, minimum length half a mile, complete with 6 electric karts, accessories and charging facilities

Coffee shop area featuring high-back leather stools

Salad Bar. (No requirement to fill, but must be present)

Hot Food station for burgers and hot dogs

Approximately fifty workstations, all wireless, with 27" screens.

Two boardrooms

Nine meeting rooms

Fully stocked bar area with forty-plus beers and lagers from around the world

Personalised hoodies for all staff

Tickets to the CES Tech Show

Android/Apple phones and tablets for every staff member

Fifteen 120" 8K colour TVs

Sandpit

Janice had seen similar lists on dozens of business plans so encouraged him to get on with it as quickly as possible. She had already organised the company formation and opened the bank account so all they were waiting for was the cash do be deposited.

Once the cash was in Luke was free to sign the dotted lines.

There was one main caveat though, which Janice was very clear about and made Luke repeat back to her:

Under no circumstances, commit to any leases or contracts for a period of more than 3 months.

She explained this was necessary due to the fast-moving pace of change in the tech world, allowing them to change specs or upgrade as newer options were introduced. She also confirmed he could draw his salary at the same time, allowing him to take the first three months pay all at once. Luke was delighted, and made a mental note to check his spreadsheet as he couldn't remember the latest figure.

Janice was delighted with his progress. She knew by the time she left for Florida it was unlikely that many of the orders Luke was placing would have been delivered. She saw another call waiting from Tod, so she cut the call short.

He wasted no time with niceties.

"Are you crazy?" he barked "You expect all the cash at once? And what about the contract? You've crossed out nearly all the terms."

"Hi Tod. Yes, I'm well thanks, and your twins are too."

Silence, so she continued, calmly and confidently.

"Tod, it was you who wanted in, I told you it would only be on the same basis as the deal I'd agreed with BFD. If you remember, we weren't looking for more funds, but you insisted, but if you've changed your mind, I'm ok with that. Say hi to your PA Candy. Bye."

Janice hung up, counted to six, and when the phone rang again, counted another six before answering.

"You better not screw-up. I'm doing this for the twins" he said, leaving Jan in no doubt he was doing it because he was a greedy, competitive, weak man who hated to think another bank would beat him at a deal.

CHAPTER 37

Marie and I have managed to avoid each other for several days. I spend my evenings Ubering and tiptoe around when I'm at home to avoid her.

I couldn't care less about interrupting her sleep, I just don't want to see that face of hers.

She's still not agreed to my offer and unless she does, I risk losing half of Project Ronald to her. I'm not entirely sure how much that's worth now, but as each day passes the thought of sharing anything with her sickens me.

I'm desperate to get her to agree to a clean break sooner rather than later, and the only tool I've got is my fictitious profile on the married dating site.

I realise it's been a few days since she sent me – or Mike - her photo and I've yet to reply.

It's gone 3am so I open google images and type in "handsome 45 year old male". I pick one of the less handsome one's as frankly they all look too good to be true, save it to my desktop, and login to my secret hotmail account. *Mikewantsmuchmore@hotmail.com* has missed talking with her.

> Hi Marie
>
> Sorry for not mailing sooner but I'm busy with work and looking after my wife. I've got so many divorce cases on, and as usual they're all squabbling over ridiculous little things when they could just be moving on with their lives. Crazy eh? I hope you and you're soon to be ex aren't racking up fees and fighting over anything you know to be worthless. I always recommend a clean break and avoid all ties (have I mentioned that?)
>
> Thanks for your photo. You look gorgeous. Just the sort of woman I'm looking for.
>
> What's going on with you? How's your divorce going? Are you planning on moving out soon? Maybe when you're living alone you can invite me over?? Lol.
>
> Thinking of you even when I'm not writing
>
> Mike x
>
> PS Hope you like my picture

Next I login to my bank. It's a depressing read.

I've breached my two thousand pound overdraft limit by £6.80, and incurred £150 in costs as a result. I've managed to pay this month's mortgage but the bank's still chasing for the three months I've missed. At least I assume they are, but I've stopped checking the post and leave the pile unopened on the kitchen counter. The only thing I've opened this month is from my credit-card company to ensure I can still pay for my hotel. I can, but I'll have to forgo Denny's, and if I want to eat I'm going to have to rely on Mickey's hospitality, or perhaps take sandwiches.

My lawyers tend to only communicate by email anyway.

It's bad enough dealing with one, but to complicate my life even more, I've got two sets of them. My divorce lawyers have gone quiet, and my other lawyers keep reminding me their patience is running out and they can only give me another month. They also inform me they charge fifteen percent interest. Bang goes my idea of tipping them as a reward for bearing with me.

I put it out of my mind as I set about preparing for tomorrows flight.

I pack two pairs of pants and two shirts.

I'm only in San Jose for two nights this time, so I should have need for little more. I also dispense with the razor, but keep the toothbrush. No umbrella this time.

Without the need for Non-Disclosure Agreements and presentations, I find I can fit everything I need for the trip comfortably into my laptop bag, which is considerably roomy and light, not least of all because I've taken the laptop out. I have no need for it on this trip.

I check the economy saver-fare ticket courtesy of Mickey. His PA's changed it twice; once because it was originally booked for San Jose, Costa Rica, and once because it was booked under the name of Benny Goodman, a musician who I believe died over thirty years ago.

I decide to arrive at the airport four hours before the flight in case there are any other issues to contend with.

As Mickey and his entourage won't need to get there until thirty minutes before the flight leaves, I won't get to spend time with him this trip.

He's already told me he needs as much sleep as he can get before the premiere, so he'll be in bed on the plane, but he hopes to see me at the event.

It's just as well. We've not spoken since the shredding incident, but I'm sure we'll discuss it at the premiere.

The flight appears much longer this time. With the constant thought of what's in store for me in San Jose, I'm unable to sleep, and there's no one to talk to. I'm squashed between a student traveller who speaks little English and a rather attractive woman who's used her perfect English to make it clear she has no interest in talking to me. She's also sprayed herself several times with an overbearing fragrance that has made my chicken and rice dish taste of lavender.

To keep me occupied, I've watched three films, one of which is an espionage film to which I've completely missed the plot.

I'm not comforted by knowing Mickey's probably snoring away on a flat-bed up front.

In a few months, when I've got more money than him, I'll make sure whenever I travel with a friend, they travel with me rather than behind me.

He was right in his thinking though. We can't be seen together now otherwise people might think we're working in cahoots.

CHAPTER 38

The Hackworth IMAX is a large complex in the centre of San Jose. It rarely sees the attention that's lavished on it before a premiere and was being suitably spruced up for the occasion.

Despite the early hour, the car park was crammed full of trucks from catering companies, safety barrier installations, security firms and florists.

Even though it was still more than thirty-six hours until the premiere, a couple of Outside Broadcasting TV trucks were already in situ with large satellites extended.

People were scurrying around with their hands full of plants or boxes, and a great sense of urgency.

There were several giant posters of Boogie Trent wearing what looked like a skimpy silver trouser suit and bright red goggles which was supposed to show her being a tech robot of the future but made her look more like an oven-ready turkey. No one knew why Mickey cast her in the leading role, it's common knowledge he hates her.

They screamed the message, 'Silicon Robots' and in smaller typeface, 'Mickey Roughton's latest blockbuster. Premieres here June 15th'.

At a little after 9:30, a large black stretched limo rolled to a halt outside the main doors, where plants, foliage and a rolled up red carpet were placed awaiting their final deployment.

A few of the contractors noticed as the rear door opened and Mickey Roughton stepped out. Everyone stopped work and followed him with their eyes.

He was hobbling slightly and looked smaller and fatter up close, and there was something strangely odd about his hair. Those brave enough to approach him were instantly waved away with a swipe of his arm.

Mickey was not a happy man. He hated the build up and anticipation as much as he hated the main event. He was also conscious he'd not written his welcome speech, which was the key part of tomorrow's performance – in more ways than one.

Word reached the cinema manager who came bounding out to greet the superstar. A couple of the organisers attached themselves to his side to pay their respects and show their humility to Mr Roughton. They never tired of meeting celebrities, and this one's as big as they get.

"Morning Mr Roughton. Welcome to the Hackworth" said the complex manager as he stooped his shoulders and extended his hand.

Mickey produced a fake smile and no hand to shake. Like all movie producers, he's a perfectionist, over-pedantic and impossible to please.

He has to see first hand the layout of where his movie's going to be shown, down to who's seated where, and whether he can arrange for the carefully arranged plants to be moved so they can block the view of some of his audience.

In a world with such fragile personalities, obliterating an actor's view with a leaf from a plant can end relationships and ruin careers.

He checked the VIP signs on the front row and moved Boogie's sign to the end, just beside a spotlight stand, and asked for a large plant to be moved to the adjacent position.

"Just checking everything's set" he replied as he held his fingers up towards the door, forming a square and squinting through it. "Make sure everyone approaches the main doors from the right" he said.

The manager had no idea what he was talking about, but nodded just the same.

Mickey started walking, beckoning for him to follow.

"Show me around kid. I'd like to know the layout. Can you give me the final running order? How about the press pack? Can you get me a fucking aspirin, my feet are killing me."

As Mickey toured the premises, continually raising his fingers and forming them into a square, he barked orders to the manager. The entourage that followed him grew. By the time he'd returned to the front of the complex to where his car waited, he was leading a crowd of twenty or so, most of whom had nothing to do with him, the complex, or the movie. People suddenly appeared next to him, grinned for a selfie and disappeared. None of the images would show Mickey smiling.

Mickey got in the limo and was waved off. As it pulled away, the small crowd turned their attention to their phones to check the photos they'd just taken, before proudly posting them on their Facebook and Instagram pages.

Suddenly, there was an almighty screech, a whirring of a car engine and once again, Mickey's limo came into view, this time approaching in reverse.

As it came to a halt, the back window lowered, and a hand stretched out. The manager rushed over.

"I nearly forgot. Take these. They're the passes for friends."

He handed over a handful of plain white envelopes with neatly named labels, and a larger brown packet with a handwritten name on it. Mickey knew it was unlikely his PA would have spelt many of them correctly.

CHAPTER 39

As soon as I arrive at the Self-Starter Inn I'm welcomed by the same musky smell. The scruffy girl is still on her stool positioned in front of the TV and has possibly remained there since my last visit. She's as unwelcoming as she was then.

Without any acknowledgement that I'm a returning guest, she processes me exactly as she had done less than three weeks ago. It surprises me little this place has not embraced a loyalty scheme.

Although it has a different number, my room is almost identical to my previous, save the colour of the bathroom, which is now a putrid green. The pungent smell of mildew is still present, as are patches of missing plaster. The view this time looks out over a back alley where the rubbish dumpsters sit, and across the way I can see Denny's, which beckons me. I've got just enough dollars left from my last trip to indulge myself.

I visit there with a body clock so confused, I don't know if I'm having an early supper, late lunch or perhaps breakfast. Whatever it is, the staff appear to remember me and choose to ignore me for fifteen minutes.

I have a free night and a free morning tomorrow, but that's it. The rest of my time is split between sleeping and attending the premiere, which I want to get to as early as possible. Of all the people I met here a couple of weeks ago, there are none that interest me enough to want to see again, other than Janice, who intrigues me, but will no doubt want nothing to do with me since my goodbye email. I feel bad for her. She's stuck in a store selling swimming trunks, and I've killed her one opportunity for success. Maybe, once I've banked my millions, I'll pop back and help her out. Maybe I'll even ask her out. Once she finds out who I am she'll probably throw herself at me.

I make a mental adjustment to my wish list and add a dozen pairs of Octajour shorts which will cost me just under four thousand dollars.

I can't afford to take Ubers on this trip, which is just as well in case it's her partner that turns up.

I wonder if he's still spouting off my idea to his passengers, and whether he ever realised the cupcake venture I told him Janice was working on was completely fictitious. Once again the sweet girl from the Oat House pops into my mind and once again I realise I need to return her hessian bag

My thoughts return to the premiere.

The biggest names in the valley are going to be there, and I may have the chance to challenge Mark Zuckerburg on why he pinched my Facebook idea. Whilst I'm at it, I'll probably see the bastards behind Uber, Instagram and the countless other ideas stolen from me, as well as a few faces I met at the Oat House.

I decide the best plan of action is to keep a low profile, watch Mickey do his thing, and leave surreptitiously before anyone has a chance to see me.

The film starts at 8pm, but the reception and pre-movie party starts at 6pm.

The Premiere Special is being broadcast live on Fox from 7pm for an hour, so the biggest names will want to arrive as soon after that as possible to ensure they get enough time to swan down the red carpet, mixing with the film's stars and making out they're all old mates, despite having never met before.

Mickey will probably arrive at 7:30pm and he'll want to talk about how fantastic his movie is, and thank everyone who helped him bring it together.

I, of course, arrive bang on six, and am amongst the first.

There's a great deal of fuss going on as the TV cameras and boom microphones take their positions along the red carpet. The few others who have arrived early are watching the cameras, watching them. They're being used for positioning shots only. There's less than zero interest in who they are. It's only ever those that have done odd-jobs on the set, or are related to the major players, that turn up at this time.

Behind the barriers, there's already a crowd assembling. I walk past them, and as I step onto the red carpet I can't help feeling slightly superior, and perhaps a little sweaty.

I notice my chest puff up, and my pace slow. From the corner of my eye, I see people hanging over the barriers watching me, and I sense their envy.

I slow further and develop a slight swagger to my walk. About half way along the carpet I hear someone shouting, and almost immediately, a security guard appears next to me ordering me stop. He points to behind the barriers, where he wants me to go.

I tell him smugly, I'm invited and watch the look of disbelief on his face, as he demands to see my invitation, which I suddenly realise I don't have. There are a few jeers from those behind the barriers as people are quick to remind me I'm no one special, and I'm escorted towards a make-shift hospitality tent, behind a truck buzzing with generators.

Both the security guard and the lady in the tent seem genuinely disappointed to find my name on Mickey Roughton's personal guest list, albeit misspelt.

When I'm handed a brown package, inscribed 'to my good mate Barry, enjoy the show' with a smiley face and Mickey scrawled across it, they become apologetic. I milk it for all it's worth and explain I'm actually Mickey's partner but I keep a low profile. It backfires somewhat as they offer me an access through the rear entrance, which I politely refuse.

As I stuff the package into my inside jacket pocket I'm escorted back to the beginning of the red carpet. I speed up. Making an entrance is one thing, but re-entering in front of the same crowd is nothing short of humiliating.

I've only watched Fox TV once before, but I instantly recognise the tanned face and white teeth of Chuck Jenkins, the over-enthusiastic host who interviewed Mickey on his last trip. He's caked in make-up and standing at the entrance to greet the VIPS and celebrities who will follow my footsteps in the next hour. He waves me on, shouting for me to walk quicker as I'm going to ruin his shot if anyone important comes along.

Aside from him, I recognise no one, so I spend time walking around on my own looking like an extra in a crowd scene, which I conclude I am.

As I wander, I see the long lines of seating, extended by the additional seats brought in for tonight's performance. There's a large marquee to one side through which I see a bar. I decide that's where I'll spend my time.

After plucking two rather pleasant cocktails - the names of which I don't know – from the bar, I find myself relaxing. Not being a drinker, I have no idea what else to order. Apart from lager and coke, I only know the names of drinks from what I've seen on TV or in the cinema. The barman tells me there's no such thing as Duff beer so I order a tequila slammer, and then an extra-dry martini, shaken, not stirred, and with an olive. Both drinks are disgusting.

The area's filling up and although I don't recognise anyone, I know these are the most powerful people in the Valley. Some of them are probably aware of Project Ronald by now. Some of them are probably ripping me off at this very moment. I'm looking out for Mark Zuckerburg when suddenly music starts blaring from a speaker on the tall post I've been leaning against for balance. There follows a buzz in the room as it fills with a wave of celebrities. They're all waving and blowing kisses. The guys are shaking hands with everyone they pass, cupping their victims hand with their other hand as if to add sincerity to their shake.

There are cameramen walking backwards as they lead familiar faces across the room. I've seen some of them before on TV. I think one was in *Mash* and another was in a film about a shipping disaster I saw last year.

Then I see Mickey. He's flanked by Boogie Trent and another star - who's name I don't know, but I think she was in a film about rock band - and he's holding their hands like they're best friends. There's a camera in front of him and one each side.

His hair looks immaculate and I think he's also wearing makeup. He's grinning and as he walks past me our eyes catch and he winks.

I have no idea what time it is, and as I drink my Singapore Sling, I realise we're live on air.

Mickey is escorted to the front.

Someone who I think was in *Cheers*, goes before him. The music stops.

"Ladies and Gentleman ... please welcome a man without who none of us would be here... my closest friend, Mickey Roughton!"

There's an eruption in the noise as the bloke from *Cheers* slips away, and Mickey replaces him on stage, with his arms stretched as if he's just scored a winning goal.

I'm finding it difficult to focus.

"Friends ..." The noise lessens, "Friends ... because that's what we all are ... I'm delighted and proud to be here in San Jose" he stops and grins, as though he's pleased with himself for remembering where he is. "This town is very special to me ..." more applause, a bit of whooping too, "... which is why I produced this movie about a robot that was built here, and why I chose this to be the first place on earth to show it."

There are two cameramen on stage with him, one of them's kneeling with his camera pointed up at Mickey as he continues.

"What you're going to see tonight is the culmination of my heart, my soul and those of my closest friends too – like Boogie Trent." He points to Boogie and winks as though he means it. The crowd starts again. Mickey continues, and the short burst subsides. Boogie looks pissed he didn't let it linger longer.

"I'd like to thank some of them now, without whom, this movie wouldn't be the blockbuster I know it's going to become ..."

More whooping, as he goes through a list of directors and actors, some of whom I've heard of, but I can't be sure at the moment.

"... and there's someone here to whom I'd like to make an apology."

The crowd quietens in preparation for what must be a quip. Maybe a film studio who missed out on the opportunity or perhaps an actor who turned it down.

"Of all my dear friends here tonight, there's one who's done a great deal for me, who's inspired me, who's driven me you might say." He looks round, presumably for me, but with everyone pushing in front of me, I'm now back nearer the bar, leaning on it for support.

He pauses, and checks to ensure the cameras are capturing his every word.

"Well, I won't mention his name so as not to embarrass him, but being in Silicon Valley, I feel this is the place to make the apology as this man is hoping to make his fortune here. Why am I apologising? Well, a week or so ago, I shred a whole bunch of NPAs or NDAs – I can't remember what he called them - but he entrusted me with them for his Project Ronald."

I try to order my thoughts. My mind might be fuzzy, but I try to get a grip on what's being played out in slow motion. I remind myself we're on prime time TV, covering every home and business in Silicon Valley, and probably the whole of America. There are probably millions of viewers, not to mention the biggest names in the online and tech world who are hearing him first hand, and, if I'm not mistaken, he's just told them all, in short, I no longer have anyone's signed Agreements protecting me from them stealing Project Ronald.

I jolt up and as I rush towards the exit, I throw up. Half of it's down me, half of it's down a woman who until seconds ago was very much more attractive than she is now.

I stop briefly, clutching hold of a post to steady myself when I hear Mickey's punchline.

"I love you B. I hope they weren't too important and I hope you'll forgive me. If it's any consolation, I've had your presentation put on my website so anyone can download it. If anyone's interested, please take a look. He's a bright guy and it's a great project. If what I hear's correct, the whole world will be using his idea soon."

As impossible as it appears, the situation's actually deteriorating even further before my very eyes. Not only does everyone know my ideas no longer protected, but in case anyone's not aware of it, they can now download the whole presentation on what it is and how it works.

I'm staggering around towards the exit as I see someone that looks like Mark Zuckerberg in the distance. I wonder whether I should go up and tell him about it in case he missed any of it, before I punch him. I realise, anything he's missed he'll catch on the re-run, or perhaps even download it directly from Mickey's website.

As I'm rushing out of the complex, I pass a TV Van and see the TV monitor allowing me to catch the tail end of Mickey's speech as he tells everyone he's already writing the script for his next movie *Silicon Hustler* but I don't need to hear what it's about.

CHAPTER 40

I don't remember how I got back to the hotel, nor when I went to sleep, but it's clear from the vomit stained shirt I'm wearing, I didn't undress.

I've got less than an hour before I have to leave for the airport, and I'm still in bed nursing a very sore head.

The memories of last night come rushing back. I grab my phone and see Mickey's had no problem sleeping. He'd sent his text at 9:12 this morning.

> Hope you enjoyed last night and my speech. The presentation's been downloaded 112 times. Is that good?

I leave my sweaty bed, undress for a shower and switch the TV on.

I'm still unable to think straight and focusing on the picture is difficult.

I'm watching someone called Stewart Weinstein on *Stews Reviews*, talking about last nights premiere.

"What's all that about?" he asks rhetorically, referring to Mickey's bizarre apology last night.

I switch it off.

I check my emails.

I see one's from Katie, so I open it first.

> Heard about last night. Do you want to talk about it?

I rush to the bathroom where I'm sick again. I'm not ready to engage with Katie yet. Maybe I'll reply to her when I'm at the airport.

I'm not sure how many times I'm sick, but to focus my mind elsewhere I open my emails and see one from *SiliconValleyNews*. It's a big news day so they've sent it early, with the promise of an updated edition later in the day.

There's a list of events in the region, a bit of gossip about a possible data breach at one of the giants, and a link directly to Project Ronald, which they've taken from Mickey's site. Below it is the heading: 'Is this the greatest ever breech of confidentiality?'

It then gives what amounts to a very positive review of the idea, and agrees with Mickey – it is the next big advancement in communications and we'll all be using it. They even have an idea that will improve it, but stop short of mentioning what it is.

The article finishes with a challenge to it's readers. Whoever launches this first is going to make billions.

I have so many emotions fizzing around my head, all clouded by my nausea.

I'm sick again.

As I pass through the now unmanned entrance desk, I pick up a copy of *The Mercury News*. There's a full page devoted to last night's premiere, half of which is a photo of Mickey, beaming on the podium either just before or just after he's told the world my idea. In the background there's a woman with a look of disgust and her arms up, partially blocked by the back of my head.

There's another half page under the heading "Mercury Comment" in which the editors spewed his thoughts on the oddity of Mickey's speech.

He pities greatly the unknown friend of Mickey's who he assumes has probably got a contract out on him by now. He considers whether there's a case for suing Mickey for all his worth and explains all the victim needs to prove is that he had the capability to do it himself and was about to do so. He's neatly summed up for me the reason I could never sue Mickey.

He goes on to say that he would like to think there's enough decency and honesty in the world that the NDA's still respected by anyone who signed it. He finishes his article by assuring his readers, much as he'd like to think there are such people, he's yet to meet any.

In case anyone's not seen or heard of Project Ronald, he's kindly printed a link to his newspaper's website from which the presentation can be downloaded.

He's managed to summarise in less than half a page that my brilliant idea is free for anyone – and everyone – to copy without risk. He's still got enough room to post a picture of himself and an email address for any comments.

I can think of nothing I want to write to him about, but decide to keep the newspaper and frame it.

CHAPTER 41

As soon as the twins were tucked up in bed, Janice switched on the TV, just in time to watch the premiere live. She recognised many faces there, having helped many of them with their business plans in their early days by playing her part in arranging their funding. Only some of them turned out to be billionaires. Most were only multi-millionaires.

Although she didn't actually see him, she was in no doubt Tod was milling around in the audience somewhere, probably with a woman draped over his arm. If they were still married, she'd have been there too.

By the time Mickey had got up to make his speech, she'd lost interest and gone to switch channels. As she fumbled for the remote, what she heard stopped her and she froze.

She was a signatory on one of the NDAs destroyed by Mickey.

Her hand covered her mouth in shock as Mickey went on to announce where the presentation can be downloaded.

Had this been a few days earlier before she'd received the banks funds, it would have been catastrophic.

She felt a sudden wave of pity for Barry wash over her. Although he didn't want to progress with her - or accept her guarantee of two million dollars, he'd never been particularly offensive.

It sickened her that someone could destroy his once-in-a-lifetime opportunity for success. She felt almost guilty for using her plan to profit from his idea, which he never could.

By the time she'd reached the shower, the feeling had passed. She was more interested in how Mickey's announcement might affect her situation. It was now more than likely that anyone who'd signed the agreement with Barry would cut him out, safe in the knowledge no-one could prove they hadn't got the idea before seeing it on TV.

She also knew that every viewer, techie and funder in the region would be downloading the presentation and working on it too.

It wasn't just Barry who had no chance. With Luke in charge, she also had no chance.

She was delighted. It couldn't have been better news. She just had to make sure the banks continued to support her.

If she hadn't felt so bad for Barry, she might have sent a letter to Mickey, thanking him for making her own plan easier to implement.

* * *

By 8am the following morning, the board was gathered around the large glass table, waiting for Tod to make his grand entrance.
They'd all received his text late last night, asking them to get in early, and few were in doubt of the reason why.
Only Sandra, a newly recruited admin assistant was curious. No one else had been instructed to wear a short skirt and heels, but she duly complied anyway. She was also in the boardroom despite having no reason to be there, or knowledge of what went on in Tod's department – but she'd fallen under his spell, and did as he asked.

Tod walked in, winked at Sandra and took his seat at the head of table.
"Morning gentleman. I know it's early, but, well, what the hell."
He signals Sandra towards the sideboard on which two bottles of Krug champagne are sitting, together with a dozen crystal glasses. As she pours and distributes the glasses, Tod continues.
"I assume by now you're all aware of the events last night?" There's a muttering of affirmatives. "Well I can tell you, it was every bit as entertaining as you can imagine."
"The Movie?" asked the CTO.
"That too" he winked.
"Was the guy with the idea there, you know, the one Mickey Roughton was talking about?" Asks the COO.
"Yep. I saw him throwing up all over the place as he walked out."
"Poor sod. You almost feel sorry for him" replies the COO.
Tod's tone changed as he addressed the CTO "Not for a minute. This is a dog-eat-dog world and we're a big hungry dog. The good news is – unless he's kept copies – which I very much doubt - no-one knows we've signed anything with him. It's now in the public domain so we can cut him out and go alone." He surveys the room. "And we don't even have to fork out the two million we were going to give him." He paused. No-one's impressed by saving a couple of million.
"... and the bad news?" asks the CFO.
"Well, the bad news is that just about every software house, funder and have-a-go entrepreneur will have seen it by now, and they'll be racing to get it out first."

He stopped momentarily to build the impact on his next bout of genius. "We're better placed than anyone though."

He scanned the room to ensure he had everyone's attention.

"We've got two edges. Firstly, we're developing a GPS component to it which no one else will be smart enough to think of, and secondly ... well I've already backed another horse in the same race."

He looked round at the blank faces. Perhaps he needed to make it clearer.

"There's another runner we've backed ..." still blank faces.

"I've lit two fireworks with one match." No reaction.

He prods himself in his chest "For fuck's sake, this genius has backed another rocket."

The penny had finally dropped.

"F.A.B" said the COO. "Who's the other rocket?"

"Well, I er ... I can't say I've actually met the guy who's running it, but we've been introduced to it by a very canny investor who's got a fantastic track record ..." He softened his voice to a whisper "... Janice."

"Who?" He hadn't heard.

"Janice ..." Said Tod, sheepishly.

"Your ex-wife Janice?" There was much surprise in the room, before the CFO turned the mood.

"She certainly is a rocket. I'd certainly like to light her blue touch paper."

There's much guffawing in the room before the COO raises his glass.

"Excellent, if we're backing two horses in the same race, and Janice is riding one of them we know we've got a winner."

"There's just one last thing guys" Tod said, eager to finish up and make his move on Sandra. "From this point on, no one but ourselves must ever know we signed an NDA with Barry. If anyone asks, we got the idea from Mickey Roughton's website."

There are nods around the table. Everyone's delighted to be part of the hungry dog team that's backing two horses in the same race and lighting touch papers for two rockets. They congratulate Tod on another of his shrewd decisions and then decide to double their investment in their own party to ensure they win.

* * *

Barely a block away, Bob Harper's in boardroom No.1 waiting to address his team at Silifunders. He's pacing up and down as Mike Kapinsky, his Head of Legal saunters in.

Not since the day he'd started Skopeez, which he'd sold for $1.8 billion, had Bob ever found an opportunity he couldn't control by throwing money at it. With the recent developments relating to Project Ronald he was in danger of losing control, and he had no intention of letting that happen.

He'd already forged ahead with Barry's idea, having tried and failed to contact him to cut a deal, and now here was the opportunity to remove him from the project altogether. Thanks to Mickey Roughton, everyone on the planet had been handed the same idea on a plate.

"Guys, it's in the public domain so we need to crack on with this immediately before every other son-of-a-bitch in the Valley's on it. Whatever you heard about the NDA stays in this room. Outside that door, no-one need ever know we didn't get the idea the same way every one else did last night. We're just lucky we've been working on it for a couple of weeks so we're that much ahead."

"Can we do that?"

"No, but we just did. And don't forget, we've got an edge by adding GPS to it so I'm even gonna up the stakes. I think we should put a team of fifty coding it so we can get this mother launched inside seven or eight months."

"That's going to cost a lot of cash."

"I know. We're going to double our initial investment. Ok with everyone?"

"But what if everyone beats us to it?"

Bob doesn't like being questioned.

"No one's going to beat us to it. Not with the vast sums of money we're going to throw at it."

It's not an answer, but no one's brave enough to challenge Bob.

* * *

At Linkosys, the team of four - Jim, Josh, Jake and Jez had all seen the daily email from *Siliconvalleynews.com* and read all about the very project they were working on. They had only a vague recollection of signing paperwork with Barry in Starbucks a couple of weeks earlier, but paid little attention to it, having no idea what it was for. They remembered the term 'NDA' and wondered what it was and how it would affect them if the guy who'd given them the idea, had destroyed them all.

Having now seen the details of Project Ronald being available freely for anyone to download, they decided it might be perhaps something they should discuss with their investor, Alan Androposa. Not being sure themselves, they knew Alan would know whether access to the idea was a good thing or not. They respected him for his shrewd mind and uncanny investments, of which theirs happened to be his biggest, making him over a billion dollars.

As always, their motivation was less about the cash rewards and more about the opportunity to create good code.

They were just grateful to be diverting some of their skills into a project they could be proud of, rather than the gambling software they'd made Andropossa billions from, and their parents ashamed.

They had their usual coffee in Starbucks at 6am, after which they squashed themselves into an Uber to the Andropossa building, arriving at 7:15am, to find it still locked.

Alan, the founder and chairman, was the first to arrive and directed them to his boardroom where they were joined shortly afterwards by two of his executives. They had all already downloaded the presentations from Mickey's website.

Alan was a large, rounded man, always suited and with a face reddened by good living and high blood pressure. Today, his face appeared redder than usual, extending across the entirety of his bald head. He looked anxious and Jim, Josh, Jake and Jez realised very quickly, all was not well. Whatever this NDA was, it didn't sound good that this guy had lost them.

Alan didn't sit. He paced up and down the length of the shiny wooden table at which they were seated. Each time he went to speak, he raised his arms, lowered them again and paced a little more. Eventually, he found the words.

"So guys, just so I've got this straight, you come to me to present your new idea. Not just any idea. An idea that we all agree is off-the-clock fantastic. You tell me you need more funding – which I might add, I released the very next day – and now I find anyone with internet access can download the same presentation. Am I right?"

Jim looked at Josh, who was looking at Jake who was looking at Jez, who finally spoke.

"Yes, but we ..." Jez looked at Josh, who tookover.

"Mr Andropossa we never actually said it was our idea. We were given it by an old man in Starbucks."

Alan completed another lap of the table, and appeared at the front of the room. Once again, he put his arms in the air, and once again, he searched for the words. His fellow executives said nothing and avoided eye-contact by burying their heads in notepads. Each took copious notes despite nothing note-worthy being said.

Alan had reached the other end of the room when he spoke.

"So, you stole an idea, you use the same - exactly the same - presentation as was made to you, and then after I write out a cheque for millions, I find, I've cut out the poor bastard whose idea it is?" He stared intently at the boys, his red face almost glowing. "Have you any idea what would happen to my credibility if it got out that I'm backing an idea and cut out the founder?"

Silence. Alan continued from his new position directly behind Jez.

"So did you ... no ... one minute. So ... I assume you're one of those that signed the NDA. Actually, don't answer. I don't wanna know... lie to me. Tell me you haven't." He softened and broke into a smile as he realised it no longer mattered as the proof had disappeared.

"So let me get this straight. All we've got is a two-week lead over anyone who's only just discovered the idea, right? So how can we make sure we stay ahead of the game?"

"Well, we've tweaked it a bit" replied Jez, relieved not to be told off.

"Go on ..."

"We added another component."

"GPS" said Josh.

"It's slower to build but it's a real game-changer" added Jez.

"How soon can you get it done if we throw more at it?"

"Six months"

"Don't sit here wasting a minute of it. You've got it, now get on with it. We can't afford to lose this, so get as many developers on it as you need. I'll deposit more funds this afternoon."

Jim, Josh, Jake and Jez scrambled out of the room like a bunch of schoolboys after hearing the final bell. When they reached the outside they discussed what had happened, and concluded they had no real idea what was going on, but they should hurry up and complete the project to keep Mr Androposa happy.

* * *

By the time the crowds were leaving the premiere, the limo had whisked the two senior executives from Seattle back to the airport where the second of their private jets awaited them.

For much of the two hours it took for their Bombardier Jet to get them home, they mused over the movie, the stars, the heads of tech companies they'd met, and of course Mickey Roughton's odd speech.

When he'd mentioned he'd destroyed the signed Non-Disclosure Agreements, they laughed – firstly at his stupidity and then at the misfortune of the creator of the idea. It was only when the name "Project Ronald" was announced, they stopped laughing and looked at each other. Each of them froze as they arrived simultaneously at the conclusion that Project Ronald was obviously what they'd been referring to as Project Donald.

Somewhere, within their vast organisation - thanks to their mysterious Uber driver, Project Donald was now under development.

His name had been immortalised in a gilt-edged frame on a sideboard in their office suite.

'Luke Palatino. Ubering - but don't need to.'

Perhaps they had the wrong man.

Was it possible that one of the biggest ideas of the decade – perhaps even the century – given to them on a plate, was actually the very same idea Mickey was talking about last night?

Who was Barry?

Within seconds of landing, each had removed their phones, searched for Mickey's website, and downloaded the presentation, conveniently positioned and highlighted on the home page.

As they swiped through the pages, seeing in glorious detail the very idea the driver had told them about, each of them rubbed the tufts of their goatee beards.

It was the taller one who spoke first.

"Did we sign a Non-Disclosure on this?"

"No idea, it's worth checking but either way, it doesn't matter now."

At that moment, both their phones buzzed as an email came in from Jane in compliance.

> Subject: Re: Project Donald
>
> Hey guys

A couple of weeks ago you asked me to check if we'd signed an NDA on Project Donald.

I didn't find anything at the time, but I was watching TV last night and saw this thing about Project Ronald.

Should I get the team searching under that? Maybe someone mixed em up lol.

Jane

Both beards looked at each other.

"Might as well tell her not to bother. Now that anyone can download it, we can say that's how we got the idea too."

"Fair enough" the taller one said, as he typed his reply to Jane.

Subject: Re: re: Project Donald

Thanks Jane. It turns out it was indeed Project Ronald and it's freely available in the public domain now - so we can't be accused of pinching it!

We'll be back after lunch

Mickey isn't on the same flight back as me. We haven't spoken since last night, and I've not replied to any of his texts.

I checked on his website and he's kindly put a counter there. It tells me it's no longer 112 downloads, it's 203.

As the presentation can now also be downloaded from the *Fox TV* website, *The Mercury News* website, and no doubt countless other sites that take their feeds from both – not to mention the bloggers and forums, I can only imagine how big the total number is. It's been less than eighteen hours since Mickey first posted it on his own site.

After the eleven hour flight, I'm relieved to be finally able to hold down my food. I opt for the veggie bolognese, described as a rich vegetarian option, but find it's just a very poor version of a meat one.

I manage to stay awake on the tube home and am further relieved to find I'm alone when I arrive.

I go through the same rituals I did less than a fortnight ago, dumping my bag, making myself a coffee and some toast, and then opening my laptop. This time, I lack the appetite and after buttering the toast, throw it in the bin.

I notice my hands are shaking, which is a reaction to last night – but I'm not sure if it's from the drink or the events.

I sit in front of the TV and open my spreadsheet to peruse the long list of contacts that I can now never prove had signed my NDA.

After an email exchange with Katie, I'm careful to include all her points in the message I craft to them.

> Subject: Project Ronald
>
> Dear
>
> I hope you're well.
>
> It was a pleasure to have met you two weeks ago, and I hope you enjoyed my presentation on Project Ronald.
>
> Due to a freak accident, all my Non-Disclosure Agreements have been destroyed and as I have no copies, I no longer have any proof that you signed it.
>
> Would you be kind (and honest) enough to confirm you signed it otherwise I have no way of proving this idea was mine.

I hope we can work together to bring this project to life.

Kind regards

Barry Goodman

I send it to all sixty-eight names on the spreadsheet, making sure to insert the correct name for each mail.

I then email the only contact address I have for the Oat House Meeting Hall Pitching event.

Subject: Project Ronald

Dear Administrator (apologies, I don't have your name)

I hope you're well.

I was present at the last Pitch & Present you held on June 3rd, during which I presented my Project Ronald.

I had enough Non-Disclosure Agreements for virtually everyone present, but not quite everybody. Due to an unfortunate incident, I am not able to confirm which of the parties signed and which didn't.

Would you happen by any chance to have a list of those parties that did?

Kind regards

Barry Goodman

I close my laptop and wonder how I would fill the 165 remaining days, which is what's left before my millions start rolling in.

I have no urge to speak to Mickey for the moment, and wonder how long it will be before either one of us makes contact.

I have no money and nothing to fill my time. In a desperate need to keep me occupied I do the one thing I'd least like to, so I switch my Uber app to available. Within minutes I've got a fare.

As we sit in traffic on the North Circular Road, I consider how different our cultures are as I imagine how my passenger will react if I tell him I'm a tech entrepreneur, just back from my second trip to Silicon Valley in a month. Would he believe I've already turned down a couple of million dollars and am holding out for the big prize. I look in the rear view mirror and see, thankfully he's asleep.

I wonder whether that would stop the Uber driver I had in San Jose and whether he'd spill my idea anyway.

It's no surprise to me that my morning emails are largely unanswered. Of the twenty one that bother replying, all of them tell me they either have no record of signing an NDA with me, or that the person I've emailed is away. I'm also not surprised – but slightly insulted - to hear most of them have no recollection of even meeting me.

I need a response from all of them, so I write eagerly. I can't progress until all sixty-eight confirm they have no knowledge of my NDA.

The Oat House administrator sends me a polite email telling me that it's my responsibility to hold on to the NDAs and she has no way of knowing who did and who didn't sign. She also tells me her name is Josie and asks whether I could get an idea she has for a film to Mickey Roughton.

Over the course of the next month, I write and re-write dozens of emails in an ever-increasing desperation to get their replies.

It takes until the end of Summer until eventually every name on my list has a tick by it.

There are several columns:-

No record of meeting me at all: 25

Vaguely remember meeting me, but not signing an NDA: 31

Not available to comment as the person I'm writing to is no longer there: 12

With every *SiliconValleyNews* email I get, I see an ongoing commentary on how my idea is progressing with an ever-growing list of companies that claim they'll be the first to launch it. They all seem to have a unique edge, which they claim will separate them from the pack, although none are willing to disclose what it is.

I salivate as I read the size of the funds some of them have raised to be in the race. Those that are big enough to use their own funds boast how much of their resource they're putting into it.

I know some of the names, but there's an ever-growing presence of names I've not pitched to before, and they certainly didn't sign an NDA with me. These are obviously those that have downloaded my presentation and started work on the project after Mickey's speech.

I diligently list them all, and add them to my spreadsheet of sixty-eight names.

I struggle to keep up with the sheer volume of coverage my idea's getting – and it's not just around Silicon Valley. Through searching on *Google* I can see it's USA wide and in much of the UK press too. There are forums of people discussing it and users who want to be the first to sign up for it as soon as it's launched.

There are several sites I can't read as they're in languages I don't speak, but they all include the words in my search term: Roughton, Project Ronald.

I even find a betting site listing a dozen or so companies who are claiming they'll be the first to launch, allowing punters to back their favourite.

Of all the people I met on my first trip to Silicon Valley, not one of them has any interest in me any longer. As unpopular as I was, at least a few had the decency to try negotiate a deal to get me out of the picture. Now, all of them assume I've disappeared back to the hole from which I'd crawled out of. Only Mickey and Katie know of my ongoing involvement.

Marie obviously knows nothing of my masterplan, but everything about the speech at the premiere. She had the decency not to confront me face to face, probably because the sight of me is as sickening to her as hers is to me.

She was however, kind enough to leave me a typed letter on the kitchen table next to the growing mound of post I no longer bother opening.

When I read her note – and remove the expletives – it says, amongst other things, that there's a video she's seen several times on Facebook which refers to how some idiot's been completely ripped off. Knowing the dates of my trip and track record, she's worked out the idiot is me, although apparently the accompanying commentary confirms it.

She's now changed her mind on what she wants from me.

She's been 'taking advice' – which I originally assume is from her lawyer, but as I read on, I see it's actually my alter-ego Mike from the married dating site, who's wording she appears to have copied verbatim.

She's happy to make a 'clean break' and to ensure there are 'no ties', so she's prepared to have no further interest in anything in which I'm involved – but she does want a hundred percent of the house. Her tone reminds me of how disappointed she is in me.

She's probably expecting a fight. No one in their right mind would allow their spouse total ownership of all the assets. She firmly believes my business interests are worth nothing, which I can understand seeing as after many years of telling her my big dreams, I've achieved nothing but big debts.

Of course, she has no idea this time it's different. Very different.

Shortly after seeing her letter, I get an email from my divorce lawyer at Barnet Family Law. Lesley's reiterated the same thoughts, without the expletives, and at a cost of three hundred pounds.

My first thought is to agree, as quickly as possible – but I worry whether that's making it too obvious that I'm up to something. I remind myself that Marie – and no doubt her lawyers – think I'm a complete idiot, and the thought of me having the ability to scheme is beyond them.

With time being of the essence, I decide I have no choice but to reply quickly.

I word my email to suggest she's driven a hard-bargain, and even though I'm likely to have nowhere to stay once it's sold, we should sell the house and break our ties as soon as possible.

My next concern is the timing. Although I'd like to think by the time the house is sold I'll have millions in the bank and be on my spree of buying houses around the world - or at the very least, living in a posh hotel planning it -

if I get the timing wrong, or the house is sold too quickly, or heaven forbid, my plan doesn't come off – I really will have nowhere to live, other than the Vauxhall Zefira. I'm only thankful I've got the LX spec.

I decide I have no choice and after a flurry of emails, a visit to my lawyer and a couple of signatures, I agree to sell the house. The estate agents must have been waiting around the corner, because by the time I return from Ubering, there are two of their boards firmly planted in the front garden.

In the knowledge that Marie and I will only have to tolerate each other until the house is sold, there's a new calmer relationship since we agreed the basis of our divorce. We even become polite.

Meanwhile, with credit card debts, screaming lawyers and the need to continue to eat and keep myself in soft toilet rolls, I'm still having to Uber. I keep myself sane by focusing on what's going on in Silicon Valley, and working on my second stage of emails, which are now ready to go.

With the flurry of opportunists that have stolen Project Ronald, my list has grown to eight-four names although it's only the initial sixty-eight I'm interested in at this stage.

Again, I email Katie before composing the email.

Subject: Project Ronald

Dear

I'm disappointed there's no record of the Non-Disclosure Agreement you may have signed for my idea. As you know, I can't prove you signed one as they've all been destroyed.

You're probably aware that it was mentioned on TV (and in the press, and online) so I'd be grateful if you can confirm you were working on it before then?

If you can that will help me prove you had seen it before.

Thanx

Barry Goodman

As expected, none reply on the first round. I spend another week or so chasing them to get a response.

I wonder how many are dismissing my emails on the basis they look like they're written by an idiot.

After constant chasing, my poor grammar and atrocious spelling eventually reaps the responses I need.

* * *

By the end of September, I've got all sixty-eight emails confirming they only started on the project after details of it were broadcast assuring me that's proof enough they had no earlier knowledge of it.

Their eagerness to acknowledge they only saw my idea once it was in the public domain is critical to my plan. Without their total greed, my plan won't work.

I feel the importance is high enough for me to email Katie again. This time, I tell her I'd desperately love to see her. I figure sitting with her, having some time alone with her would be very comforting - but she disagrees.

I must have asked a dozen times or more to meet her. I've invited her for coffee, lunch, drinks at a pub – but she's adamant this is something we can discuss by email and text.

She does however suggest some ideas on how I should reply to drive my message home, and I can't help agreeing with her.

Subject: Project Ronald

Dear

I really don't want to keep bothering you, but I just want to clarify the position.

If you hadn't heard about my idea from me, then presumably you heard it from one of the following.

- Broadcast on *Fox* at 7:38pm on June 15th
- Posted on *Mickeyroughton.com* website from June 15th
- Posted on *Fox* website from June 16th
- Featured in *Mercury Newspaper* on June 16th
- Featured in several hundred blogs and other websites since then

Please tell me as it will help prove if you signed an NDA.

Barry Goodman

I knew this was a risk. I was now not only feeding them with their excuse, but pandering to their laziness so they needn't bother researching where they might have found Project Ronald.

I hope by giving them the exact times and channels, I've made the job so easy that they might respond sooner rather than later.

Whether it's that - or because I'm now becoming a nuisance, the replies come through much quicker – and much more succinct.

Their emails are short and sweet, telling me they've heard about the idea in the media.

A few bother selecting their preferred media outlet.

Either suits me fine.

As the emails pile came in, I forward them directly to Katie. I also print them out, twice and store them in two separate locations. There's no risk of these being lost – or shredded.

Katie emails me back, acknowledging receipt.

Subject: Prior Art

Barry

Great work.

Now tell them to prove it. Get a letter from their lawyers ;-)

Katie

Once again, I return to the mailing list, sending yet another batch of emails. This time, I'm trying to sound more

assertive, perhaps even threatening. I tell them - in short – their word isn't good enough, and that I need something formally, from their lawyers.
It takes a couple of days before they arrive, but sure enough I start getting emails from posh sounding law firms, each attaching their response on a posh letterhead. Somehow they seem far less impressive when I print them on my inkjet printer – possibly because the yellow cartridge has run out.
Whilst their answers vary in the wording, they all tell me in far too many words, that their client has retained them to confirm they have no knowledge of ever signing an NDA with me, and that they had started work on the project only after it was broadcast, and therefore it was in the public domain, which is why they're free to pursue them as they wish. And by the way, how dare I suggest otherwise unless I have supporting evidence, being the signed document.
Unless I can do the world's most complicated puzzle and reconstitute tens of thousands of strips of shredded paper, they're pretty safe.
Finally, they ask me to 'cease and desist' from any contact with their clients.
They've all been polite, firm and direct – and presumably at extortionate cost to their clients. Most of them are patronising enough to summarise the situation for me. I have no NDA and the idea was free for anyone to exploit. They therefore consider the matter closed.

A couple of the more commercial lawyers have added a paragraph asking me if I've considered taking legal action against Mr M Roughton, as they'd be delighted to quote me for taking on the case.

I think back to my experiences a few years ago and how devastated I'd been when I'd shown everyone my ideas, only to be told they'd already had them and my NDA was worthless. It seems strange how hard I'm working to achieve a similar outcome.
This time, having been spoon fed with the actual times, dates and outlets from where they could have got the idea for nothing, they just had to ask for proof they ever signed an NDA, and then get their lawyers to do the same.

I forward the lawyers emails directly to Katie, and wait with baited breath for her feedback.

Subject: Prior Art

Barry

You've just proved there's no prior art.

I'm so excited for you.

Katie

I feel a tingle travel up my legs and through my body. I like it when Katie's pleased with me.

Before I close my laptop, I open the brown package Mickey had left for me at the IMAX Ticket Office, and remove the CD from it.

It whirs for a while before the database of the 622 invited guests to the premiere open into a spreadsheet. As I scan down the rows, I see many of the names I'd presented to at the Oat House.

I also see Mark Zuckerburg's entry, but avoided the temptation of sending a separate email asking him why he stole my idea for Facebook.

I send each one a mail with a presentation on Project Ronald.

Subject: Project Ronalc

Dear

You will have heard Mickey Roughton discussing this project at his recent film premiere.

In case you missed it, here's the presentation.

CHAPTER 43

Luke was thoroughly enjoying his role of CEO despite the inability to advise his staff on what they should be doing.

He'd moved from his dump of an apartment in Tenderloin to a detached house with pool and four-car garage in the prestigious neighbourhood of Silver Creek. Within a week he'd handed out almost three hundred of his new business cards, to neighbours, his local stores and the dealer where he bought his new Mercedes.

Each time, he watched the amazed reaction of the recipient as they read back his title:

Luke Palatino. CEO of $84m Tech Company

There was no description of what the business actually did nor what it was called. He was still in disagreement with Janice on the name. She had flatly refused all of his favourites: Luke Industries Inc, LukeSoft, Lukebook, Lukeoogle. For the moment, the company was called simply by its incorporation number: 436573532 Inc.

When he'd been asked what his $84m Tech Company actually did, Luke had been vague and dismissive, varying his stock answers from "a large comms co" through to "I can't divulge that information".

Nevertheless, he'd been dutifully going to his new office - several blocks from his new house- every day, to welcome new staff and make sure they each received a personal welcome and a signed business card.

His own office, situated on the upper East Wing of the vast space, was filled with quality oak furniture, picture frames – still featuring the autumnal landscape photos with which they were sold– and several wall prints of well known business leaders, alongside his own.

In the two months since he'd been there, he'd called board meetings twice a week, in which he'd sat as little more than an onlooker, carefully avoiding any discussion that might indicate the holes he had in his understanding of what the business actually did.

The first meetings were rather more awkward as initially it was just himself and his HR Director, but now, with five directors – each responsible for a handful of staff – he considered the meetings were purposeful.

The directors had commented on how refreshing it was to have a CEO that didn't push them to limits they were incapable of, or question them too deeply – or indeed at all – on what it was they were doing. They'd never worked on a board that was so laid back.

Luke's main focus was on the cash burn, and how long he would last before there was no investment left, at which point, he assumed the party would be over.
With only three million of his eighty-four spent, he figured it would be a while yet.
He dutifully followed Janice at her word and avoided entering into any agreements that would commit them to more than three months expense. His board were all on rolling contracts and his lease had break-clauses every quarter.
Even Janice would only visit once a week. Despite understanding what the business did, she had surprisingly little interest in attending board meetings, and also focused her visits solely on the amount of cash they were spending, and preparing positive reports for her investors.

All appeared to be going well. Coders were coding, directors were directing and the offices were filled with the buzz of people focused on bringing Project Ronald to life, and make 436573532 Inc. – the success it was destined to be.
Everyone knew the urgency of a launch, especially as the whole of Silicon Valley was awash with other companies working on a similar project – all of them boasting how their own version had a secret edge and bragging on how soon they'd be launching.
Internally, everyone knew they were at least ten months away from even the most basic beta launch, so just like everyone else, they lied. The countdown on their website displayed the amount of time to launch, and it was currently 186 days, nine hours, seven minutes and thirty-two seconds.

Part of Luke's daily ritual, after checking the progress of the men laying the GoKart track and logging in to see the company's bank balance - then his own -was to look at the websites his sixty or so competitors to see what their countdown clocks showed. The shortest was under four months, and the longest over nine months. Several of them were reset daily.

His daily report to Janice gave her three sets of information. How much was in the bank, how much cash was committed for the next month, and what their realistic launch date was estimated to be.
He spent the rest of his day excusing himself from the various meetings he'd arranged with important people. Most of the time he returned to the office with freshly coiffured hair, polished nails or an orange glow.

It was during Janice's visit in early October that Luke first became aware there might be a problem.

Having now left her job at Octajour, he had no idea how she'd been keeping herself occupied, other than a couple of trips she'd made with the twins to Florida, taking them out of school to do so.

He was disappointed she'd not spent more time with him. He'd certainly put the effort in with his constant offers of dinner or a private viewing of his new house – both of which she always politely declined. When he'd upped his game and sent her texts asking what she was wearing, she'd told him to mind his own business.

She was certainly on edge, which Luke presumed was down to the stress of her remortgage and her need to please the banks.

When – as he was sure it would – the venture failed, it would be down to his fellow directors, certainly not him. He had already penned his letter of resignation and had it ready for when all the cash was spent and he could no longer draw his salary.

As usual, Janice had visited Luke to discuss the latest cash burn report for the bank.

Luke's PA escorted her into his grand office suite, grateful for something to do other than arranging his haircuts, manicures and spray tans.

He was at his desk admiring the bronze bust of himself that had just been delivered. He quickly placed it on the floor by his desk and welcomed her in.

"Hey Janice. Good to see you. Great tan!"

"Thanks Luke. You too" she said, ignoring his orange glow, bright white teeth and rigid hair. She paused.

"Hey are you ok? You look troubled" he asked

"Luke, let me get straight to why I'm here. I need to tell you, I'm worried about our launch date" she said as she toyed with the glass paperweight on Luke's desk noticing his image was etched into it.

"Nothing's changed. Still looking at April" he said confidently as he leant back in his rich leather chair.

"Is it April, or is that just a blag?"

"Come on Janice, everyone's blagging it. We had a board meeting yesterday and we're up to ... Well ... whatever's on page 19 of the schedule. Everyone tells me they're doing very well and although no one knows exactly when we'll launch, everyone agrees we're doing fine. In fact I was considering us all getting a bonus at the end of the quarter."

"Well Luke, we don't know who is and who isn't blagging, but there are plenty I'm reading about who intend to launch sooner than April." She hardened her tone "...and do not pay out any bonuses."

Luke smiled, and rested his chin in his palm, not dissimilar to the pose in the picture on the wall behind him.

"Oh dear. So what shall we do? Give up?" he said sarcastically.

"Yes" she replied, looking him in the eye. "That's exactly what we should do."

"Jesus, I was only joking" he said, bolting forward in his chair.

"Luke, if we're being realistic, and we know we can't beat these others, then let's not burn the cash for the sake of it."

"Janice, don't give up now. I beg you. I'm telling you we can do it"

"Luke, the sooner we close down and move on, the quicker we can get on with the cupcakes."

Luke went silent. He certainly loved the opportunity the world of cupcakes offered, but on the other hand, he was on a little under twenty-grand a month and had no real work to do. He quite liked his apple-cart as it was and didn't want her upsetting it.

"Do I get to keep drawing my salary?" he asked sheepishly.

"No. I'm too upset at the moment, let me make some calls and we'll catch up next week."

She returned to her car and made two phone calls. Both recipients had never received a call like it before.

CHAPTER 44

One of the For Sale signs in our front garden has been uprooted, but the agent seems not to care – there's plenty of interest without it.

We have a steady stream of people visiting our house, prodding our walls and looking inside our wardrobes. How I hang my trousers or where I put my belts has no bearing on the value of the house, but nevertheless, it seems to interest many and deters few people from making an offer.

It's humiliating to show people around the house to see that two bedrooms are in use especially when they realise it's just the two of us that live here.

To avoid conflict, Marie and I take it in turns to escort couples around, as we listen to their plans to rip walls, re-decorate or remove carpets they consider to be outdated and ugly. They tell us about the children they either have or plan to have, and how happy they'll be in our home. The contrast to the life the house has led with us, saddens me.

As the offers come in, it's clear we're going to have to accept less than our asking price, but frankly as all the money's going to Marie, it makes no difference to me.

Nevertheless, I suggest to Marie we hold-out for an offer nearer to our original price, which she takes as a gallant effort for me to help her maximise her money. Actually, I simply want to delay the sale for as long as it takes for me to start seeing some of my fortune pour in. If we accept the first offer, I'll still be skint when it's time to leave, and I have the prospect of living in my car to face.

Unfortunately, one of the buyers comes back with an offer near the asking price, and the assurance he can transact quickly as he wants to be in for Christmas.

I call Lesley at Barnet Family Law to see what can be done and am advised, frankly, nothing, and by the way can I please settle her invoices otherwise she'll have to stop advising me and call in debt collectors.

By now it's the middle of November and I can hardly sleep. I'm not quite sure if it's excitement or stress but either way, in the next four weeks I'm going to be moving out of my home. I'm wondering whether it's better to live here with Marie than face the alternative.

As I tick the days off in my diary, I notice for the first time the date on which my big plan is due to kick-off actually falls on a weekend.

I'm left with a sinking feeling, probably not unlike how a prisoner feels to find the staff aren't available to set him free on his release date.

I have no idea whether my plan requires it to be a normal working day, or at the very least a weekday, to be implemented. I'd hate to spend two days longer than necessary.

As always, I look to Katie for answers on all my problems, so I email her.

I'm blown away by her response.

I read it twice.

> Barry
>
> It doesn't matter which date it appears. The fact that it's going to appear is enough. You don't have to wait.
>
> K

I think back on all the events of the past eighteen months. If I had known I didn't have to wait for the actual date to arrive, perhaps I would have done things differently. Perhaps my impatience would have ruined everything.

Perhaps Katie knew that, and didn't tell me on purpose. Or perhaps it was obvious but I was – on this occasion – being an idiot.

Now I know there's only a few days left, I feel there's nothing more to wait for.

I email her back.

> Katie
>
> Shall we do it now?
>
> Barry

When the reply comes, I feel another shiver spread through my entire body. I start shaking because I know what it's going to say.

> Absolutely. We're ready. I've got the list. I'll send them over for you to check and verify before they go out.
>
> K X

I feel the bile rising.

I can't sit down. I can't *not* sit down. I have no idea what to do.

I don't want to be alone. I don't want to be with anyone.

I run myself a hot bath.

I stop it halfway through and take a shower instead. It's cold because I've used all the hot water.

I phone up Marie and ask if she wants to have dinner with me.

I have absolutely no idea why I did that.

She also has no idea why I did that but accepts the invite.

Despite both leaving from the same house, we arrange to meet at the pub, which avoids the requirement for small talk in the car but makes for an uncomfortable exit as we both fumble for our keys, and pull off in convoy.

We sit in the small gastro pub where I once took her when we were single. The difference now is that the pub has replaced their microwave for a full kitchen and charges five times the price. And Marie and I are talking about the past rather than the future.

We're both civil, even warm in our approach, but my mind's elsewhere.

She tells me she's found a flat in Oakwood, a couple of miles from where the house is, and her offer's been accepted. She asks where I plan to live and when I tell her I have no idea, I sense the pity she's feeling.

She then surprises me by asking me if I've met anyone. The thought hadn't even crossed my mind. The last woman I'd shown any interest in was Marie, and I don't particularly remember being over-enthused even then.

I return the question, and am even more surprised to hear about a relationship she says is 'blossoming' online with a chap called Mike. I want to tell her that actually Mike is me, but in the interest of keeping on good terms, I listen as she tells me how handsome he is, how successful he is as a divorce lawyer, and how he loves dancing.

I have no idea where she got the last bit from. I'd never mentioned dancing in any of the emails I'd sent, but in her imagination he's her perfect match, and for the moment it works better for her to believe in him. She appears to be having a better relationship with someone in her imagination than she's capable of having in reality. I'm not about to burst her bubble, so to feign interest and avoid her suspicions, I indulge her.

"Where's he live?" I ask, knowing he's not told her, and there are no addresses in Imagination Land.

"Clapham" she says, with no doubt in her voice. "He lives with his wife who's dying from a rare tropical disease. And he's got a Lexus."

"How many times have you seen him?"

"Just a couple."

I briefly wonder if she's talking about another divorce lawyer called Mike, who's also handsome.

It's when she asks me about my work that I start gibbering rubbish.

She asks me about my venture, skillfully avoiding any mention of Project Ronald or the humiliation I suffered.

I can't tell her the true story as I don't want her to know of the vast sums she's about to miss out on, but with our new found civility to each other I'm starting to feel bad for her so I think perhaps I might give her a million or two from my jackpot. I still can't tell her my plan though, or about Mickey, who she knows I've met. I've never told her how close we are – mainly because a large chunk of our friendship was based on our mutual hatred of our wives. The only person who knows the full story is Katie and she's never met her or heard me mention her name.

After we've toyed with our food for a bit, we agree to stay as civil to each other as possible, for the sake of our son Danny, even though he doesn't speak to me and appears to hate me anyway. She leaves as she has important people to see whose nails aren't going to varnish themselves.

I'm delighted to get home, and even more delighted to see the email from Katie.

> Barry
>
> Please check the attached. If you get back to me by close of play, I'll have them out today.
>
> Exciting isn't it?
>
> Katie

The attachment consists of ninety-three letters, all exactly the same, the only exception being the name and company to which they're addressed.

I open the first one. Perfect.

I throw up again.

The emails are sent at 5:02pm London time, and the hard copies posted by UPS on their next day service to the USA. If any of the recipients miss their email, the letter will be on their desk by the time they get to work tomorrow.

CHAPTER 45

I'm so immersed in relaying my story; I forget Howard the journalist has to keep up with me.

I'm suddenly aware of where I am. The plush surroundings of the posh hotel and the subtly piped classical music that forms the backing track to my events.

Howard's in the midst of copious note-taking, desperately trying to keep pace of my story with no inkling of what's about to unfold. I excuse myself and run to the lavatory where I throw up. I had no idea how re-living the experience would bring such vivid memories and the same bilious reaction.

Being only a few weeks on from the event means it's still fresh in my mind, and I need to keep reminding myself of how I actually find myself here today.

As I return to the lounge, I see Howard flicking through his notebook and shaking his head. I can tell he's puzzled.

"You're probably wondering what's in the emails and letters Katie sent" I say as I sink back into the body shape I'd carved out in my armchair.

"I'm still wondering what Janice was up to?" he says, as though my story's not the headline here.

This rather breaks my flow, but as we've finished our sandwiches, which I've now disposed of in a manner rather more violent than I'd hoped, I'm wondering if, by backtracking, I can stretch out this meeting to include dinner.

Before continuing, I check he's ok with the timing.

"How much longer do you think this is going to take?"

I have no idea whether he's trying to tell me he's exhausted the time he wants to spend on this, or whether he's prepared to stay longer. I figure if I keep talking, he'll let me know which it is.

I explain to Howard one of the greatest pressures on a creative genius is the ability to find a way of leaving a trail of clues to show the outcome's been planned and nothing's accidental. He doesn't look the least bit impressed.

I decide to fill him in on the back story which starts when I first meet Mickey Roughton.

I'll also fill him in on Janice, but I'm now regretting ever telling him about her in the first place. I don't want any attention deflected from me, and the last thing I want is to be feeding him a story in which I don't have the lead role.

I'm tempted to tell him I've made Janice up, but he'll probably question the credibility on the rest of my story so I consider other options. I could tell him she just closed the company and that was the end of the matter, or that she was struck by lightening on her way home and died instantly, or that she went on to become a hairdresser and lives in Billericay.

I decide I should tell him the truth and the brilliance with which she pulled off her plan, hoping she'll be long forgotten when I move onto finishing what happened to me.

CHAPTER 46

The call to GalactInvest from Janice was timed at 14:06 and had lasted less than five minutes.

As usual, she'd started the conversation by telling Tod his twins were well and he should make a point of seeing them, and then, for the remaining four minutes she discussed the reason for her call. By the time she'd hung up, Tod was totally confused and slightly bewildered.

In the sixteen years he'd been at GalactInvest, in the course of making billions for the bank, Tod had made plenty of disastrous investments. The small losses didn't bother him. They were nothing more than battleground scars, and with each war he'd won, they'd been forgotten.

He'd also overseen plenty of investments that had run out of cash, or collapsed, losing up to a hundred million in the process – but he'd never heard of one shutting down whilst they still had cash in the bank.

"What do you mean you're closing? According to last week's management report, everything's on track and you've still got almost seventy-five million in the bank."

"We do, and that's why I want to close it now, before we blow any more cash" Janice explained.

"But ... well ... why ... how do you know it's not going to work? You haven't even launched yet. You know the game Jan, if you've run out of money, we'll just keep giving it to you until you get it right."

"Tod, you know as well as I do there's a hundred companies looking to launch the same idea as us. They'll all come out with it before we do, and there's will all be better. Apparently we're the only one without a secret edge."

"Jan, if this is a rouse for us to invest more, you don't need ..."

Janice interrupted

"Tod, it's final. We're closing down."

"Jan, I have no idea why you're doing this but you realise you have to return the monies, right?"

"Sure I do. I'll let you know the amount when we close."

He wondered whether Janice had lost her nerve – or perhaps her mind. Who returns money to a bank when the banks happy for them to carry on spending it? Obviously she couldn't pay herself the *whole* amount in salary – after all that was why clause 5.2.4a was in the contract, and she'd not changed it – but she certainly had enough funds to take a decent salary and stretch the business out long enough for her to have nothing to worry about for the foreseeable future.

In an industry that works on wins and failures, Tod had no idea where this one stood. Getting an investment returned was probably best described as a draw. He certainly wouldn't get a bonus for it. The few million dollars they'd have lost on running the business so far was insignificant.

Their investment had been a total waste of time and energy. Like thinking you're number's about to come in on a spin of the roulette wheel, only to be told it's a miss-spin. Even the bank's shareholders would prefer them take a bet and lose it rather than not take it at all.

He looked at his new cute blonde assistant sitting across from his desk and in an instant his attention turned elsewhere. Getting the cash back from Janice was something his compliance department would work on, and he would return to having as little to do with her as possible.

* * *

The call to BFD-TechBank from Janice was timed at 14:12 and was terminated at 14:16.

Ray was surprised to hear from her, particularly as she'd ignored his texts and calls following their memorable night only weeks ago.

Actually, he'd concluded, it wasn't particularly memorable. Most of the night was nothing but a blur. He was however starting to have flashbacks of lying horizontal, looking up at a toilet bowl, and being driven to his apartment, but little else. As he had no recollection of their night of passion and she'd shown no interest in meeting him again, he could only assume his performance had been below par.

He certainly wouldn't want to give her the opportunity of raising the issue so he'd content himself with the souvenir pair of her knickers and a single stocking.

All communication was focused solely on the bank's investment and the progress reports. Since the opportunity had been available to everyone, this was a race they hoped to win by backing an early runner – and Janice was certainly there at the beginning.

It was unusual for them not to take a seat at the board but with Janice's track record and good judgment, they'd accepted her changes to the contract and continued to have every faith in her ability to ensure the team delivered.

Ray had not expected to hear from her, especially as everything appeared to be on track. If anything, they were spending less cash than he expected, and the launch date was on target.

When Janice sprung her intention to close the company on him, Ray was gobsmacked. When she mentioned she'd be returning monies to the bank, he was staggered.

Janice had never been wrong about an investment, so it was ironic that the one time she'd invested her own money was the one time she'd got it wrong.

He wondered if perhaps it was having her own skin in the game that had created the additional pressure and clouded her judgment. Whatever it was, he had no idea how to set about collecting the returned funds from a failed investment. He'd dealt with money coming in from dividends, he'd dealt with money coming in from the sale of companies in which he'd invested, but he'd quite simply never dealt with money coming in from the return of his funding.

On the contrary, he was used to having desperate executives begging him to invest more so their business could continue burning cash, and they could continue drawing a salary – even though it was clear to all it was doomed to failure.

He hung up the phone and walked over to the large whiteboard in his office. Halfway down the long list of company names was 436573532 Inc. He picked up a red marker to cross it out, then realising it wasn't a loss, went to pick up the green marker, which he promptly replaced again.

He picked up the rubber and carefully erased the entire entry, as he wondered how the board would react.

* * *

The final day at 436573532 Inc. was as uneventful as all the days that preceded it. No one had been there long enough to be emotionally attached, and no one was impressed by Luke's farewell speech, which was little more than a self-tribute. No one appeared to appreciate his parting gift of a signed photo.

One by one, the workforce filed out the glass doors for the last time. Only a couple of them had brought enough of their personal belongings in to warrant a cardboard box.

The pay-offs were generous considering the short time the business had been in existence, and the mood was light. Every one of them would likely find a new job within a week, and none of them would miss the perks - not least of all because most had yet to arrive.

The Go Karts had yet to be installed, as had much of the other equipment. The Bar area had only ever been stocked with bottled water. The forty plus beers and lagers from around the world failed to materialize, and the sand had never arrived for the sandpit.

All outstanding orders were cancelled by the Chief Financial Officer who stayed on for another week in order to straighten the accounts, implement break clauses on all contracts and oversee the return of the funds.

The only other person in the office was Luke, who'd worked out he had enough money for another two months, after which he'd be reliant on income from the new cupcakes venture – or back to Ubering.

He was just shredding his remaining several hundred business cards, when Janice showed up.

"Hey Luke. Got a minute? I may have something to make you smile."

She seemed far more relaxed than their last encounter for which Luke had apologised several times for hanging on to her leg, begging her to change her mind.

"Sure" he replied, hopeful it was news on the cupcake venture and more importantly, his new salary.

"Luke, how much cash is there to return?"

"About seventy-two million, four hundred thousand" It was the only fact Luke was sure of.

"Ok … it might be a good time to tell you a little about the investors' contracts"

It took several explanations before Luke finally grasped what Janice was saying.

She'd scribbled her way through four sheets of his personalised notepads headed with 'From the desk of Luke Palatino– CEO $84m Tech Company'. Finally, he realised what she was saying. He jumped up and punched the air in excitement.

"It's genius" he beamed.

Janice had to agree. The small but significant changes to the contract had never been questioned, and with so many clauses, probably not even noticed.

The bank had been focused on the milestones and too busy arguing over their loss of a seat on the board to spot section 4 (term 3 sub-section 23a), and if they had, it would have seemed fair enough.

The contract was seventeen thousand words, of which the most common were "Director" (seventy-four mentions) Shareholders (seventy-one mentions) and Investors (sixty-eight mentions). Everyone was so blind to the three words, that the replacement of one for the other was almost undetectable.

All Janice had done was subtly cross-through one of the mentions of 'investors' and changed it to 'shareholders'.

The original clause had read:-

'In the event of the business closing with cash in the bank, the cash would be returned to the investors.'

The banks were not the only shareholders.

Luke picked up one of the sheets to check the figures.

BFD-TechBank	25%
GalactInvest	27%
Janice	43.2%
Luke	4.8%

Luke was tapping away on his calculator.

"So I get 4.8% of all the cash we're returning? That's almost three and a half million dollars?"

"Yep" Janice nodded.

As little as she thought of him, Luke had been worth every cent to her.

She had needed a great idea but more importantly, she needed someone to front it that both looked the part and had no hope of making it work.

The quicker she pulled the rug, the more money she'd be left with – although even she was surprised to find it was as much as thirty-one million.

She couldn't help thinking of the other idiot who'd helped her pull it off. Poor Barry. He'd declined her offer of a couple of million, and now he had no proof she'd signed an NDA, he couldn't claim anything. Of all the idiots she'd met, Barry was without doubt the biggest.

* * *

It took several weeks for the dust to settle.

Both GalactInvest and BFD-TechBank were paid back their share of the remaining cash, and both subsequently appointed lawyers to reclaim the rest.
Both banks felt compelled to do so, if for no other reason than to demonstrate to their shareholders this was an exceptional case.
Neither wanted to win in case it deterred other opportunities from being presented to them, especially if word got out that they were suing over such small losses.
The only significant outcome for them was to ensure they didn't allow minor changes to their contracts to go unchecked for future deals.
As expected, and fortunately for everyone, including the highly paid lawyers that delivered their opinions, both banks were told they had no case, and there was no proof that the business was set up with the intention of failing so soon.

Ray sat in his office resenting BFD-TechBank's policy of no alcohol, precluding him from pouring a glass of champagne and toasting Janice.
Recognising an alternative option, he cleared a pile of paperwork from his perfectly shiny desk and buffed it with his hanky.
He unwrapped the neatly folded paper from his pocket and generously poured out three perfectly straight lines of cocaine. With his finger tightly against one nostril, he sniffed the lot, then, looked up, and shouted.
"This is for you Janice. I love you" before keeling over and collapsing behind his desk.

Over at GalactInvest, Tod was fuming. As the bank's top investment manager, his best ever year, including bonus, was eight million dollars. It was enough to cover his growing harem of women, his Ferrari, Range Rover and exotic trips and wild nights – as well as the wild times in bed.
Since Janice had left the bank, his fireworks had become less frequent, less colourful and less explosive.
He was now pulling in less than four million a year, which lost him both his spot as top performer and his kudos.
He'd never seen a payday like he'd just watched Jan get.
His pride was hurt, but nothing else. The bank had laughed it off, and so too would he.
He returned to the brunette who was delivering his post. He needed something to commiserate with, and her shapely legs looked perfect for the job.

CHAPTER 47

Howard stops writing again. He appears suspicious of Janice's story, and I'm deeply offended.
"So she made thirty-one million dollars on a legal scam?"
His pencil's up by his lips, as though he's wondering if he should jack in being a journalist and do the same. I realise it's not suspicion he's feeling – it's envy.
"It's never going to happen again" I say, "That loophole's well and truly closed." hoping he'll stick to his vocation and write about me – which is, after all, why we came here in the first place.

"Look, I appreciate your time" he says as he closes his pad and stops his recording. I feel like the bride that's gone to her wedding only to find she's a bridesmaid.
"Whooa... don't you want to hear about me? You don't know how my story ends. It might be even better" I say, regretting it straight away.
"Is it?" he asks curiously.
I scratch the back of my head as he sits there waiting for a response. I'm disappointed he's not on the edge of his seat begging me to tell him the content of the letters my lawyer sent out.
He's in danger of leaving here thinking Janice is a blockbuster movie in the making and I'm the idiot who came away with nothing.
I wink. Unfortunately, because I've never mastered the movement of closing a single eyelid, both close and it looks like a patronising smile, or that I've been temporarily dazzled by the light.
"I think you're going to realise what a creative genius I am" I say, softly, but it sounds more like I'm threatening him.
However he's taken it, it's worked. He restarts his recorder, re-opens his notepad, and positions his pencil ready again - although not before drawing a thick line below where he last wrote, presumably so he can return to the interesting bit later.
"So what's next?" he asks, with no attempt to hide his boredom.
I think now's a good time to tell him the background to how I ended up in Silicon Valley. I'll leave the content of the letter sent by the lawyers to the end, when he's most likely to run out of patience.

* * *

After the vending company I worked for went bust, three years ago, I found it difficult finding another job in the industry partly because I wasn't particularly good at it, but mainly because I wasn't looking. I wanted a change in career - ideally somewhere I could put my creatively genius mind to good use, and avoid being with Marie as much as possible. The longer the hours I could work, the less time I'd have to spend with her – so I was open to anything.

After several disastrous interviews with ad agencies and design houses, most of which lasted a matter of minutes before I was escorted off the premises, the need for income overtook my need for job-satisfaction and I ended up answering an ad for work as an executive chauffeur, which is basically a mini-cab driver in a suit.

The clients also tend to be VIPS and executives rather than sales reps and drunks.

It was only through luck that I got the position. When I turned up for my interview, the receptionist told me that no one of my appearance had ever worked for the company and – to coin her words – "it would be a dark day, when someone as unpleasant looking as you ever drove for us".

Fortunately, they had several contracts and were desperately short of chauffeurs. Their only criteria were their drivers spoke English, had less than nine points on their licence and presented well.

In their desperate state, they settled for two out of the three, and once I'd promised to address what they termed as 'hygiene issues', I was in.

I was fast-tracked through their training program - all six hours of it - and given the keys to a brand new Mercedes S Class, a mobile phone, and a print-out of an address in Holland Park where my client lived. I was told to hang around near his house and whenever my phone rang, pull up majestically outside his front door, appropriately attired, open the door for him and take him wherever he wished to go.

I was also told to buy two of the same dark suits from Burtons and rotate them, ensuring both were clean and neatly pressed. I later found everyone else required just one suit and no-one else was given antiperspirant and aftershave as part of their 'welcome kit'. Nor were they required to sign a contract agreeing to change their shirt daily.

They dispensed with the chauffeurs cap as the only size they had merely balanced on top of my hair.

Two days later, I met Mickey Roughton for the first time.

In my role as a vending machine mechanic, I'd never come across anyone famous, although I did once install a Vending Master VM30 in Alan Sugar's reception although I didn't actually meet him. I did however see his Rolls Royce in the car park, and I also heard him shouting.

For the first two weeks, I never actually conversed with Mr Roughton. I was too star-struck, and he only ever grunted instructions of where he needed to be taken.

On a couple of occasions, I drove him to premieres or TV studios and had to navigate through crowds of screaming fans, but mostly the trips were to regular haunts; his tailor, the studios, his favourite massage parlours.

One day, I'd forgotten to turn my personal mobile phone off, and Marie called me. In my fumbling attempt to cancel the call, I pressed the loudspeaker button and subjected Mickey to several seconds of her hurling abuse at me before I finally managed to find the end-call button.

Horrified, I looked in the rear view mirror - and saw him in hysterics.

We ended up chatting and he told me how much he loathed his wife, and I was probably the first person who's was as bad as his.

From then on, we chatted about anything and everything. We planned fantasy disasters for our wives, we laughed at the same things, and we both hated driving - although fortunately for Mickey, his career didn't rely on it. Turns out we're very similar. We're both creative geniuses. He just happened to be a very rich and successful one, and, well, I was neither – but we were both very lonely and happy to spend time together.

He talked to me about the plots in his movies, the aggravation he had with his main stars and all the gossip on them - and occasionally, he'd take his wig off, and we'd go to Pizza Express for dinner together like two mates. He loved being able to order dishes he could understand, he loved the feeling he wasn't be ripped off, and most of all, he loved being incognito so he could enjoy his meal without being hounded by packs of selfie-seeking fans.

Howard's writing furiously. I notice every time I mention Mickey Roughton's name, he appears to listen more intently.

"...and what sort of gossip did he give you?" he asks.

"Well, did you know Boogie Trent was in rehab?" I offer.

"Yes. But only because she wrote a book about her addictions and was in a documentary about drug abuse" he says sarcastically.

I ignore him and continue. I know if he's going to bother with my story I have to keep peppering it with Mickey's name. Fortunately, he's a starring role in my plan so I continue.

I move on to how I was Mickey's driver when he released his blockbuster *Bank Busters*, after which he became embroiled in a copyright case with a guy in Oklahoma who claimed the film was based on his book *Rich Rewards*.

The similarities were striking.

Mickey's film involved a gang calling themselves Parkers Army, whereas in the book they were called Peppers Army. Mickey's head of Police was called Sergeant Walker; in the book he was Agent Walker.

The stunning woman that worked for the bank was called Angelina in both the book and the film.

Frankly, it was a direct rip-off. Even Mickey couldn't believe how little he'd tried to hide it.

The man from Oklahoma ended up suing Mickey, and despite Mickey knowing he was in the wrong, he counter-sued for damage to his reputation. He hired the best Intellectual Property lawyers to work on the case, explaining to me it doesn't matter who's right or wrong – just who's got the best lawyers, and who can keep paying them the longest. Mickey was confident he could score in both, just like he'd done on many previous occasions.

For the next few months, much of my time was spent ferrying Mickey to and from his Intellectual Property lawyers in Holborn. He'd always plan his meetings for 9:30 am so we were always sitting in rush hour traffic for an hour or more, despite it being less than five miles away from his home.

After a few weeks of me talking to him through the rear-view mirror, he suggested he sat up front with me.

I'd drop him at the lawyers, like a dutiful husband dropping his wife to work, and then invariably spend most of the time he was in there looking for somewhere to park.

When he finished his meeting he'd call me and often wait ten or fifteen minutes for me to get back there to pick him up.

* * *

Howard's stopped writing again.

Realising I've stopped talking, he stops and looks up. His tone is somewhere between pity and frustration.

"Look, I don't want to appear rude – and much as I'd love to hear what the emails and letters you sent were about, but ... well, with the greatest respect ..." He pauses, and a look of sympathy spreads across his face as his eyes wander up and down me. "... things obviously didn't work out... *this* time. I mean, don't get me wrong - it's great hearing all about how you drove Mickey Roughton about but, frankly, I need to sell stories and unless there's some juicy gossip – which the rest of the world didn't know before you - no-one's going to be interested in buying it. If you can give me Janice's number, I might be able to sell her story.

I sort of understand his point. Maybe I should have left out the bit about dropping Mickey off at Squiffy Myers, the lawyers that fought his copyright case, but how else do I get to explain how we ended up ditching the car and going up there together by taxi. Mickey asked me to accompany him just so we could chat, and seeing as I got paid by the time rather than mileage, I was happy to. Besides, I enjoyed his company.

Instead of wasting time searching for somewhere to park, I sat in reception waiting for him to come out of his meeting.

"Howard, believe me, you're going to love what I learned."

He raises his eyebrows as he looks at his watch, suggesting he's missing out on something more important, but will allow me the benefit of the doubt. Without saying anything, he huffs and opens his notepad. He slowly flicks through page after page, exaggerating each turn to demonstrate the copious notes he's taken, and the laborious efforts he's made, which have so far resulted in nothing.

He's hoping I'm about to reveal something that happened to Mickey in his meetings, but as I wasn't in any of them I have no idea. I'm about to tell him how, in 1982, I came second in the school speed-reading test. Fortunately, I stop myself as he'll probably think I'm wasting his time again. It's a moment of glory I'll have to sacrifice, even though it will give him an understanding of how I managed to read every pamphlet, every law magazine and every case-study on the glass table in the reception area of Squiffy Myers, the world's leading Intellectual Property & Patent Lawyers. In the eight months it took Mickey to reach a settlement, in his favour, from the Oklahoma man suing him, I'd become an expert in how to protect an idea.

I continue my story at the point when I've learned everything I need to know about patents, how to register them, how they work, and how to ensure no one can take an idea owned, registered and proven to be from someone who had it before them.

Of critical importance were two terms I'd learned; Prior Art, which means, in short, if someone's already working on an idea, another party can't then patent it.

The other term's 'Public Domain', meaning if something's been made public, no one can protect or patent it.

As someone who was over-flowing with ideas, I was sure I could use both these to stop another of my ideas from being stolen.

I read the only way to protect an idea was to ensure anyone told signs a Non-Disclosure Agreement. This would allow me to prove I had the idea first, and stop anyone patenting it as their own.

The NDA also stops them from telling anyone else – or putting the idea in the Public Domain. It's probably an anomaly in law in that the title says exactly what it's for.

It goes without saying (but I see Howard still writes it down) until anyone signs an NDA, they have no idea what the idea about to be divulged is, so a standard clause within the agreement is that if they can subsequently demonstrate they had the idea beforehand, then the protection of the NDA is invalid.

I waited for Howard to recognise that I'd not given anyone my contact details after they signed my NDA. He didn't, so I spelled it out.

As no one could contact me, they couldn't lie to me that they knew about it, or pretend they'd started work on it in order to cut me out.

By the time I contacted them, they'd already heard the idea in the public domain so it was easier for them to claim that's where they'd first seen the idea.

By putting my idea in the Public Domain, anyone could claim a right to use it, and for my plan to work, I wanted as many companies working on it as possible. I also made sure I left out one vital -but obvious- ingredient from my idea so they would all think of it and assume they had an edge over each other.

By broadcasting it on national TV, Mickey certainly put the idea in the Public Domain. By announcing the Non-Disclosure Agreements had been destroyed gave the parties who'd signed one with me, an opportunity to deny it.

Simply put, all they had to do was deny any knowledge of having signed an NDA with me, and claim they'd first got the idea from it's broadcast.

Every one of those that signed the Agreement with me was so desperate to prove to me they'd got the idea from Mickey's broadcast, they even got their lawyers to confirm it in writing.

It also proved one other vital fact: because each lawyer had been so adamant their client had only got the idea from the publicity it got, they were proving to me there was no Prior Art. No one had been working on the idea previous to Mickey's announcement.

Judging by the way Howard's plumped up his cushion and sat forward, I can see he's finally realised there's a twist – although I'm not entirely sure he's grasped the enormity of what it is.

"So Mickey destroyed the Agreements on purpose?" he asks.

"He not only destroyed them on purpose, he also told the whole world what he'd done, and then allowed everyone access to the idea on his website."

"So everyone thought they could nick your idea without needing to find a way of wiggling out of the NDA to cut you out?" he says. Yet again he stops writing, which I'm not sure is a good sign. Fortunately the tape's still whirring.

"And what no-one knew ..." I stop and point to his notepad, "... you may want to write this bit down. It's the most important bit" I stop to add drama and clear my throat. I lean forward, and in a voice much softer than I intend, continue, "... what no-one knew... was that I'd already patented the idea a year earlier."

I lean back, observing his reaction. His mouth is open.

"It takes eighteen months to publish a patent" I said, "so I waited to make sure I could prove no-one had the idea before"

"So why didn't you just tell everyone you'd patented the idea, and sell it to the highest bidder?"

"Aha!" I say as returning to the brilliance of my plan. I'm a little over-excited, and wipe the dribble before answering.

"There are a few reasons. I was handicapped from the start. As I think you've realised, there was no way I could do this on my own. I was skint, I can't code and no one would ever back me. All I really had was an idea and a shitty presentation. At best I would be offered a couple of million to walk away from it – which is exactly what happened, twice - and whilst that kind of money was beyond my wildest dreams, I recognised it was a drop in the ocean of the potential I could make."

He'd already mentioned he wanted some emotion in his story, so now's a good time to introduce some.

My eyes start to water as I tell him that even with the greatest laid plans, things can fall apart all too easily. If the plan didn't work in its entirety it was completely useless.

I feel my voice croak as I tell him of the costs involved in preparing, checking and filing patents, and how, until it's final filing eighteen months after the initial application, it's as good as worthless.

He's about to hear how my world turned upside down. I bring the back of my hand to my forehead. I wonder if he thinks I'm hamming this up just for him. I watch as Howard increases the intensity of his scribbling, then stops suddenly and waves his pencil.
I've confused him. I decide to jump back to when I had the epiphany.

I tell him how, although I knew I could probably sell the idea and my patent to one company, because they're such greedy bastards, if they didn't know it was patented and they could cut me out, they'd all have a go at it.
They'd actually compete with each other to see who could launch it first.
I was no longer paranoid about being cut out, in fact I'd *want* to be cut out because I couldn't possibly partner with them all.
Finally, I'd get them all to prove the idea was mine, and that's when I would wave my patent in front of them and demand my fees.
The result would be loads of partners, all paying to use my patent.

Howard's staring at me. I wait for him to congratulate me on my brilliance, but since nothing's forthcoming, I wonder if he understood what I'd been talking about. His notes look rather illegible to me, and in case they're equally illegible to him, I wonder whether I need to repeat it.
"Ok" he said. "Tell me about the letter."

Apparently not.

CHAPTER 48

It was the end of the working day in London, and just beginning in Silicon Valley when Katie sent the emails.
By mid-morning, all had reached their target's inbox, been opened and created havoc. There wasn't a lawyer in the city that wasn't on the case.
In particular, the three firms that specialised in Intellectual Property were in meltdown.
By lunchtime, scores of PAs and secretaries from the banks, software houses and internet giants that were on my list, had busied themselves arranging sandwiches and drinks for urgently schedule boardroom meetings.

The whispers started around the office water-coolers and permeated through the small clusters of cigarette smokers congregating outside, on to Starbucks and finally through the radio stations, newspapers and local TV stations.
Switchboards were in meltdown as reporters frantically went through the lists of companies claiming to be working on Project Ronald, seeking reaction from their management.

* * *

Everyone's seated when Tod Damar marches into the crowded boardroom at GalactInvest. He doesn't sit. He's clearly stressed and he's removed his jacket revealing the patches of sweat as they seep through his shirt. The air conditioning's on it's coolest setting.
"Is there anyone in here who hasn't heard about this?" he says waving several pieces of paper.
Everyone nods. There's no-one within thirty miles that's not heard about it.
Nevertheless, he reads the main paragraph aloud in summary.
"blah blah ... I refer to the above patent, blah blah was registered in June 2015 blah blah ... and is due for publication November 2016."

He stops, looks up, then reads the next line, louder and stressing each word.
"This patent forms an integral part of what has widely become known as Project Ronald."

He looks up again. No reaction. The email's been circulated. They know what's coming next, but Tod continues anyway.

"It includes a communications platform ..." his voice loudens "... together with GPS capability ..."

There's a cough from the back. Someone leaves the room.

"We require you, within 7 days of receipt of this letter to confirm which of the following options you undertake a commitment to:-

1. Cease and desist from any further involvement or development of the project in which this patent is breached, or alternatively
2. Send a payment of £10m (ten million pounds sterling) or equivalent in US dollars, together with a 10% transfer of shares in the project, registered with Mr B Goodman as the beneficiary, as compensation and the license for the ongoing use of the patent."

The CFO picks up a sandwich from the platter in the centre.

He needs to eat when he's anxious.

"Gentlemen, how the fuck did this happen?"

No response. Everyone's looking down.

"Ok ... let's be logical" he looks to Steve, head of strategy. "Steve, we can tell them the patent's useless as we were already working on it, right?"

Steve looks uncomfortable when he replies.

"Tod, we already confirmed we didn't start work on it until after it was broadcast on TV."

"And we did that because....?" Tod's stare was intense.

"Because otherwise Tod, we would have had to admit we'd signed the NDA with that guy and acknowledge that's how we got the idea."

Tod marched round the room.

"What the fuck do we do?" His voice had changed from anger to desperation.

Everyone looked to Steve. He was the only guy brave enough to respond.

Steve cleared his throat. He wasn't about to deliver good news.

"Tod, a patent isn't published for eighteen months, but it's valid from when it's filed. He must have filed it in June last year. Apart from that, we've made a point of telling him we'd only started working on it after we saw it on TV. We've actually assured him of it. In writing, and what's more, he's asked us to clarify it – which we did. Through our lawyers!"

Tod turned to his CFO, who was mid-way through a bite on his chicken surprise sandwich.
"Jack, how much have we spent so far on this?"
"Well, we announced we were committing an initial thirty to forty million on it. We've spent probably less than five so far."
Steve butts in with his point.
"If we stop now, we may save a few million, but that's it - we're out of the game for good and we'll also lose face. That's why we wanted it so badly in the first place. If we pay, we've still got a chance of hitting the jackpot." He played with his sandwich for a bit as though waiting for the courage to speak "And don't forget Tod, we've er ... well, there's no second horse in the race since the Janice incident"
No one needed reminding of the Janice Incident, which was now part of the bank's folklore.

The sandwiches are replaced with donuts as discussions continue through late afternoon. By the time they leave, everyone fully understands the laws surrounding patents.
Quite simply, Barry had made sure they'd jumped through every conceivable hoop necessary to ensure his patent was bulletproof.

Tod's last words before he left the room were to Steve.
"What a clever bastard. See if you can negotiate."

* * *

The Silifunders website was unusually slow to load. With the company switchboard being permanently engaged, shareholders and journalists were visiting in record numbers. When it finally appeared, the image of Bob holding his chin had been replaced with a hurriedly prepared statement designed to reassure.

November 27th: Many of you may be aware that a project in which Silifunders has invested is subject to a claimed patent breach. We would like to assure our shareholders that both parties are negotiating over a settlement and we fully expect this to be resolved within the next 48 hours. We are confident of a positive outcome and the launch date remains unaffected as of March 18th.

* * *

Jim, Josh, Jake, Jez are on their way to meet with Alan Androposa following they're meeting with the company lawyer, who's recommended they either close-down the project or pay off for use of the patent.
Androposa is at his desk dictating an email to Messrs Squiffy Myers.

* * *

In Seattle, Jane Witham, Head of Legal, was in Boardroom 9 of Building G, surrounded by eleven representatives of Berkley Munsford, the prestigious law firm drafted in for issues that couldn't be dealt with in-house.
They had been instrumental in successfully fighting - and winning - the dozens of class actions brought against their clients by users, suppliers and staff.
With a reputation for making any problem disappear, their swift response and deadly punches often resolved any issue before it reached the media or damaged a share price.
Having been forwarded the email from Squiffy Myers within minutes of it's arrival, the tier-one team had been scrambled to the Seattle HQ, arriving in a convey of four cars.
En route they made calls, searched on their tablets and discussed strategy.
By the time they'd arrived, their battle-plan was fully prepared.
"We can win this" said lawyer No.9
"Thank Gd" said Jane, grateful their unblemished record would remain intact.
"It's simple. We'll have a claim for false representation filed by first thing in the morning."
"Okay. Against who?"
"The Goodman character."
"What was false?"
"We're not sure yet, but it's a good first step."
Lawyer 6 cleared her throat.
"We're also going to contest the patent" she said.
"How? They've proved no one was working on anything similar."
"We're not sure yet, but it's a good second step."
"How much and how quick?"
"Difficult to say. Between two and three years. We can't cost it yet."

"Don't bother."

The lawyers filed out of the room like a badly choreographed troupe and Jane opened her laptop and sent her recommendation to her bosses.

> Guys
>
> We need to settle with Squiffy Myers.
>
> Jx

CHAPTER 49

Mickey takes my call within its first ring.

"Well?" he sounds excited.

"The letters went out last night" I say, my voice quivering.

"Fuck. That's fantastic. How many?"

"Ninety-three ... but ..."

"Holy shit. How much are you asking for?"

It's about now I should be telling Mickey about Janice, and how indebted to her I am – or would have been if I hadn't received the bombshell this morning.

If I overlook the fact that as of an hour ago, my plan was bulletproof, he'd still have another blockbuster movie on his hands. I wonder whether I should share the small detail that my plans are now collapsing around me. I decide not to.

I may end up a penniless laughing stock, but at least I'll still have the kudos of having a film made from my story.

I hold back on telling Mickey the amounts whilst I talk him through how I first met Janice in a swimming shorts store and how she'd given me two lessons - both of which were to prove far more valuable than she'd ever know. I remember them exactly as she delivered them, and repeat them to Mickey verbatim, even though my mind's elsewhere.

"There are two things you have to know about the Valley. Firstly, in an industry where the currency's measured in billions, millions is nothing more than small change."

I'd let Mickey digest it, before continuing with the second rule.

"And secondly, it doesn't matter whether you think an idea can work or not. It ALWAYS works if there's enough money thrown at it, so the important thing for any investor is to own it before anyone else can. They can be ruthless in making sure they do. So what I'm trying to say, is, however much you think you want to raise, ask for more. Much, much more."

My mind's elsewhere. Mickey's still on the phone.

"Barry? What the fuck are you warbling about? Just tell me how much you're asking?"

I can't bring myself to tell him what I've discovered, so I carry on as though everything's fine. I try not to let my emotions get in the way of telling him what he needs to make his movie.

"Mickey, when the letters were originally drafted, they were asking for a million each."

"Jeees-sus, that's a pile of money."

"Mickey, after what Janice taught me, I changed them to ten million"

Silence.

It's been almost six months since the ninety-three companies had started working on Project Ronald. Within a couple of months, many would be ready to launch, complete with the GPS function.

Having invested so heavily, they were unlikely to throw the towel in now.

Ten million may have an enormous impact on me but to these vast corporations and heavily funded opportunists, it's less than the alternative, which would be wasting what they'd spent to date and leaving the race.

Mickey needs no explanations. Although patents and copyright differ somewhat, he knows the game better than anyone, thanks to his vast experience in ripping-off others' scripts.

I had worked hard to keep my expectations as realistic as possible, though even my lowest estimates blow my mind. If only ten percent settle, and each only offer me fifty percent of what I'm asking, I can make thirty plus million.

There's also the small percentage I'll end up owning in a bunch of companies hoping to launch my idea – and one of them has to be the successful one, which they'll probably sell for billions – and even that's conservative according to Facebook's cheque book.

"Let's celebrate" says Mickey "I'll send a car for you now."

"Maybe later" I say. "I've got a pressing issue to deal with right now"

"Barry, are you alright? You sound shit"

I can't bring myself to tell Mickey about the letter I opened less than an hour ago.

It was only when, in preparation for the sale of our house, I'd come across the huge stack of envelopes I had avoided opening. I knew they were mostly final reminders and debt collectors letters which I'd learned to ignore, but as I thought I was about to come into huge riches, I thought it might be prudent to see how much I owed. I thought it might even be entertaining.

The letter from Squiffy Myers, the world's leading Intellectual Property & Patent Lawyers, was dated exactly two weeks ago.

Dear Mr Goodman

We're sorry to find there's been no movement to the debt you have built with us. As of today, the total outstanding is £42,461.00, of which a significant part is now over twelve months due.

Regrettably, unless we receive payment to bring your account with terms within the next seven days, we will no longer be putting any further resource into dealing with your patent. We will also be unable to cover the filing of your patent No. 26638923820/A

As the final filing date is now only ten days away we would urge you to address this immediately to ensure your patent application doesn't breach the Patent Office deadlines, in which case it will lapse.

Yours faithfully

Accounts Dept.

They've been responsible for preparing, filing and monitoring my patent, which is in danger of becoming entirely worthless.

I wonder if Katie knew the patent had already lapsed before the letters and emails were sent. I conclude she couldn't have, otherwise she would have known what a waste of her time it was.

I'm not sure how many times I call them but they've still not called back. I can't even get hold of Katie. I leave a message with the receptionist that I'm coming in, and demand to meet with Mr Myers himself. I don't need to tell them how desperate I am, their answerphone messages are filled with my dribbling, sobbing and woeful begging in the hope they can extend the deadline on the patent. On one of them, I don't think I actually said anything, but just wailed.

After the brief interruption from Mickey, I leave for Holborn. I should have taken the tube, but with what's going on, I don't want to be without a phone signal for a minute. I have no idea why, as other than from the very people I'm on my way to, I'm expecting no calls and no emails.

I spend another age looking for a parking space, and when I find one, I'm shocked at the cost. I don't have enough change or any credit cards I can use, so I leave the car. My mind's in a blur. If it's towed away I could have nowhere to sleep next week.

By the time I check in at reception, I'm sweating profusely.

Although the receptionist has changed, the surroundings are familiar to me from the times I used to sit there waiting for Mickey.

She's on a phone call, but seeing the state of me, she covers the phone with her palm and looks up at me, unable to hide her look of pity. She also looks scared.

"I'm guessing you're Barry" she says.

"Yes." I say, lacking the breath to add anything else.

I lean on her desk as she casually apologises to the person on the phone, and then without any urgency, pushes a button placing her call on hold.

She presses more buttons, and after a couple of seconds, announces "he's here" before replacing the receiver.

"Mr Myers will be down in a moment" she says outstretching her arm to point me to the seating area. She has no idea how familiar I am with the waiting area. I've probably spent more hours in this building than she has.

My breath is coming back, but the panic doesn't subside. As I sit with my head in my hands, thoughts rush through my head. Am I about to be homeless, am I destined to be poor for the rest of my life. Why didn't I ask Mickey for help? He'd always told me he'd be there for me – but I'd never considered myself as desperate as I am today – and now it's too late.

I look up as I hear the footsteps approaching.

Although I've never met Mr Myers before, everything about the man approaching me shouts successful lawyer and whispers he's never struggled in his life. His smart pin-striped suit, perfectly complemented by his whiter-than-white starched shirt, with his tie and hanky perfectly matching, together with his half-moon gold-rimmed spectacles – looks straight out of a book.

There's not an ounce of warmth in his face, and he doesn't extend his hand. He's clearly more interested in my debt than the millions I've lost.

"Mr Goodman, I'd like you to accompany me please" he says with no emotion in his voice, but still managing to sound patronising.

As we walk to the lift, I find myself gushing an endless flow of questions, but mostly 'why'. His face remains stern and he talks slowly and deliberately, punctuating every syllable.

"Mr Goodman, I appreciate your concern, but please understand. Our practice cannot survive unless our clients pay us. We can't just continue disbursing funds endlessly on our clients' behalf." He stops, then quips "After all, we're not investors" he sniggers, as though he's entertained himself.

I lose control in my reasoning as I spew an array of promises I'll make if he can extend it. Even I know a patent can't be extended.

"Mr Goodman, regrettably, the Patent Office offers little flexibility. Once a deadline has been passed, it's ... well, it's passed. I'm not sure why they'd call it a deadline otherwise". He gives another little snigger. I'm delighted he sees my situation as an opportunity to show off his skills in humour.

The lift doors open on the third floor, and I follow him to a corner office, in which there are four people seated around a large table.

One of them, a grey-haired woman, probably in her seventies, is in a wheelchair. She's the only one whose face looks remotely friendly, probably because her false teeth fix her mouth in a permanent smile.

"Mr Goodman, please take a seat" he says pointing to a chair in the centre. "It's important our clients understand what's entailed in producing a patent, and the costs - which is why we just can't extend endless credit. I'd like you to meet the people whose time and expertise is reflected in our fees."

I really don't need a lecture in why he's ruined me, nor do I want the additional humiliation of the others around the table pointing their fingers at me, telling me their pay packets are lighter because I haven't settled my account.

I feel my mouth opening, with no idea what's going to come out. Fortunately, nothing does.

He goes round the table, standing behind each individual, holding their shoulders as he tells me their name.

"This is Darren Martin. He translated all your presentations and emails into legalese patent speak. He also speaks Spanish, French, German and of course, Latin – which comes in handy." Darren nods. He looks really pissed.

Mr Myers shifts one pace to the left.

"This is Arthur Rankin. Arthur made the application, searched to see if there was anything similar already filed, and followed it through the entire process. He's got a wonderful collection of African Warrior Dolls."

Arthur Rankin doesn't even look at me. I don't give a shit about his dolls.

"Sharon Gail, looks after the finances here. Sharon loves dogs, and has two miniature poodles."

"Actually they're Standard Poodles" she says proudly, as though they alone could solve my problems.

"Yes, Standard. Anyway I'll let her go through some of the figures with you" he says, pointing towards the stack of paperwork and a calculator Sharon has in front of her. She briefly looks up at me before clearing her throat.

"Mr Goodman, according to the latest statement, there's forty-three thousand, four hundred and twenty one pounds outstanding, including interest. I'd like to discuss how soon we can clear this, and draw your attention to the final invoice we submitted last Tuesday."

Her gall staggers me. She clearly knows my situation; surely she's not expecting me to suddenly produce a cheque book.

I stand there motionless.

The woman in the wheelchair can see my world's collapsing and wheels herself round to me. An awkward silence descends on the room as everyone acknowledges she's on the move and watches to see her destination.

As we follow her progress, Myers points to her.

"And that's Katherine. She's responsible for relationship management, so she's at the sharp end, dealing with our clients directly ..."

When she finally pulls up at my side I can see she looks far gentler than the others.

"Barry, I really think you should look at the last invoice" her voice is soft and comforting.

As Sharon thrusts it in my hand, I scan it. It's for eight hundred pounds plus VAT, totalling nine-hundred and sixty pounds.

As I read what the charge is for, my eyes water.

"Charge for filing of final patent fee, and granting of Patent. Completed within deadline."

At that very moment, the lady in the wheelchair extends her frail arm.

Myers approaches both of us.

"... but we all call her Katie."

She takes my hand "Barry, it's an absolute pleasure to finally get to meet you."

My eyes are tearing. I find myself holding Katie's hand, as though she's a long lost friend, which I have no doubt she is. I've spent the last two years exchanging emails with her, and I'm overwhelmed to meet her at last. I'm only slightly put out she's not the blonde bombshell I'd hoped her to be.

Mr Myers comes to where I'm sitting and puts his hands on my shoulders.

"Mr Goodman, I want you to know it was Katie who insisted we make the payment for the filing fee, and I think she's done you a great favour, as Sharon will now tell you."

Sharon is still fumbling with paperwork, and clears her throat again.

"Mr Goodman, it appears the recipients of the letters Katie sent out were rather desperate to conclude matters as speedily as possible, so I can confirm we're in funds to your favour."

I can hear her, but I'm not really following much of what she's saying. I'm still coming to terms with the relief my patent's actually been filed.

She continues.

"After I convert them into sterling and of course deduct our fee, I can tell you ..." she stops momentarily as she punches the keys on her calculator, "you're left with ..." more punching. Katie squeezes my hand "three hundred and twelve million, six hundred and twenty two thousand ... and about four hundred pounds."

A waitress approaches our table and Howard shoos her away. He's scribbling in his notepad with an enthusiasm I haven't seen since I mentioned the name Mickey Roughton. I tell him the actual amount has increased since last week to £352m.

I'm told there are a couple of stragglers still negotiating, but as Katie pointed out, anyone who's not settled by now is likely to be out of the game.

In a rush for everyone to continue in their battle to be the first to launch, all of the monies were transferred, converted to sterling and are being held in a client account in my name at the lawyers. They'd tried to transfer a million to me, but my bank rejected it due to money-laundering regulations – and possibly the presumption that the money had been sent to me in error, probably because my account's never been in credit.

Katie's helping me sort the paperwork to ensure they accept future transfers, but until then, Mickey's given me one of his credit cards and told me to spend whatever I like on whatever I like until my money's through.

Since our house was sold ten days ago, I've been living in the Presidential Suite of this hotel, which is why I asked Howard to meet me here. It's also near Bond Street which is handy as I've got a whole new wardrobe to buy – and pack into my Louis Vuitton luggage - before my 2pm flight to St Lucia tomorrow, where I'll be spending Christmas with Mickey. He's told his wife he'll be away for a couple of weeks working with the main character in his future film.

Knowing I'm sitting on several hundred million, Howard seems a little less abrasive with me.

I catch the waitress's eye and make a squiggle in the air to indicate I'm ready for the bill.

"Would you mind if I asked you another question?"

He's not bothered asking my permission for any of the others.

"Sure."

"Did Mickey pay up for the film rights?"

"No."

"Will he?"

"What makes you think he should pay me?"

"I thought you'd agreed a figure on the plane on your first trip." He opened his notepad and flicked back through his mounds of notes.

"Here it is. You said you'd haggled over it. To quote you, 'The first figure is five million, countered by zero etc ... and you settled on a measly hundred thousand."

"Yep. That's right" I say. "The only reason there would ever be a movie was if the plan came off, and as Mickey's the only person I trusted to help me, I felt five million was a fair reward but he wouldn't take it. Eventually, after I insisted, he agreed to take a measly hundred thousand. I told you – he's a real friend"

He slumps back in his chair, chewing his pencil and looking at me.

"Do you mind me asking why you picked me to interview you?"

"You were the only one of the eight that responded."

"Who were the other seven?"

"They were the others on my son's journalism course at Nottingham."

I watch as Howard mentally scans the members of his class until the penny drops. He points his pencil towards me.

"Danny?"

"Yep."

The waitress returns with a silver tray on which is a book-shaped wallet, a pen and several mints. I remove the slip, write my suite number and sign it.

"Thank you Mr. Goodman" she says as she reverses away from the table.

I return my attention to Howard.

"I need you to do something for me" I lean forward "I want you to get in touch with Danny and tell him everything I've told you - and then rip up your notepad."

"Why?"

"Because I want him to know I'm not such a klutz, and that I love him."
"Why can't I sell the story?"
"I don't want anyone knowing."
"But what about the movie?"
"It ends with no one offering to settle, and me losing the patent."

I remove two envelopes and a folded sheet from my back pocket and throw them to Howard. He looks stunned when I tell him his envelope contains a cheque for twenty-five thousand. Danny will be even more delighted when he opens his and sees a cheque with a large number followed by seven zeros.
I unfold the letter and present it to Howard for his signature.
He assures me he'll comply with both points; he'll repeat the story only to Danny, and he'll destroy his notes.
I tell him it's one of two sets of agreements Squiffy Myers had prepared for me since we'd starting receiving the settlement offers, and for which they'd made no charge.
"What was the other one? he asks.
"A Non Disclosure Agreement I had to sign for each party to ensure I never told anyone about their settlements. But you know the value of NDAs, eh?"

THE END

23702340R00129

Printed in Great Britain
by Amazon